THE TULIP VIRUS

Daniëlle Hermans

THE
TULIP
VIRUS

Translation by David MacKay

MINOTAUR BOOKS

NEW YORK

This is a work of fiction. All of the characters, organizations, and events portrayed in this novel are either products of the author's imagination or are used fictitiously.

THE TULIP VIRUS. Copyright © 2008 by Daniëlle Hermans. English translation copyright © 2010 by David MacKay. All rights reserved. Printed in the United States of America. For information, address St. Martin's Press, 175 Fifth Avenue, New York, N.Y. 10010.

www.minotaurbooks.com

This edition published by arrangement with the Sebes & Van Gelderen Literary Agency, Kerkstraat 301, 1017 GZ Amsterdam, the Netherlands.

Library of Congress Cataloging-in-Publication Data

Hermans, Daniëlle, 1963–
    [Tulpenvirus. English]
    The tulip virus / Daniëlle Hermans. — 1st ed.
        p. cm.
    ISBN 978-0-312-57786-5
    I. Title.
    PT6467.18.E76T8713 2010
    839.31'364—dc22

                                    2009047496

First published in the Netherlands by A. W. Bruna Uitgevers B.V., Utrecht, under the title *Het Tulpenvirus*.

First U.S. Edition: May 2010

10 9 8 7 6 5 4 3 2 1

For Taco

THE TULIP VIRUS

Alkmaar

She brushed away the fly and scowled at the empty shelf. The bread she had baked the day before was gone, and she knew exactly where it had ended up: in the bellies of the drunkards who came there to squander their meager wages on liquor.

She wiped her damp hands on her apron, undid the bow under her chin, and gave the fly, which had now settled on the shutter, a swat with her cap. The blue-green bug plummeted to the counter, its legs flailing helplessly in the air. She picked up the pestle, clenched her teeth, and brought it crashing down. Then, setting aside the heavy tool, she wiped the sweat from her forehead and left the kitchen, hoping there might still be bread in the taproom.

As she opened the door, she was overcome by a wave of stench. She staggered back into the doorway. Gaping at the form that lay sprawled in front of the cupboard, she reached for the door frame behind her to steady herself.

"Mr. Winckel?"

She let go and stepped into the room, approaching him warily. Then she clasped one hand to her mouth and the other to her belly, as her nostrils were assailed by the foul odor of urine and the metallic tang of dried blood. She took a deep breath to keep from retching, but her stomach heaved so violently that the vomit ran down her fingers and out of her nose. She turned away, resting her hands on her knees, and gasped for air. The spasms gradually subsided.

With the corners of her apron, she wiped the strings of slime from her mouth. Slowly, she turned toward him. Pursing her lips and exhaling, she peered out of the corner of her eye.

Dangling halfway out of its socket, Mr. Winckel's right eye stared back at her. The left side of his head had taken such a heavy blow that there was almost nothing left of it. A gaping hole. Blood, splinters of bone, and pulped brain had mingled into a pink jelly on the floor. The fluid had seeped into the porous joints between the tiles.

As she bent over, the swarm of flies rose and began to circle her head. She dropped to her knees and reached out her trembling hands, but swiftly pulled back. A sheaf of papers had been rolled into a tube and stuffed down his throat with so much force that the corners of his mouth had ripped open. The hideous grin on his face brought back her nausea. Her gaze drifted downward. His torn shirt rippled over his colossal abdomen, which protruded unselfconsciously, with something like pride. Not knowing where to look, she followed the chestnut-brown line of hair on his belly to the waistline of his trousers. Around his crotch the shade of the black fabric darkened, and she cast her eyes down, embarrassed.

When she looked up again, the sun had found him. Its beams shone through the half-open shutters and glinted on the silver buckle of his shoe.

"Oh, my God, Mr. Winckel," she whispered, "what have they done to you?"

Half stumbling, she ran out of the room.

In the early morning calm, the flies made an infernal racket.

ONE

He sat up with a groan, turned on his reading lamp, and checked his watch. Who would be crazy enough to come by at four in the morning? Flopping back onto the bed, he stared up at the ceiling. By this time, he could have drawn its every ornament, crack, and bump from memory. He'd hardly had a moment's sleep for weeks, and now this.

Well, worrying wouldn't help, he knew that much. And he knew his lack of sleep made everything seem worse—even more final, somehow. Still, he couldn't stop his mind from churning. Around and around it went, a cement mixer loaded with problems that would not blend into a manageable whole. It was driving him out of his mind.

The relentless chime of the doorbell was punctuated by loud thumping.

"I'm coming, I'm coming."

He swung his legs over the side of the bed, probed for his slippers with his feet, and slid them on. After pushing himself up slowly from the mattress, he struggled with his bathrobe. Once it was on, he went to the window and pulled aside the curtain. What he saw outside made him gasp.

It was as if the glass had been sandblasted. The outside world had almost disappeared. He squinted into the night, but all that was visible of Cadogan Gardens, the private park for his row of houses, were the vague contours of the gate and hedgerow. The Cadogan Hotel across the way, usually a beacon of light, had disappeared. Even Sloane Street, which he could normally make out from where he stood, had been enveloped by the London fog.

He craned his neck forward as far as he could. As his cheek pressed against the cold glass, a shiver ran through him. He looked down. The two columns flanking the entrance to his eighteenth-century home gleamed in the dim light of the streetlamps.

From the window he could generally catch at least a glimpse of whoever was waiting in the portico. But not tonight. He couldn't see a thing. For the thousandth time, he cursed the city government for not installing new street lights since the Industrial Revolution. "Stupid limeys think the world hasn't changed since Dickens."

His breath had clouded the glass; he wiped it away. The pounding, and the doorbell, went on uninterrupted and seemed to grow ever more insistent. The heavy curtain chafed against his back and neck. He pushed aside the thick fabric and then pulled the curtain shut again with an irritated tug. Silence fell for a moment, as if the person below had heard the jangling of the curtain rings against the copper rod. After a few seconds the noise started up again.

Sighing, he headed out of the bedroom. In the doorway, he tightened the belt of his bathrobe. Running his hand along the wall, he found the light switch and flicked it on. For an instant he was dazzled by the glare of the chandelier on the white-tiled hall below. As he made his way to the staircase, the noise stopped. Dead silence. He cocked his head, like a dog hearing an unfamiliar sound. Nothing. He swore under his breath. But just as he was about to turn around, again he heard the pounding.

"Mr. Schoeller, are you there? Mr. Schoeller?" a muffled voice said.

Hesitantly, he descended the first few steps.

"Who's there?"

"Police. Open up, please, it's about your nephew."

"Alec?"

With a trembling hand he took hold of the banister, and as fast as his stiff legs could carry him, he made his way downstairs. On the bottom step, his foot slipped, and he flailed his arms, cursing. Once he'd recovered his balance, he raced to the hall table and snatched up his keys. The pounding had started again.

"Hold on, I'll be right there," he shouted, out of breath, as he opened the panel next to the front door. He punched the security code, then rose to the tips of his toes, peeping through the small pane of glass. The light from the hallway shone onto the reassuring metal badge of a police helmet. He turned the key in the lock and opened the door.

TWO

Alec woke with a start to the sound of his ring tone. He reached down to the floor, groping for the source of the blue glow. There on the tiny screen was Frank, staring him straight in the eyes from the Piazza San Marco, with a smile on his face and so many pigeons perched on his outstretched arms that he looked as though he might keel over. It was five thirty.

"Frank? Hello?"

The phone at the other end of the line fell to the ground with a bang, followed by a scraping sound. Alec pressed his cell phone tight to his ear; in the background he heard labored breathing. Then a cry of pain, so close, so loud, and so inhuman that he nearly dropped the phone. Alec shot to his feet, wedged the phone between his shoulder and his ear, and reached for his clothes.

"Hello, Frank? Is that you? Can you hear me?"

"You have to . . . come here."

Frank's voice was so soft that Alec barely recognized it. His moaning swelled into a tortured scream.

"What's wrong? Are you sick? Should I call an ambulance?"

"No!" came the sharp reply, followed by inaudible whispers.

"What? What's that?"

"Come here." Frank spoke with a rising inflection, like a small child who knows only a few words.

"I'm on my way. Don't hang up, all right? Stay on the line!"

Alec threw on some clothes and raced out of the room, grabbing his leather jacket from the banister as he passed. He rushed down the stairs and threw open the front door.

The fog shrouded him like a veil and eddied around his feet. He could barely see the other side of the road. The Victorian lampposts along the bank of the Thames shed an eerie light, and the smog muffled every sound but heightened the odors of the city, sharpening Alec's sense of impending doom. His heart was in his mouth as he pressed the phone to his ear.

"Are you still there?"

He heard nothing but faint panting.

"Hang in there, Frank. I'm getting in the car now. I'll be there in five minutes."

The empty streets gave his fears free rein. What on earth had happened? Why didn't Frank want him to call an ambulance? He floored the pedal, and the car shot forward.

In all the years his uncle had taken care of him, Alec had never experienced anything like this. His panic stemmed not just from the fear that something terrible had happened to his uncle, but also from his sudden awareness that he was responsible for Frank. It was a fact he had never faced up to before; after all, Frank had always been in perfect health. Alec was the one who got roaring drunk, tried to paint, and woke up Frank with late-night phone calls, in search of inspiration for the ultimate work of art. From the moment at the airport when that total stranger had lifted the seven-year-old Alec in his arms, the terms of their relationship had been fixed. For years, Alec had been taking advantage of his uncle's unconditional love. Nothing seemed to faze Frank. When Alec's reckless lifestyle had almost destroyed him, it was Frank who had been there for him, never scolding, always sympathetic.

The blinking amber traffic signals were like beacons in the foggy night. He tore down Kings Road, swerved around a group of drunken tourists, crossed Sloane Square, and entered Sloane Street at the same breakneck speed. Seconds later, he lurched to the left and hit the squealing brakes, bringing the car to a standstill on the sidewalk in front of 83 Cadogan Place. Flinging himself out of the car, he darted up the four steps to the entrance and was putting his key in the lock when the front door creaked open.

He stepped into the dim front hall. In the half darkness, the men and women in the eighteenth-century portraits that lined the walls seemed to be gazing down at him with proud, reproachful stares.

"Frank?"

His voice, more pinched than usual, echoed in the silence of the house. No answer. The door to the study was the only one open. Light shone through the crack, forming a triangle on the tiled floor. With quick strides, Alec went to the door and swung it wide. Then he stopped, rooted to the spot.

Frank was lying in front of the fireplace. His small, bright blue eyes caught Alec in an unswerving gaze. As his nephew rushed to his side, Frank moved his lips. He had managed to pull the duct tape off his mouth, and it was now dangling from his cheek. His fingers clasped the telephone. When he relaxed his grip, the phone slid across the wood floor, leaving a trail of blood.

Alec dropped to his knees and carefully removed the tape, taking in his uncle's condition. Frank's pajama top was torn open, and his torso was grooved with deep cuts. His stomach and his chest were smeared with blood, and with his left arm he clutched a book to his lower body, his knuckles white with effort. Alec took Frank's hand, provoking a howl of pain. Then he saw the blood oozing out of his uncle's nailless fingertips.

"My God, who did this to you?"

Frank rocked his head back and forth, a shudder running through his body. The look in his eyes was desperate.

"Everything's ruined, everything. They . . ."

"Take it easy. Wait."

Alec grabbed a cushion, which he slid underneath Frank's head. When he pulled his hand away, it was covered in blood. Gingerly, he turned Frank's face toward him, revealing a gaping wound on his temple, a perfect circle, as if someone had thrust a rod into his head with such force that the skull had caved in. Alec collected himself, choking back his emotions.

"I'm going to call an ambulance."

Frank slowly shook his head. "No . . . look. Here."

With a tremendous effort of will, Frank slipped his hand beneath the cover of the book. Alec cautiously opened it. Frank's hand lay fluttering on the yellowed paper.

"It'll be okay," said Alec. "Here, give it to me."

"No, look."

Frank dragged his hand off the page, revealing a drawing. Alec looked at the flower, its white petals flamed with red, as red as the bloody fingerprints that Frank had left on the page. The stem curved under the weight of the tulip in full bloom, as if its own beauty were too much for it.

"I see it. Now let go," Alec said, carefully prying the book out of Frank's hands and laying it down at his side. He leaned in close to Frank, whose breathing sounded shallow. His uncle's eyes were glazed, and a tremor passed through his body as he lifted his head and pointed a trembling finger at the book.

"Tulipa, tul . . ."

Frank's hand dropped to the floor with a thud. His head sank back, and he let out a moan. Still holding Alec in his piercing gaze, he took a deep breath and said, "The book, take the book. No police."

His eyelids began to droop.

"Frank?"

Alec could see the life seeping out of his uncle, flowing away down the contours of his body with each muscle that went slack. He grabbed him by the shoulder and shook him hard.

"Can you hear me?" he shouted. "Please, don't let this happen, Frank. Don't leave me here alone."

Muttering curses, he took out his cell phone and dialed the emergency number. He could barely choke out the words. "Help me, please, it's my uncle. He's badly hurt. Eighty-three Cadogan Place. Hurry, please hurry."

He tossed away the phone, tears streaming down his cheeks, and buried his face in his hands. Feeling Frank take hold of his forearm, he looked up.

"I'm so sorry," Alec whispered. "For everything."

"Careful . . . dangerous. I love you—"

The pain in Frank's eyes ebbed away, and his face relaxed. Though he was still staring at Alec, his eyes were now dull and lifeless.

Alec summoned all his courage, trying not to lose control. What was it Frank had said to him? Something about the book. What was he supposed to do with it? Get it out of there; no police, that was it.

He snatched up the book, ran outside, and jumped into his car. A frantic pull of the lever and the front trunk of the Porsche flew open. No sooner had he put the book inside than he heard sirens wailing in the distance. As they approached, he slammed the trunk shut, raced back into the house, and kneeled at Frank's side.

THREE

The man parked his car as close as possible to the railway bridge. As he climbed out, he wrinkled his nose in disgust. The stench of the river, copper mixed with decay, brutally invaded his sensitive nostrils. He buttoned up his coat and buried his nose deep in his scarf.

The trunk popped open, light spilling out of it. He unzipped the sports bag that lay there, filled it with the bricks heaped beside it, picked it up, and calmly made his way to the steps that led up to Grosvenor Bridge.

For the moment, the bridge was quiet and deserted. In an hour, the chaos of the morning commute would burst loose: crowded, foulsmelling train cars screeching past hurying pedestrians, all rushing to their offices like lemmings. To bosses they would have to satisfy, to coworkers they couldn't stand, to their dull, pointless lives.

He sniffed, a sense of superiority rushing through his veins and filling him with scorn. The supreme pleasure of watching people suffer, watching the life drain out of their bodies, was like nothing else in the world. He could never get enough of it, and he even got paid for it.

Halfway across the bridge, he peered over the railing, down into the surging waters of the Thames. After a few seconds, he tore his eyes from the hypnotic current and looked up. Through the dense fog, he tried to make out the Millennium Wheel on the opposite bank of the river, and managed to discern its faint outline. It reminded him of the scene in *The Third Man* in which the hero, Holly Martins, meets Harry Lime, a mercenary killer, on the Ferris wheel at Vienna's Prater Park. As they reach the top, Martins asks Lime how he feels about his victims. "Victims?" Lime says with a sneer. "Look down there. Tell me. Would you really feel any pity if one of those dots stopped moving forever?"

I'm just like Harry Lime, he thought. They don't mean a fucking thing to me. Not from a distance, and certainly not from close by. The smell of their bodies, the sounds they make, even the way they move—it makes me sick.

He ran his fingers through his short brown hair, which was damp with fog. As he looked down, he wondered how many pounds of human tissue, how many gallons of mucus, bile, and blood, the river had swallowed in its day. How many body parts—arms, legs, heads, trunks? Puzzle pieces. How many bloated purple corpses had bobbed to the surface and washed ashore on the slick brown banks of this watery grave? Always room for more, he said to himself. The more, the merrier. Then he reined in his wayward thoughts. He had to get out of there before the dots started swarming again, confronting him with their nauseating presence.

He opened the bag, sliding a brick into the far corner, and dropping another one into the police helmet. After zipping the bag shut, he grabbed the handles, took a quick look around, and flung it into the Thames. Far below he saw the splash; a little white spot appeared and was gone again. He turned away from the railing, listening intently. The sounds of the waking city reached his ears. The stink of exhaust fumes was growing fouler by the minute.

He thrust his hands in his pockets and strolled back toward his car, trying to imagine how the man would react when he found out it had all been for nothing.

FOUR

At the entrance to the Metropolitan Police Service, the New Scotland Yard sign turned swiftly on its axis, as if to suggest that the Met fought crime at the same dizzying pace. The silver letters gleamed against the gray stone background. A group of Chinese tourists were having their picture taken in front of the sign. As the photographer called out instructions, they spun along with it and burst into giggles.

Fifteen stories up, Inspector Richard Wainwright was swiveling back and forth in the chair at his desk. Holding a mug of tea in front of his face, he stared at his own image. WANTED, DEAD OR ALIVE! read the words under the photo. He knew that just then his wife would prefer him dead. It hadn't escaped him how insufferable he'd become, but his most recent case had left him shaken. He cleared his throat. A few days' leave, yes, that would be just the ticket. A long weekend at the seaside, Blackpool, maybe, where the salt wind could blow away the gruesome images he'd stored up over the years. On the other hand, seaside resorts always depressed him. Heaving a sigh, he scratched at the words OR ALIVE.

He put down the mug and started up his computer. With a click, he opened his mailbox, glumly watching it fill with messages sent to him since eleven P.M. the night before. He scrolled past minutes he would never read, press releases dotted with red exclamation marks and urgently requiring his approval, internal newsletters devoid of news, and a slew of forms he'd have to fill out. Then he clicked on the next-to-last e-mail, sent at 2:03 A.M. by the forensic pathologist who had performed the autopsy on Frank Schoeller. He opened the attachment and hit Print.

Half an hour later, he'd managed to wrestle his way through the medical jargon. Schoeller had died of a brain hemorrhage and internal bleeding. He also had five broken ribs, and the nails of three fingers had been torn off. The injuries to his upper body were too superficial to have caused his death.

"So it was something he knew? Or something he had? What the hell were you up to, Schoeller?"

Toward the end of the report, the pathologist noted that she'd discovered tiny flakes of gold foil on Schoeller's hands, which she planned to examine more closely. As for the source of the flakes, her working hypothesis was that he'd been holding a book, considering the clearly visible right angles in the blood on his two palms. Some of the blood on his fingers had also come off, and she'd found fibers suggesting that it had been absorbed by paper. There were no fingerprints on the body except those of the victim's nephew, Alec Schoeller.

Wainwright stapled the pages together and glanced out the window. The wind was propelling the raindrops slantwise across the glass toward the narrow, rusty gutter. More than a hundred feet below, a long line of cars crept by. Umbrellas floated down the streets like rainbow-colored circles.

He looked at his watch and stood up. A bulletin board covered much of the wall to his left. With his short nails, he pried out the thumbtacks. Five minutes later the floor was littered with photos, charts, maps, Post-its, and page after page of scribbled notes. He bent over, gathered them all together, and put the whole pile on his desk.

The girl in the topmost photo exposed her braces in a broad smile. She was tipping her head slightly to one side, and her brown hair fell to the shoulders of her school uniform. Her eyes were still puffy with sleep. Her name was Isabelle White.

"Izzy," he said softly.

She was the first of the six girls found in the past two years along the banks of Thames, their bodies viciously mutilated. They'd been treated like garbage, their expiration date depending on when their captor chose to deflower them. He'd tossed them out afterward, like spoiled goods.

In time they had caught the killer. He drew up schedules for secondary schools, constantly moving from one place to another. At each one, he chose a victim. He kept their uniforms in his closet, washed and ironed, as if it were the most normal thing in the world.

What had most disturbed Wainwright were the photos the killer had taken after abusing the girls. He had drawn makeup on their faces with indelible marker—red smears bloating their lips, wild streaks of blue covering their eyelids, and false lashes that curved up to their foreheads and down below their cheekbones. Staring into the lens, the girls looked like dolls, except for the heart-wrenching fear and pain in their eyes.

That was the first time in his career that a case had given him nightmares. "So pack it in," his wife said. "Take early retirement. You're getting too old for this sort of thing."

With a heavy sigh, he opened the Schoeller file. As he pulled out the photos and laid them in a stack, he decided to change his tactics. He would drop the courtesy he'd shown Alec the night his uncle died. Young Schoeller was hiding something, he was sure of it, and he'd find out what before the day was out.

He lined up the photos in order and left the room.

Alkmaar

The end of the Little Ice Age had reached the Low Countries. For centuries, the winters had been long and cold and the summers brief and
humid. This year was different. The heat had been unbearable for weeks,
and the nights were hardly cooler. The odor of sweating bodies drifted
out through the open shutters and hung in the streets like a vile blanket
smothering the town.

Cornelius flashed an irritated glance over his shoulder. The boy kept
slowing down and was now lumbering along about ten feet behind him.
They had no time to waste, and besides, he felt uneasy on the streets after what had just happened. He stopped and turned.

"Hurry up, Jacobus, we're late."

He gave the boy a moment to catch up, and they walked on together.

"You think he's still up?" Jacobus asked. "Maybe he's gone to bed."

"Don't you worry, he'll be awake, all right."

"You're sure?"

"Do you really think he would retire for the night without even knowing what happened? Mark my words, he'll wait. Now step lively, boy, we
must make haste."

"Yes, of course he wants to know, but I . . ."

Cornelius glanced at his companion's smooth chin. The boy had never
before shown any signs of fear, but now there was apprehension in his
voice. The orphanage had a good reputation, but of course you never

knew what went on behind closed doors. What Cornelius did know was that Adriaen Koorn, the director, ran his institution with an iron fist, maintaining the strictest order and discipline.

"Must I spell it out for you, Jacobus? Surely you understand that this was the only way to stop him?"

Cornelius wondered if they had made a mistake. Could Jacobus really keep silent about the act that now weighed on his conscience? If he spilled their secret, the consequences would be disastrous. Not just for him, but for others as well. He had wondered whether Adriaen had made a wise choice by assigning Jacobus to accompany him, for the boy was a bit naïve and slow-witted. But he had accepted the offer, because Jacobus was tall and as strong as an ox. In any case, there was no point in worrying about it now. The deed had been done, and there was no way back.

"No, I understand," Jacobus said. He bowed his head and gazed at his outstretched hands. Turning them over, he splayed his fingers and stared at the dried-up rivulets of blood that ran down the lines of his palm. With a groan, he rubbed his hands together, and minute specks of red dust whirled to the ground.

"I want to wash my hands."

"Come along, then, don't fall behind. The sooner we get there, the sooner you can wash them."

Cornelius ran his hands through his hair, reached back, and pulled a few damp strands out of his collar. Sweat was pouring down his face. The boy's petulant voice was starting to get on his nerves. He rubbed his belly, still feeling queasy.

How hard it had been for him. Wouter Winckel was his second cousin, and despite their differences, they'd been good friends. Four years earlier, when Elizabet had died in childbirth, of all those who'd been there to support Wouter, it was Cornelius who had found a wet nurse for the infant. They had shared many confidences. That was why it had come as such a shock when the orphanage director told Cornelius what Wouter was up to. Cornelius had dismissed it at first, thinking it no more than a rumor, for he'd always seen Wouter as a wise man. And more important,

Cornelius had always thought that he knew Wouter inside and out, that they kept no secrets from each other. But Adriaen had showed him proof of the contrary.

At first, Cornelius had been filled with disappointment, but in time that feeling had swelled into rage. How could Winckel have so betrayed his trust? Their years of friendship had evidently been a mere miscalculation, a farce, based on nothing but lies. In all their conversations about faith, and about their own beliefs, it seemed unlikely that Wouter had ever meant what he said.

Cornelius sighed. He knew God's hand had guided him and forgiveness would soon follow, but he hadn't expected it to be so hard. It wasn't the horror of the deed that shook him; no, that meant nothing to him. But he would miss Wouter's vitality and foolish jests, how freely he gave to others, and how he could laugh at himself. Cornelius had knocked on his old friend's door with hatred in his heart, but now he walked away aching with sorrow.

FIVE

The little elevator smelled of cigarettes and fried bacon. The menu for the week, loaded with carbohydrates and saturated fats, was on display behind a grimy sheet of plastic. Alec read the death notice next to the floor buttons: the detective had been buried five weeks ago; his wife and children would miss him; the family asked that no flowers be sent. Next to the card was an urgent appeal from the Scotland Yard rugby team, which was searching for new players. It included a phone number in case anyone was interested.

The elevator doors slid open to reveal a woman. As he stepped aside so that she could enter, she turned toward him and held out her hand. "Good morning," she said. "I'm Dawn Williams."

He came out of the elevator. The woman smiled. She was tall, almost as tall as he was, and her skin was the color of mahogany.

"You're here to see Inspector Wainwright?"

"Yes, I have an appointment."

She nodded. "I'm helping him with the investigation. Follow me, please."

Dawn led the way at such a rapid pace that he had to scurry to keep up with her. At the end of the corridor, she knocked on a half-open door.

"Mr. Schoeller's here to see you, sir." She backed up against the door to let him pass.

Wainwright was standing by the window, in front of a bulletin board so full of holes it looked like a woodworm colony. Daylight shone through his protruding ears, making them glow bright crimson and seem to float alongside his head. In his left hand, he was holding a box of thumbtacks.

"Mr. Schoeller, good to see you. Take a seat. Coffee, tea?" Dawn stood waiting at the door.

"No, thank you." Alec sat down, his eyes drawn to the bulletin board.

"Ah, yes, I was just getting started."

Wainwright bent over his desk and jotted down something on a piece of paper. Alec heard the door click shut behind him, and the little office filled with the pungent smell of ink and the squeak of the felt-tip pen.

"There." Wainwright pinned the note onto the board.

When Alec saw what it said, he grimaced and rose to his feet.

"'The Schoeller case,'" read Wainwright, folding his arms. They both stared at the words. Wainwright glanced at Alec and saw that his teeth were tightly clenched.

"I don't know why you wanted to see me again," Alec said crossly. "I don't know anything more than what I've already told you."

"Hmm. All the same, I'd like to go through it again, step by step, just in case we missed something—or perhaps I should say, in case you missed something."

"You're wasting your time."

"Why don't you let me be the judge of that, Mr. Schoeller?"

Wainwright turned toward Alec and took a step forward. He was standing so close that Alec could see the broken veins on his nose.

"The more we learn from everyone connected to your uncle, the sooner we can get this investigation under way and catch the culprit. I presume we have a common interest in finding out as soon as possible who committed this crime. You've probably read enough murder mysteries to know that the first few hours of the investigation are critical."

Wainwright's voice kept rising as he moved in even closer. Alec recoiled.

"Am I in your space, Mr. Schoeller? Well, you had no qualms about getting into mine with your friendly advice about how to spend my time. So if it's all right with you, I suggest we get down to work. Why don't you hand me those photos—one at a time, please—and I'll put them up."

Wainwright pointed at the pile on the desk. Alec went over hesitantly and picked up the one on top, a picture of the front door at Cadogan Place. A detective was crouched there, wiping the doorknob with a brush. Through the doorway, Alec could see himself standing in the hall. Wainwright plucked the photo out of Alec's hands, pinned it to the board, and tapped it with his index finger.

"One more time for the record, Mr. Schoeller. When you arrived, was the front door open?"

"Yes."

"We're assuming your uncle let someone inside. There's no trace of a break-in. We would even go so far as to say it was someone he knew. I don't suppose he was in the habit of opening the door to all and sundry in the middle of the night?"

"No, of course not."

"Any idea who it might have been?"

Alec shook his head and shrugged his shoulders.

"Mr. Schoeller, did your uncle have a lot of . . . hmm, how shall I put it . . . casual encounters? Might he have phoned someone to come over and, er, keep him company that night?"

"He didn't go for that sort of thing," Alec said, glaring at Wainwright.

"No, no. Fine. Next photo, please."

Alec put the picture in his outstretched hand.

"Right, the hallway. When you arrived, was the light on or off?"

"Off."

"And then what?"

Alec sighed. "We've covered all this before. The light was on in the study. That's where I found him."

"Dead?"

"Yes." A lump rose in his throat.

"Your uncle was tortured; you saw that for yourself. Any idea why? As far as you know, was he involved in anything . . . dubious?"

"How can you talk such rubbish? A seventy-five-year-old man dabbling in crime? What exactly do you have in mind? Let me guess. Drugs. I can just picture my uncle hopping from club to club with a briefcase full of cocaine, in search of customers. Or hang on, here's an even better one. He was into child pornography, or maybe he sold children into slavery. That's it. He smuggled Thai boys across the border, stole their passports, and set them to work in brothels until they dropped."

"Mr. Schoeller, I really—"

"No, no, wait." Alec held up his hand. "I'm not finished yet. But I am quite finished with your insinuations. This man was esteemed in the highest circles. He had friends in politics and the diplomatic corps. He taught me the meaning of respect and love. In fact, he taught me everything I know about living decently in this wretched world. And now you're suggesting he was some two-bit crook. Who do you think you are?"

"All right, all right, I know who I am," Wainwright said in a placating tone. "But what about Tibbens?"

Alec found himself momentarily speechless. "What about Tibbens?"

"What can you tell me about him?"

"I suppose you've spoken to him."

"Of course, but I'd like to hear more about him from you."

"What can I say? He's been in my uncle's service for more than thirty years. I've known him ever since I first came to live at Cadogan Place. He started out as a driver and never left. The only thing I really know about him is that he would have done anything for my uncle. That's how loyal he was."

"Anything? How far would he have gone?"

"What are you driving at?"

"This."

Wainwright went to the windowsill and picked up a brown envelope. Inside it was a photo, which he pinned to the board. It was Tibbens, staring straight ahead with a stoic expression and holding a sign with a number printed on it.

"What on earth . . ." Alec went up to the bulletin board and peered at the photo.

"Wilbur Tibbens has a criminal record. He was once arrested for assault."

"Assault? There must be some mistake." Bewildered, Alec looked at the photo again.

"No mistake, he beat a man half to death," Wainwright said sourly. "Not a pretty picture. I was thinking maybe he and your uncle had quarreled, and things got out of hand."

"Quarrel? Those two? If they had, my uncle would certainly have told me."

"Hmm. A different question. Had you noticed anything peculiar about your uncle lately? How was he doing? How was he feeling? Was his behavior out of the ordinary in any way?"

"No, not really."

"Not really?"

"I mean, no."

"Could his death have had anything to do with blackmail? How had he been acting recently? Did he seem upset about something, or easily distracted? Was he unusually irritable, perhaps, or nervous?"

"You don't have to spell it out for me; I get the picture."

"And?"

"And what?" Alec snarled.

"Was he being blackmailed?"

"For what? For being homosexual, you mean? That's impossible; he was always very open about that."

"Right. Give me those photos, and you can be in charge of these," Wainwright said gruffly, thrusting the box of thumbtacks into Alec's hand. He took a photo, held it up to the bulletin board with one hand, and extended his other hand toward Alec, waiting for a thumbtack.

Without turning around, he asked, "After you entered the study, what happened next?"

Wainwright stood motionless, blocking Alec's view. Then he stepped aside, and Alec felt his breath catch. He could feel Wainwright's eyes boring into him as he stared at the lifeless body on the parquet floor. He gulped and rubbed his eyes with his fingertips, then turned to Wainwright with a scowl.

"I told you all about it. He was lying by the hearth, and I ran over. When I saw the state he was in, I called the emergency number right away."

"Did you move the body or touch anything at all?"

"Well, obviously I touched him. I'm sure you can see that. I put his head up on a cushion and checked for a heartbeat. I . . . I tried to re-suscitate him, but it was too late."

"Are you sure about that?" Wainwright raised his voice and waved a finger at the bulletin board. "Look at his expression. Does he seem scared to you? Is that a look of fear? Is this a man who is staring his killer in the face? Here, look at these, and these."

The photos he tossed on the desk showed Frank's corpse from every conceivable angle. Wainwright moved in closer to Alec.

"Mr. Schoeller, I'll be perfectly plain. I've read the reports from the pathologist and the scene-of-crime officers. There are a couple of things that just don't match your version of events. I think you haven't been quite straight with me. I believe you're hiding something."

Alec swallowed. "Why would I do that?"

"Well, that's what I don't understand." He jabbed his finger into Alec's chest. "But you know all too well that some things don't make sense."

"Like what?"

"Like the bloody fingerprints your uncle left on one of his book-shelves. Just in one spot. That suggests he took something off the shelf after he was attacked. Presumably a book. The strange thing is, we couldn't find a single book with bloodstains."

"So supposing you're right about this. Why are you assuming I was the one to find it? Why not the murderer? Besides, given the state my uncle was in, do you really think he got up and fetched a book? It sounds pretty implausible to me."

"Is it possible he said something to you?"

"Said something? Is that the latest Scotland Yard investigative technique? Asking the corpse who killed it? He was dead when I found him. How often do I have to tell you that? I put a cushion under his head and gave him mouth-to-mouth and chest compressions."

"Why would you put a cushion under his head?"

"Sorry?"

"Mr. Schoeller, why would you put a cushion under his head? You enter the room, and there's your uncle, dead. The first thing you do is reach for a cushion and slide it under his head? It's simply absurd."

Wainwright saw Alec blink as he said, "Listen, it was just the first thing that popped into my head, to make my uncle as comfortable as possible."

"You wanted to make a dead man comfortable? Interesting. So you put the cushion under his head before you tried to do mouth-to-mouth."

"Yes."

"Because you thought he was still alive?"

"That's right."

"Is that helpful, putting a cushion under someone's head before you perform mouth-to-mouth? Is that what they taught you in your first aid course? First a cushion, then the kiss of life?"

"I don't know; I've never taken a—"

"The paramedics say you knew just what you were doing. Too bad, I was hoping you could help us work this out. Oh, well."

Alec shrugged. "I did say you were wasting your time on me."

"Mr. Schoeller, there's something you're not telling us. I don't know what it is, and I don't know why. But I'd like to make a deal with you. If you think of any way at all you could help, please contact us. Sleep on it, why don't you? Who stood to gain by your uncle's death—besides yourself, of course? Who would he let into the house at night? As soon as you think you have any information that might be useful to us . . ."

Wainwright fished a tattered business card out of his inside pocket and held it out to Alec.

"You mentioned in passing that I stood to benefit from his death." Alec slipped the card into his pocket. "If you suspect me of something, why don't you tell me to my face? I assume you've checked me out pretty thoroughly by now, so you know I don't need his money. I do quite well for myself, if I may say so."

Wainwright looked at him. It was true: He'd instructed Dawn to find out everything she could about Alec, and earlier that day he'd studied her report. Alec had been seven years old when his parents died in a plane crash. Frank Schoeller, Alec's paternal uncle, became his guardian and brought the boy to London. In later years Alec had studied history, but he never graduated, instead throwing himself into painting, a decision that proved financially rewarding. Since then, Alec Schoeller had become one of the top-selling artists in Western Europe. His paintings were hot items, fetching an average price of about two hundred thousand pounds apiece. Dawn Williams had also discovered that just a few years earlier Alec had spent six months in rehab, battling a cocaine addiction.

"Money's an odd thing, Mr. Schoeller. Not many people ever think they have enough of it—though it depends on their needs, of course." Wainwright shot Alec a meaningful look. "Besides, money's not the only possible motive. You know that as well as I. By the way, have you been told you can go into the house again? They've finished examining your uncle's body. I understand the funeral will be in Holland, so you can go ahead and make the arrangements."

He held out his hand. "See you around, Mr. Schoeller."

After the door shut with a bang, Wainwright went to the bulletin board and put up one last thing: a photo of Alec.

SIX

Standing beneath the awning at the entrance to Scotland Yard, Alec buttoned his coat and flagged down a cab. As he settled into the back-seat, he was suddenly overwhelmed by such a powerful wave of lone-liness that he thought he was going to scream. He dug his nails deep into his palms and pressed his weight into the cushion behind him. Calm down, he thought, calm down. After taking a few deep breaths, he leaned forward and closed the little window between himself and the driver.

His sense of powerlessness hung over him like a dense cloud, too impenetrable to breathe. It was back: the rage he'd thought was gone forever, that had haunted him since his earliest childhood. The rage at the thought of everything taken from him, at the desperate loneliness to which he was condemned. Wainwright's vulgar insinuations that he'd had something to do with his uncle's death only made it worse.

Alec pressed the switch, and the window slid down. The cold air rushed over his face as he closed his eyes.

Images of his life with Frank flashed through his mind. Alec's first, illegal driving lesson, late at night: maneuvering the stretch Mercedes around the empty parking lot of a soccer stadium and almost dozing off at the wheel, while Frank, in the seat beside him, was brimming with energy. Frank rushing out ahead of him in the twilight at Ber-mondsey Market, where he combed the antiques dealers' stalls with a flashlight in search of "hidden gems." His profile as he read to his nephew by the dim light of the bedside lamp. All the times Frank had held him and comforted him. These moments of happiness were burned into his memory.

He opened his eyes and felt his body crying out for something to ease the suffering, for a moment of oblivion. The need preyed on his weakness, and he felt himself plunging into the hollow, insatiable depths of his craving with such force that the pain was almost physical.

His cell phone bleeped; someone was texting him. He picked it up and saw a message from Damian: *Call me if there's anything I can do, and let me know what time you're getting in. I'll pick you up.*

Alkmaar

JULY 21, 1636

The Old Archery Hall was the most popular tavern in town, the pride of the Alkmaar Crossbow Archers' Guild. Its shutters were normally wide open, the aroma of a hot meal tempting passers-by. But now it was deep in the night, and the inn looked deserted.

Wouter Bartelmieszoon Winckel looked up with a start when he heard the pounding on the door. Before closing his ledger, he scribbled one last entry. Then, with a groan, he bent down to pick up the pouch that lay on the ground beside him. He filled it with the guilders stacked on the table, then hurried down the steps and crossed the taproom to the tavern door, where he undid the latch and threw open the shutters of the cross-casement window.

"Who goes there?" he asked, poking his head outside.

He saw the silhouettes of two men, one tall and broad shouldered, the other short and squat.

"Good evening, Wouter. It's Cornelius," the smaller man said, stepping forward and removing his hat.

"Oh, Cornelius, I didn't recognize you. What brings you here at this late hour?"

"I must speak to you. I know it's late, but this is a matter of great importance."

"All right, give me a moment. I need to finish up here."

Wouter closed the shutters and went to the open cabinet at the back of the taproom. The shelves had been removed and propped against the wall, and the pitchers, plates, and dishes were stacked on the tiled floor. He stepped into the cabinet, turned the key in the lock of the oak panel in the rear, and pulled it open.

The space was five feet high, five feet wide, and six feet deep. Wouter shuffled in on his knees, with a candlestick in one hand and his pouch in the other. The shelves on the right-hand wall sagged under the weight of the coins. He put the pouch on the bottom shelf and moved the candle to his left, illuminating a chest with dozens of tiny drawers. On the front of each drawer was a slip of paper inscribed with words and a few numerals.

Wouter smiled. Stretching his upper body as far forward as possible, he pressed his nose against one of the drawers. Through the perforations in the wood, the scent of damp earth reached his nostrils. He opened the drawer cautiously and cast an affectionate glance at the small, onion-shaped bulb inside it.

"The scent of freedom. The future of the world in a drawer," he muttered, carefully sliding it shut with his index finger. He crawled out of the hole feetfirst.

Before shutting the panel, he leaned forward again, holding out the candle as far as he could reach. The pamphlets lay stacked against the back wall. Again, Wouter smiled.

SEVEN

"Would you hurry up, Em? We really have to get going. It starts at three o'clock."

Damian's deep voice boomed down the long corridor of their canal-side town house, echoing from the marble wainscoting.

"I'm on my way. Another two minutes," a distant voice replied.

"Another two minutes? My God, she's taking forever. Why do women always take forever?"

Sighing, he checked his watch and turned to his chauffeur, who was standing beside him with his arms crossed and a faint smile on his lips.

"What are you smirking about? Care to let me in on the joke?"

"It's nothing, sir."

"Well, you can wipe that smile off your face. You'll have to work miracles to get us there on time."

He was worried. Alec had arrived in the Netherlands the previous morning. His appearance as he entered the arrivals hall had startled Damian. He had dark circles under his eyes, and his unshaved stubble cast shadows over his face. But what worried Damian most was his friend's look of furious determination.

He thought back to the moment many years ago when he'd seen Alec for the first time, on orientation day at their English boarding school. The new pupils were gathered in the courtyard of a medieval castle transformed into a finishing school for the children of well-to-do parents who envisioned international careers for their little darlings. Damian spotted Alec immediately, keeping his distance from the cliques that were forming with dizzying speed. The courtyard was mobbed with loud polo shirts and fresh faces, as if it had been overrun by a pack of young dogs, all the same breed. Alec, on the other hand, was nearly drowning in his gray-blue army coat, the fur collar turned up so high you could barely see his face. With his duffel bag at his feet, he looked more like a Russian soldier on his way to the front than a fifteen-year-old pupil at an elite British boarding school. Damian went up to him and held out his hand.

"Hello, I'm Damian Vanlint."

"Alec Schoeller."

Alec's broad, paint-flecked hand felt rough in Damian's.

"Where are you from, Alec?"

"London. How about you?"

"Oh, I'm from Holland."

"That'll come in handy," he replied in Dutch. "We can speak Dutch when we don't want to be understood."

Alec grinned at the startled expression on Damian's face.

"I've been living with my uncle in London since I was seven, but I'm originally from Holland too."

"Is that Dutch I hear?" said a soft voice with a slight French accent.

The two boys stared at her in surprise.

"You're Dutch too?" Damian asked.

"That's right," she said. "Well, half Dutch, anyway. How do you do? I'm Emma. Emma Caen."

Damian was jolted out of his reverie by the sound of approaching footsteps. The door at the end of the hallway opened, and his wife came walking toward him, her high heels clicking on the marble floor. He gazed tenderly at her, recalling Frank's speech at their wedding.

"My dear friends Emma and Damian, I have a confession to make. I'm jealous. Or, rather, I'm envious. What's the difference, you ask?

Let me explain. I wish you all the happiness in the world. But I'm envious because I don't have the love that you share. I'm delighted you found each other, I truly am, but I'd like the same thing you've got. That's what I'm trying to say. Your love for each other, the love that shines within you, has touched all our hearts. Just take a look around you."

Frank held out his arm and gestured toward the guests in front of the stage. Hundreds of faces were beaming up at them, full of expectation.

"But love entails responsibility," Frank continued. "You'll have to make a life together. And I do mean together. Don't let each other down. Good times are sure to come; you can take that as a given. But don't forget that sooner or later there'll be bad times too. And then you can look back to this moment and remember . . . me."

Hooting with laughter, Frank raised his glass.

"But now it's time for a toast. To the bride and groom!"

"Come on, we have to go." Damian's voice was subdued. Emma looked him in the eyes and caressed his cheek.

"Worried?"

"Mm-hmm."

"About Alec?"

He nodded. Standing on tiptoe, she gave him a kiss and nuzzled his chin with her nose.

"It'll be fine," she murmured. "He'll pull through."

The chauffeur opened the side door in the hall, and they passed through a narrow corridor into the private garage. He took the key ring out of the box that was mounted next to the door and pressed on the car key. The doors of the Maserati Quattroporte parked next to the silver-gray Aston Martin opened with a click.

EIGHT

Right, now Schoeller and then I'm done for the day, the funeral director thought as he made his way to the men's room. Zorgvlied was not his favorite place to work; something about the cemetery put him on edge. Most funerals went well, but in recent years it had been so busy that mourners occasionally found themselves weeping over a total stranger, as if they'd walked into a cinema and found out after fifteen minutes that they were watching the wrong movie.

Zorgvlied's popularity was growing, and there was precious little they could do about it. It was partly the country's aging population—and of course, the beauty of the place—but it was also the management's willingness to tolerate ostentatious obsequies and eccentric headstones.

Two hours had been reserved for the event. Because the mourners would include dignitaries and celebrities, he'd been forced to check the route to the grave earlier that day with a clutch of security guards, who goose-stepped after him in black two-piece suits and headsets. A few were now waiting at the open grave.

He pulled the door of the men's room shut behind him.

"Are you there?"

The hiss of static. "Yes, I'm in the parking lot," his assistant said. "Over."

"And? Is there space for everyone?"

"Well, most of them have chauffeurs, so we should be okay. Over."

"Lucky for us. I'll see you inside."

Schoeller was lucky too, he thought as he looked into the mirror, lucky there was still a place for him. He straightened his tie. The section of the cemetery designed by landscape architect Jan David Zocher was in great demand—unsurprisingly, given the charm of its magnificent trees and the sandy paths that wound between the graves.

He pulled his cuff links out of his sleeves and headed for the main entrance, passing through the assembly hall on his way. When he reached the door of the hall, he looked back. On the far wall, the little red light was weaving back and forth. The other camera was in the lobby, just inside the building, above the table where friends and relatives would come to sign the register.

Half an hour later, every seat in the hall was filled. Tight rows of mourners stood packed along the walls. All eyes were on the coffin, adrift in a sea of flowers. On an easel next to it was a picture of Frank, gazing out at all his guests in black and white with a smile on his face and a skeptical twinkle in his eye, as if wondering whether he really merited so much attention. Tango music issued from the speakers.

The murmuring died down when the first speaker stepped to the microphone. Thirty minutes, three speakers, and dozens of superlatives later, Alec came forward. He was quick to debunk the myth of the paragon of virtue in the casket.

Frank, he explained, had been stubborn as a mule, a know-it-all, fiercely loyal, full of energy, and possessed of a sense of humor that some people thought too dark, too cynical. He'd been a bon vivant who knew no limits, a materialist with a heart of gold, a ruthless businessman, and a loving uncle. At the end of his speech, Alec gazed into the crowd with fire in his eyes.

"Everyone here knows that Frank moved to England because his parents wouldn't accept him for who he was. He never once regretted his decision, but that doesn't mean it was easy. The first few years were especially lonely for him. Yet he pressed on and eventually achieved what he'd hoped for when he went to England: a life of beauty, happiness, and freedom. When I was seven years old, Frank took me into his home and into his heart, and became like a father to me. Now it's my turn to be there for Frank. I will press on, just as he always did, until I find out who committed this ghastly crime. I will not rest until the killer has been brought to justice." He paused for a moment and pointed at the people in the room. "You are my witnesses."

After a few seconds, the shocked silence gave way to uneasy shuffling and scattered coughs. At a sign from the funeral director, the guests rose to their feet, and the doors of the hall opened. Six men surrounded the coffin, slid it onto a bier, and solemnly wheeled it out. The guests slowly filed toward the exit, each taking a glass of champagne as they passed the table by the door, and followed the coffin out into the cemetery.

Alec felt as though he had shaken thousands of hands. All he was conscious of was the palms of those hands, some limp and sticky, others firm and dry. He could feel every callus, the moisture, the pressure, as if all his senses were focused on those moments of physical contact. Little else penetrated his consciousness.

He couldn't shake off the image of Frank sprawled on the floor as he had found him. He felt suffocated and longed to get away. Away from the crowd, and the sickly sweet miasma of perfume and aftershave. Away from all the people who were smothering him with kisses— their saliva mingling on his cheek—and trying to console him, or looking for consolation he couldn't give. The only thing he wanted was to walk back to the grave with Emma and Damian—and nobody else—to bid Frank one last farewell.

"Mr. Schoeller?"

He looked up.

"Mr. Schoeller, first of all, my condolences on your loss." Wainwright spoke without emotion. "I'm really very sorry." Dawn stood behind him and off to one side, nodding in agreement.

"Thank you."

Wainwright coughed. "About what you said in there. I hope you'll leave things to us from here on in. People can't just go conducting their own investigations; I'm sure you understand that. We're trained professionals. This is our job. Maybe your emotion got the better of you, but—"

"Of course," Alec interrupted, "I just got carried away. I wouldn't dream of starting my own investigation. I'll leave everything to you." He underlined his words with a dismissive wave of the hand.

"Good, good, that's what we're here for, just wanted to get that straight. No room for amateurs in this line of work."

Pulling out a handkerchief, Wainwright pretended not to notice the look in Alec's eyes. He blew his nose intently.

"Oh, and I wanted to mention that we'll be taking the video of the service back with us, so that we can start analyzing it."

Dawn nudged Wainwright, murmuring, "The list."

"Ah, yes. Have you had a chance to get that list for me?"

"Yes. I have it right here."

Alec reached into his breast pocket and pulled out four folded sheets of paper. His eyes followed the two detectives as they left the reception hall.

"Who were they?" asked Damian, who had joined Alec with Emma at his side.

"My friends from Scotland Yard."

"Scotland Yard?" Damian stared at him in surprise. "What are they doing here?"

"They asked if they could come. They wanted to film everyone who came to the service, and they also asked for everybody's name."

"Why?" Emma asked. "Do they think Frank's killer could be here, now? It was a burglary, right? That's what you said."

Alec said nothing.

"Alec?"

"Well, actually, there are a couple of things I haven't told you yet."

"What sort of things?" Damian asked.

"I'll tell you later, when we get back to the house, okay?" Alec looked around. The last remaining guests were headed out the door.

"Come on, let's go say good-bye to Frank."

Alkmaar

Just as Cornelius was growing impatient, he heard a metallic jingle, followed by the scrape of a key in the lock. He pressed his hand to his thigh to stop its incessant trembling. Sweat ran down his back, soaking his undershirt. He could smell the fear on the boy, Jacobus, who was standing just behind him.

The door of the inn swung open. Wouter Winckel's stout form filled the doorway.

"Cornelius, come inside, my friend," he bellowed. "Good to see you. And who's this you have with you?"

"Evening, Wouter, good to see you too," Cornelius said, stepping to one side. "This is Jacobus, Jacobus Riemers."

Wouter gave the young man a friendly smile. "Welcome," he said and waved them inside.

Cornelius slipped past Wouter's ample paunch. As Jacobus went by, Wouter wrinkled his nose. Even after the boy had entered the inn, the foul odor of sweat lingered by the door as if it hated to see him go and hoped to draw him back outside again.

Jacobus was the first to enter the taproom. The smell of pipe tobacco and stale beer assailed his nostrils. He looked around, surveying the paintings and prints that filled the walls: ships at sea, landscapes, portraits, and still lifes. The dark brown, black, and gilded frames were closely packed together, and the walls seemed to groan under the weight of it all.

The left-hand wall was filled with a single group portrait, militia guards in full regalia. It was clear that each guard had paid for his own portrait. The wealthier guildsmen had been portrayed in full, while the less prosperous ones were visible only from the shoulders up. As Jacobus walked past the painting, the men's eyes seemed to follow him.

"Have a seat." Wouter was standing at one of the tables in the middle of the room, moving the stools from the tabletop to the floor with practiced ease. Then he pulled the two candlesticks toward him and lit the candles.

"Something to wet your whistle?" he asked, making his way to the bar. When he returned to his guests, he had three mugs in one hand and a pitcher of beer in the other. After filling the mugs, he sat down.

"So, gentlemen, how can I help you?"

Wouter's light blue eyes gazed amiably at them, his copper-colored curls spilling over his shoulders and cascading down his broad white collar. The ends of his chestnut-brown mustache curled proudly upward. His goatee came to a sharp point, the result of constant tugging and twisting.

Wouter Winckel was one of the richest men in Alkmaar. At first sight, he was dressed no differently from the town's other innkeepers, but the fabric of his trousers and his smock was of a much higher quality. The silver buckles on his shoes proclaimed that he was very wealthy indeed.

Jacobus had not yet said a word. He kept his eyes fixed on Wouter, like a cat getting ready to pounce. Sweat trickled over his temples, pearled on his downy upper lip, and collected on the pimples along the edge of his mouth.

Cornelius glanced at Jacobus, and seeing the look in the boy's eyes, gave him a sharp kick in the shin. If Wouter smelled a rat, it would make their job that much more difficult, and it was hard enough already. They had to avoid raising the slightest suspicion.

Jacobus's face clouded for a moment. Then the boy slumped back and began to look around with a semblance of interest. His eyes lingered far too long on the large cabinet against the back wall of the taproom, and Cornelius gave him another kick, keeping his eyes on Wouter.

"To your health, my friends. I bid you welcome on this beautiful, warm summer night," Wouter said, taking a swig of beer.

"My apologies for bursting in on you at this hour, but I have something to ask you, something of the very greatest importance. I hope you will answer me frankly."

Wouter's eyebrows shot up.

"Rest assured, Cornelius, I would never lie to you. Now, out with your question."

Cornelius cringed imperceptibly. Even now, he hoped it wasn't true, that the whole story had been made up by some despicable rogue jealous of the fortune that Wouter had amassed in recent years. Or perhaps there had been some mistake. Yes, he hoped with all his heart that it was just an idle rumor. That the guilty party was not Wouter but somebody else. That the whole affair actually had nothing to do with him. Then he wouldn't have to go through with this business.

"It's about the pamphlet," Cornelius said softly, looking Wouter straight in the eyes.

"What pamphlet do you mean? New ones come out every day, and they drop them off here by the dozen. You know how it goes. Sometimes they're full of nonsense or outright lies, but sometimes they tell the truth. Which one are you referring to, precisely?"

"I think you know exactly what I mean, so there's no point in feigning ignorance," Cornelius said with sudden vehemence, narrowing his eyes. "I mean the pamphlet everybody's talking about, the one that has the whole town up in arms. The pamphlet they say you wrote and distributed. That's the one I'm talking about."

"I still have no idea what you mean. You're being awfully vague," Wouter said calmly.

"The pamphlet in which you deny the existence of God and idolize science instead. In which you not only equate nature with the Divine but glorify nature as if it were God himself. And in which, worst of all, you claim that man can take God's place!" Cornelius made the sign of the cross. "That's what I'm referring to. Is that blasphemous pamphlet really your work, as people say it is?" His face was contorted with anger and his eyes flashed fire. As Cornelius spoke, Wouter leaned farther over the table. His face was flushed.

"Ah, now I understand which pamphlet you mean. Yes, I'm familiar with it. In fact, I read it with great interest. There's no law against that, is there? But what makes you think it denies the existence of God? Either you haven't read it carefully, or you haven't understood it properly. And besides, what gives you the idea that I have anything to do with it—let alone that I wrote it myself?"

Wouter regained his composure and laid his hand on his friend's.

"Cornelius, you know better than anyone else what I think of the church, but that's never hurt our friendship in the least. As far as I'm concerned, you can believe whatever you like. I believe freedom of thought is mankind's greatest treasure, and I always had the impression you felt the same way."

Cornelius jerked his hand away from Wouter's.

"Can we possibly be talking about the same country?" He spat the words across the table. "The same republic? Are you really so short-sighted? Don't you see where this will lead? Nothing is permitted to us, do you realize that? Nothing. We cannot move freely or talk freely. We are under attack from all sides. We cannot think or write or be who we wish to be. When we pray to our Lord, we must do so in secret so as not to offend anyone. So we huddle together in clandestine churches no bigger than closets, in musty, stinking attics, always behind closed doors. They treat us like animals!"

"I know, I know," Wouter said reassuringly. "It hasn't gone unnoticed. I'm aware of all the obstacles you face. They're certainly troubling, but on the other hand—"

"There is no other hand. What you don't realize, what no one seems to realize, is that things are getting worse every day. Soon we'll have nowhere left to go. Nowhere! And that pamphlet of yours will only make things worse. It's a weapon in the hands of our enemies. You know that perfectly well. Better than anyone."

"What do you want me to say?" Wouter asked, seething with rage. "That I wrote it? You must have a very high opinion of me. Imagine me, an innkeeper, a man of humble birth, writing a pamphlet that inflames all who read it, whether they agree or disagree. I'm actually flattered you'd think I'm the author, because I have little quarrel with its contents. In truth, I agree with almost everything it says. But it does surprise me that you, of all people, were persuaded to confront me about this. Couldn't they find anyone else? Who put you up to it? What are you hoping to achieve with this conversation? Or did you volunteer for the job? You should be ashamed of yourself."

With these words, Wouter stood up, kicking aside his stool. He slammed his fist on the table, and the heavy keys on his belt clanged against the wood.

"We are family, Cornelius, but I thought we were friends too. It seems I was wrong. And now I would like you to leave my inn."

By now, Cornelius and Jacobus had risen to their feet, and in the faint glimmer of the candles the three men glared at one another.

NINE

They made their way through the deserted cemetery to the grave. In just a day, the late summer had flown. The trees were bare and leaves lay underfoot—a moist, colorful carpet. Toadstools had appeared in the most unexpected places. It was six o'clock in the evening, and the sky was almost dark. Despite the maze of footpaths, it was easy to find the place. The women mourners wearing high heels had sunk into the sandy ground with every step, and trails of little holes now showed the way.

"How're you holding up?" Damian glanced at his best friend's ashen face and wondered whether Alec was really up to this.

Alec met his eyes. "Don't worry, I'll be all right."

"What you said back there about going after the murderer, did you really mean it?" Emma asked, slipping her arm through Alec's.

"Yes. There's a lot more to this than the police realize, but I can't tell them everything, not just yet."

"What are you talking about?" Damian stopped abruptly in the middle of the path. "Hold on a second. What do you mean, you can't tell them everything? Don't you want them to catch the culprit as soon as they can?" He gripped Alec firmly by the shoulder. "If you're withholding information, the police won't be able to track down Frank's killer. Can't you see that?"

Alec twisted angrily out of Damian's grip.

Emma said, "He's right. For goodness' sake, whatever you know, you should tell them. There's no point in keeping things to yourself. I mean, why would you?"

Alec rubbed his forehead. "I wish you two would have a little more faith in me. Can we just drop it for now, please?" His tone was brusque. "You don't know enough about it to jump to conclusions like this. But I don't want to go into it here. When we're back at the house, I'll tell you everything I know. All right? Then you'll understand. Then you can tell me what you think I should and shouldn't say to the police. That's what you want, right, to second-guess every decision I make? Well, you'll have your chance soon enough."

"Listen to me, Alec. The only thing Emma and I want to do is help you. You know as well as I what kind of trouble you could get yourself into. Don't try to tell me you've got it all under control."

"Tell me, Damian, how long will I have to put up with this? How long are you going to to keep putting me down?"

"Oh, come off it," Emma said, exasperated. "Let's not do this here. If you're determined to have it out, at least wait until we get home. You're acting like children, both of you. And Damian, don't drag me into your arguments, all right? Come on, it's this way."

They stood together in silence. The grave was ringed with flowers, and empty champagne glasses stood at odd angles on the uneven surfaces of the surrounding headstones, as if in some macabre wine bar.

After Damian had adjusted the ribbons on some of the wreaths, Alec lowered his head and said, "Frank, I'm sorry for everything I put you through. For all the grief I caused you. I'm so very sorry." Then he lifted his face and clenched his fists. "I'll get you, you bastard. You just wait."

"Alec, please stop this, I'm begging you. What would Frank say if he could hear you now? He wouldn't want you putting yourself in danger. Leave it to the police. Tell them everything you know, and let them do their job."

Alec spun around to face Damian. "Damn it, would you cut the condescending bullshit? Frank was murdered. I found him. He called me, asked for my help, but I got there too late. I was just . . . too late. If I'd made it there faster, maybe he'd still be alive, maybe they could have still helped him, but it took me too long to get there. If I'd still been living with him, this would never have happened. Never."

"All I'm trying to say is—"

Emma lifted her hands. "Shut up, both of you. Alec, there's no point in that kind of thinking, and anyway, it just isn't true. It's over and there's absolutely nothing you can do about it. Frank would hate to see you like this and hear you talk this way. You did everything you possibly could."

"No, that's just it, I didn't. I could have done so much more." Sorrow tinged his voice, and his eyes grew moist. "You should have seen him, it was terrible. The state he was in, lying there on the floor. I can't just let it go. This is nowhere near over. Besides . . . I'm doing it because he asked me. He asked me to help him."

Damian's mouth dropped open. "He asked you? You mean he spoke to you?"

Alec slowly shook his head.

"Alec?"

"Later, back at the house. I'll tell you the whole story."

He had seen them heading toward the grave and started after them. The thick layer of leaves absorbed the sound of his footsteps. While they stood by the grave, he hid behind a nearby tombstone, following their conversation word for word.

Now he crept back silently. As fast as he could, he headed for the assembly hall. He'd heard enough; it was time to act. Alec Schoeller knew something, but what? He hoped that it wasn't too late, that it would still be there.

TEN

Dawn gripped the back of the passenger seat and pulled herself forward. "Alec Schoeller has nothing to do with the murder. Everything points away from him. It's obvious the man is beside himself with grief. No, my intuition tells me that—"

"Just a minute. That's not what I call professional. I'm not used to seeing you like this." Wainwright turned to face her. "Don't give me one of those whatever-you-say looks. I'm on to you. Believe it or not, my instincts are every bit as keen as yours; it's not as complicated as all that. I can see straight through the lot of you."

"The lot of you? What are you talking about?"

"Listen, here's how it works. You take a man, a nice tall one with broad shoulders. Then put some muscles on him, all in the right proportions, of course. Not too large, not too small—just right. Then add two big brown eyes and a full head of dark brown hair. Make sure there are no thin patches or, heaven forfend, bald spots." He ran his hand over his own head. "No, what you need is a good crop of hair covering the whole head. A few tears running down his cheeks and voilà! You're all eating out of his hand. Especially if he's filthy rich, like Schoeller."

"Right," Dawn replied, "because even though research has shown that women are more empathetic than men, everyone knows we're blinded by appearances. I honestly hadn't expected such simplistic reasoning from you."

"Simplistic? I'll tell you what's simplistic. You don't even realize when you've been taken in by someone's looks. How simplistic is that? You know how many born actors there are in this world who've never set foot on the stage? Simplistic. Come on, I'd expected more of you. How many years have you been on the job? Well?"

She shrugged stoically and stared out the window. The low, flat fields of Holland were racing by. In the distance, a yellow train with blue stripes sped across the landscape. She narrowed her eyes to slits, and the yellow and blue faded into the green of the pastures.

Wainwright rubbed his nose. The cardboard fir tree hanging from the taxi's rearview mirror gave off a chemical odor that irritated his sensitive nostrils. If anyone stood to gain from Frank Schoeller's death, it was Alec. Frank was leaving his nephew a fortune.

Wainwright turned to face Dawn. "Got the tapes with you?"

"Yes, sir," she said, still staring out the window as she held up a plastic bag.

"Oh, hurt your feelings, have I? You do understand what I'm getting at, though, don't you?"

"Understood, sir."

"Good. As soon as we get back, I want you to take a very good look at those tapes. Let's put a name to every face and run every name through the computer."

"Do you really think the murderer was wandering around there? All the evidence suggests it was a professional, right? Every fingerprint found on the scene has been identified. And if you look at what he did to Schoeller, it seems perfectly clear that—"

"Just do what I say, okay? I want you to concentrate on the guests. Pay attention to what they do, how they react. The smallest details could be crucial."

Dawn turned back to the window. Wainwright had an excellent record, and in the four months that they'd been working together, she'd learned more than in all the years before, soaking it all up like a sponge. But for the past few weeks—in fact, ever since they'd caught the serial killer—she'd sensed he was off his game. He seemed distracted and quick to anger—quicker than usual, anyway.

The week before, entering his room without knocking to pick up a file from his desk, she'd found him standing in front of his bulletin board. He didn't notice her when she came in and stood running a finger over the photo of the first murdered girl.

"Don't you think it's time to put them away?" she said carefully.

Without turning around, he said, "That won't be necessary." His voice had a defeated tone. "They're already gone."

Dawn had shut the door softly behind her.

ELEVEn

It was hot in the car, and no one spoke. Dim light filtered in through the tinted windows. From the backseat, Emma stared at Damian's profile. He turned around.

"You all right?"

"Yeah, sure."

He reached back and she took his hand.

"You two have no idea how happy you made Frank by getting married," Alec said softly, gazing out the window. Then he smiled at Emma. "Took you long enough."

Emma's face turned red. She lowered her eyes and withdrew her hand. A pang shot through her stomach. She'd never thought she had it in her to love two men—so much, but in such different ways. From the moment she'd seen Damian on the schoolyard fifteen years ago, she'd known he was the one for her. With his solemn, almost aristocratic bearing, he seemed to have stepped straight out of a nineteenth-century novel. She introduced herself. He brushed back his long blond hair and extended his hand. His light gray eyes regarded her with friendly curiosity. His face was calm and thoughtful, and he exuded a natural authority. When she looked into his eyes, all her worries about the first day of school melted away like spring snow. She felt as if she could take on the world.

After shaking Damian's hand, she'd turned to Alec, and her breath had caught. His eyes were so dark they seemed black. His gaze penetrated her soul, probing all her weaknesses and frustrations. In the blink of an eye, he understood her, knew everything about her. Her hand trembled as she put it in his, and the blood rushed to her cheeks.

But she'd been only fifteen years old then, a starry-eyed teenage girl who devoured English novels and fell hopelessly in love with their heroes: Heathcliff, Mr. Darcy, Mr. Rochester. So after all these years, why couldn't she get him out of her mind? Every time she knew she'd see him, her stomach tied itself in knots and wouldn't come untangled until he had left. It drove her crazy. It stood between her and Damian, even now. There was no way she could keep this up for the rest of her life. The less she saw of him, the better. Every time they met, she hoped from the bottom of her heart that the old feelings wouldn't flare up again.

The car sped through the narrow streets along the canals, skimming past the rows of reddish-brown bollards that lined the sidewalks. Now and then, the chauffeur slowed down to pass a cyclist or pedestrian. As they made their way down the Herengracht, Emma looked across the canal and watched the three-hundred-year-old buildings glide past. The chauffeur hit the brakes again, coming to a stop in front of a whitewashed house. He tapped the remote control, and the garage door slowly slid open.

A few moments later, in the live-in kitchen, Alec took a seat in one of the two chairs by the fireplace. Emma plopped down on the large cushion beside him and pulled off her shoes. On the dinner table were trays of hors d'oeuvres and a silver ice bucket that held a bottle of wine.

"Right, now you can tell us exactly what happened that night," Damian said, pouring three glasses of wine.

Alec stared at the floor. Emma got up and perched on the arm of his chair.

"If we can help, we will. You know that," she said. She ran her hand over his back and felt his muscles quiver at her touch. Pulling her hand away, she said, "But we can't do anything until you tell us what's going on."

"Yes, you're right, but I needed some time to think it over." He cleared his throat. "I'm afraid the things I know could put you in danger. On the other hand, maybe that's just my imagination. I know there's something wrong, something strange going on. But . . . I don't understand what. I can't figure it out."

His elbows on his knees, Alec went on. "What I'm about to say is for your ears only. Will you promise not to say a word to anyone? Not just because of what Frank told me, but because I think someone was after him, someone who wanted something he had. Now, that same person is probably coming after me."

"Why do you think that?" Damian asked.

"Because Frank gave me something."

TWELVE

After Alec had told Damian and Emma about finding Frank and described the marks of torture on his uncle's body, their eyes grew wide and a hush fell over the room.

"He must have been in agony," Emma said, breaking the silence. "How could he stand it?"

Alec turned to face her. "We don't know whether he could. Maybe he broke down and told them something. The question is, what?"

He got up, threw a log on the fire, and prodded the embers with a poker. "Just a couple of weeks ago, I had dinner with Frank. I could tell he was worried about something. I even asked him what was wrong, but he said it was nothing." He looked at Damian. "Did he say anything to you?"

Damian shook his head. "What kind of filthy coward could do a thing like that to an old man? Why didn't you call us right away? Then we could've—"

"No, I wanted to think about it first, get everything clear in my mind." He sat down again. "A few minutes after I called, the police and the ambulance arrived. They tried their best, but it was too late." He heaved a deep sigh. "That's when the whole circus began. A couple of hours later they took him away. Wainwright, the one from Scotland Yard, showed up at some point and started giving me the third degree, asking whether I had seen or heard anything, whether I had any idea who had done it or why. There was no stopping him. It nearly drove me insane. Around eight A.M., Tibbens got there, and they started interrogating him too.

"What did you tell them?" Damian asked.

"Everything I knew, which wasn't much."

"You said Frank had given you something."

Alec rose to his feet. He picked up his weekend bag, which was next to the chair, and set it on the kitchen table.

"Yes, he was holding on to it. I'd like you to take a look." He opened the bag. "Frank wanted me to hide it from the police, so I put it in my car. I don't know what he was trying to say by giving it to me. I can't make head or tail of it."

Damian unfolded the newspaper.

The bookbinder had let his imagination run wild. In each corner, two leaves were impressed into the red morocco and filled in with gold. Their stems met in the middle. Along each side there was a subtle inward curve, interrupted by a whorl of gold. At the center, the leather was tooled with a gilt wreath of flowers. The curves, flowers, and garlands formed a magnificent golden frame on the supple kid leather.

"Oh, my God," Emma said when she saw the streaks of blood. She clapped her hand over her mouth.

"He was holding it so tightly I had to wrest it out of his hands," Alec said in a choked voice.

Damian stared at the binding. When Emma reached for it, he seized her wrist. "No, wait. Don't touch it. I'll be right back."

As he hurried to his study, Damian's heart was racing, and he knew it was not only because of Frank's blood on the cover. The sight of the book had excited him. He could tell it must be an exceptional find. Frank's taste had been impeccable, and he'd passed on his love of antiques to Damian during the boys' many visits to Cadogan Place, when the three of them would comb London's antiques markets in the hours before dawn. Frank would arm his protégés with a flashlight, and the game was afoot. He'd noticed right away that Damian had a knack for finding the rare treasures hidden among the trash. The boy drove a hard bargain too. Meanwhile, Alec would trail behind them, bored and peevish, listening to his Walkman.

If Damian had not met Frank, he would never have become an antiques dealer with two thriving shops of his own. Books weren't his specialty, but he knew a thing or two about them. Enough, at any rate, to see that this one was a few hundred years old.

He opened his desk drawer. When he returned to the kitchen, he had a pair of white cotton gloves and a V-shaped book cradle. He found Alec and Emma bent over the book.

"The oils on our fingers could damage it," Damian said, slipping on the gloves. He carefully picked up the book.

"I'd say it's damaged already." Alec pointed at the blood on the cover.

Damian didn't respond but held the book loosely in his hands to determine the angle of opening. The pages fell open, and as soon as he saw the illustration he realized what he was holding. He lowered the book gently into the cradle, which he had adjusted earlier, and closed it again. Then he lifted the cover, holding the upper right corner between his index finger and thumb. The leather creaked softly, and the first page clung to it. Carefully, he took a corner of the page and very slowly started pulling it free. Alec muttered a curse and shot forward. He snatched the book out of the cradle and pulled the page loose in one swift tug, almost tearing it in two.

"Christ, what are you doing?" Damian said. "Get a grip on yourself."

"What do you mean, take it easy? I don't give a damn about that book. Do you really think I care how much it's worth? Here," he said, tapping his finger on the page. "Here it is. This is what Frank was pointing at. I think this is the key to the whole thing."

They stared at the bloodstained page.

Alkmaar

At a sign from Cornelius, Jacobus shot forward, grabbed Wouter by his goatee, and pulled him so far across the table that their noses almost touched.

"You heard him, Winckel. We know what you have on your conscience. You're going to get what blasphemers like you deserve."

Wouter gripped the corners of the table and tried to pull himself free. His chin felt as if it were on fire. He yelped with pain, his eyes fixed on Cornelius, who stood beside the table with a shocked expression but made no move to help him.

"Cornelius." Wouter heard his own voice like the voice of a deaf man, barely comprehensible because his mouth was being pulled open. "Aaargh . . . help me . . ."

Cornelius sneered. "I'm sorry, Wouter, but I can't understand a word you're saying."

Wouter turned to look at Jacobus, whose face was contorted with the effort of holding on to Wouter's beard. Suddenly, he let go with one hand, seized Wouter's arm, and gave a violent tug, slamming Wouter down flat on the table. As Wouter reached out to tackle his assailant, Jacobus let go of Wouter's beard and grabbed his other arm. Then he pressed Wouter's wrists together and trussed them up with a rope that Cornelius handed to him.

Wouter struggled to pull himself upright, but the floor tiles were too smooth. Instead, his feet left the ground and Jacobus dragged him farther across the table. Jacobus bound the rope to one leg of the table and walked to the other side. Then, forcing Wouter's legs apart, he took two more pieces of rope and lashed Wouter's ankles to the legs of the table.

As Wouter struggled, the cords bit into his wrists and ankles. Suddenly two hands closed around his head and turned it to the side so forcefully that for a moment he thought this was the end. His time had come; they were going to break his neck. Jacobus's hand pressed hard against the side of his face. Out of the corner of his eye, Wouter saw something moving. Before he knew what was happening, drops of burning tallow were dripping into his ear. He squeezed his eyes shut and opened his mouth wide in a scream that never emerged. A rag was stuffed into his mouth, so deep that the fabric scraped the back of his throat. He let out a stifled groan. Then he tried to calm down and breathe through his nose. But panic welled up inside him, and he felt as if his lungs were about to burst.

A deranged cackling came from very close by, though it sounded far away. Wouter felt Jacobus's lips against the tender flesh of his ear. "Those who refuse to hear God's word will feel God's wrath."

Again, two hands closed in on his head and wrenched it around. The tallow that Jacobus poured into his other ear sealed out all sound. All he could hear was the rush of his blood and the pounding of his heart. He caught sight of Cornelius, staring at him in almost stunned horror. Hearing the muffled sounds he was producing, Wouter tried to put all he had to say into the look in his eyes. Cornelius slowly shook his head and turned to Jacobus. Wouter could see his lips moving. He tugged at the ropes, but they only tightened around his wrists and ankles.

Jacobus grasped Wouter by the hair, twisting it around his knuckles and yanking his head down to the tabletop. He raised the candlestick high into the air and brought it hurtling down.

THIRTEEN

They all looked at the old Dutch title printed in elegant type on the first page of the book.

COLLECTION
OF A MULTITUDE OF
TULIPS
RENDERED TREW TO LIFE
WITH THE NAMES AND WEIGHTS OF THE BULBES,
AS SOLD TO THE PUBLICK AT ALKMAER
IN THE YEAR 1637

Damian looked up. His eyes shone with excitement.

"How did Frank get his hands on this?"

"I have no idea. I'd never seen it before."

"Unbelievable, the condition is stunning. This is an extraordinary specimen. The only other copies I know of are in museums or buried in archives. I can hardly imagine how much it's worth." Damian ran his fingers over the page. "Books like this were made in the seventeenth century, when the tulip trade was booming, and they were sold to generate interest in tulip bulbs."

"Like catalogs," Emma said.

"Exactly. There was a time when tulips were auctioned off not as flowers but as bulbs." He carefully turned the page. "Here, look how beautifully this was done."

The colors leaped off the page. The tulip's petals were white flamed with red, on top of a gently curved stem. One of the three curled leaves was a little ragged on top, as if an insect had been nibbling at it. The other two petals each came to a point, one upright and proud, the other arched gracefully outward. The illustrator's work was so skillful and precise that you could almost count the veins in the leaves.

"Some of the artists became quite famous," Damian continued. "To promote sales of their bulbs, tulip traders commissioned pictures of the flowers in bloom. It was costly and time-consuming, but worth the trouble because it advertised their merchandise. At auctions, they could show potential buyers the flowers that were hidden in the bulbs. These illustrations are worth a fortune."

"Could this book be what the killer was after?" Alec asked.

"Could be."

The tulip on the page in front of them was planted in a mound of soil with a little nameplate protruding from it.

"Look." Damian pointed. "Here's the name of the tulip: Admirael van der Eijck. The amount shown here is the sale price. See, this handwriting is different. When a bulb was sold, the trader made a note of the price it fetched. At the next auction, he knew how much had been paid for the bulb in the past, so he knew how much he could ask for."

"That price can't be right, can it?" Alec peered at the figure in surprise.

"Yes, that's right, one thousand and forty-five guilders," Damian said. "And that's nothing. Look at this one, here."

The flower he pointed to was rounder and fuller than the last, and it too had flamed petals. The color started at the base of each petal in a solid area of deep purple and fanned out toward the top as if a feather had been dipped in paint and pressed lightly against the snow-white flower. The tips of the petals were streaked with just a few thin lines of purple.

"Look what it says here. This is a Viceroy, and there are two figures underneath it. It was sold once for three thousand silver guilders, and then a second time for forty-two hundred."

"My God, forty-two hundred pieces of silver for a flower bulb," Emma said. "But how much would that be in today's money?"

"There's no way to say exactly, but you can make a rough estimate. Skilled laborers earned about three hundred guilders a year in those days. These days, they might earn about twenty-one thousand euros after taxes. So you have to multiply the three hundred guilders by seventy to get the equivalent in euros. If you used the same formula, a bulb that cost forty-two hundred guilders back then would now cost . . . let's see . . . two hundred and ninety-four thousand euros."

"How can a tulip bulb be worth two hundred and ninety-four thousand euros? It's crazy." Alec crossed his arms and frowned at the book. "Anyway, this is all very interesting, but what was Frank trying to tell me? Why did he want me to hide the book? And why didn't he want the police to know about it? I don't get it."

Damian looked at him. "What was it you said about Frank? Was he pointing at something?"

"He put his hand under the front cover, on the title page."

Damian shut the book and carefully opened the front cover again. The page was blotted with rust-colored stains and streaks. Right beneath the date was a bloody fingerprint, so clear that each groove was visible.

"Sixteen thirty-seven," Damian read aloud.

"Maybe Frank was trying to tell us his death had something to do with the tulip trade," Emma said, "or with the seventeenth century. I certainly can't think what else he might have meant. Alec, didn't Frank ever talk to you about this?"

"Never. As soon as I see Tibbens, I'll find out what he can tell me. Maybe Frank said something to him."

"Let's hope so. Frank must have had a reason for giving this to you."

Damian leafed carefully through the book. "It must have some meaning."

"Frank and the seventeenth century—what's the connection?" Wandering over to the fireplace, Alec thrust his hands into his pockets. Then, casting a sheepish look at Damian, he said, "Sorry I was so short with you. I know you're trying to help, I know you mean well, and I appreciate it. Please don't worry about me. I've never felt so powerless in my life, but this time I'll get through it clean and sober. I want you to believe that. Just trust me."

Damian went over to Alec and threw his arms around him. The two men slapped each other's shoulders awkwardly.

When Emma saw them standing there with adolescent grins on their faces, she cursed herself and wondered, not for the first time, whether they would all be better off if she disappeared from their lives completely. She knew the tension between Alec and Damian had a lot to do with her. In all the years they had known each other, they'd had their share of conflicts, but their friendship had never been as fragile as it was now.

Clearing her throat loudly, she said, "I know of one connection between Frank and the seventeenth century."

They stared at her in surprise.

"But of course I can't say whether it'll be of any use to us."

"What connection is that?" Damian asked.

"Dick Beerens."

"How stupid of me!" Alec clapped his hand to his forehead. "I should have thought of Dick right away. I even saw him at the funeral. Of course he knows all about that period."

"And the tulip trade," Damian added.

Emma nodded. "Just what I was thinking."

FOURTEEN

Tara switched on the light and kicked the bathroom door shut behind her. With a wild gesture, she swept her blond hair back into an elastic band and studied herself in the mirror of the medicine cabinet. The ponytail was so tight that her swollen eyes seemed almost slanted. After loosening the band a little, she massaged her temples with her fingertips and wiped the greasy mascara from under her bloodshot eyes.

Turning on the cold water, she splashed a handful of it into her face. Water dripped off her skin. With both hands, she leaned heavily on the sink, which groaned under her weight. Swearing, she clutched the sides and tugged until a wide crack opened between the sink and the tiled wall. Then she let go, panting.

"This is more than you'd bargained for, isn't it, Frank?" she said, wiping a hand across her nose. "You had everything under control, right? So what's next? What am I supposed to do now? Did you ever think about that? What was I supposed to do if you ended up like this?"

She snatched the towel off the heater and vigorously scrubbed her face with it. Then holding open her toiletry bag, she swept the contents of the shelf into it. Before leaving the bathroom, she took one last look in the mirror. Cold blue eyes under dark blond eyebrows, a flawlessly straight nose, high cheekbones, and a mouth pinched into a line. Her lips were bloodless and pale. She leveled a finger at herself and said, "You are going to work this thing out."

Coming out of the bathroom, she went over to the bed, where she dropped the toiletry bag into a larger one. The newspaper lay beside the travel bag, open to page 3. For the umpteenth time, she read the bold headline above the photo of Frank in a tuxedo: DUTCHMAN MURDERED IN LONDON. The article left nothing to the imagination, describing in gruesome detail how he was tortured. According to the reporter, the police were still in the dark about the killer's identity, and the motive was just as baffling, considering that nothing had been taken from the house. There were also a few words about Alec Schoeller, whose photo was next to Frank's. The article noted that he was an artist and mentioned the rumor that he stood to receive a large inheritance.

Tara sank to her knees at the foot of the bed. Hunched over the newspaper, she stared at Frank's photo, mumbling, "What did you tell them, Frank? How much did you give away? Did you say anything about me? Well, did you?"

When she'd last seen him, two weeks earlier, they'd reviewed their progress and decided their budget would stretch to at least two years of research. At last, everything was settled, and she could start. They finally had the money, and now this? Cursing, she slammed her fist into Frank's photo. Would she have to abandon the project? From the moment he'd offered her this opportunity, it had utterly consumed her; it was the only thing she could think about.

She stood up, went to the closet, and tossed some clothes into her travel bag, then added her laptop. Thank goodness it held a copy of all the data, she thought. After what had happened to Frank, she didn't dare go back to the lab. In the streets, she had the feeling everyone was watching her, keeping her under constant surveillance, as if they knew she was up to something.

No, she would press on, whatever happened. This was her chance to show the world what she was capable of, to show she was at the top of her field. She wasn't about to let anyone take that away. No, all the energy she'd put into the project would not go to waste, whatever the cost.

Straightening her back, she picked up her bag from the bed and left the room. As she shut the front door behind her, she glanced around nervously. Then she hurried across the street and got into her car.

FIFTEEN

Alec and Damian stepped into the lobby of the Faculty of Arts, a glass, steel, and concrete structure built in the 1980s. They gave their names at the reception desk and were told where to go. Dick Beerens's office was on the second floor. When they got there, Alec knocked and pushed the door open.

The two men were surprised to see Dick standing on the swivel chair next to his desk, using a pole to push open a small upper window. A cigarette dangled from his mouth.

"Dick?"

The professor of Dutch history turned around, causing the chair to wobble precariously. His short legs trembled and he stumbled backward, flailing his free arm. Alec started toward him, but with a few improbably elegant motions of his short, stout body, Dick managed to steady the chair.

"Ah, you made it. Alec, Damian, welcome. Gentlemen, welcome. One moment, I'll be right with you."

His cigarette wagged as he spoke, and a clump of ash dropped to the floor. He leaned the pole against the wall and carefully shuffled around on the seat until he had his back to them. Then he took hold of the armrests and stepped down from the chair. With the tip of his shoe, he ground the fallen ash into the carpet before coming over to greet them. His face, still flushed with exertion, looked mournful.

"What a tragedy, boys, what a tragedy. Breaks your heart, doesn't it?"

He stood in front of Alec, grasped him by the shoulders, and hugged him firmly to his chest.

"This must be a nightmare for you, son. We'll all miss him terribly." His eyes grew moist.

Dick took a step back and looked him in the eyes. "I'm glad there's something I can do, some way I can help—at least, I hope I can." Then he extended his hand to Damian. "How's life treating you?'

"Fine, thanks."

"How's Emma?"

"She's doing well too."

"Glad to hear it, glad to hear it."

"Thanks for seeing us on such short notice, Dick."

"Sure, Alec, don't mention it. Er, I hope you don't mind me asking, but have they made any progress with the investigation?"

Alec shook his head. "Not as far as I know. They haven't arrested anybody yet. I think they're still groping in the dark."

"I couldn't believe it when I heard," Dick said, his voice betraying his emotion. "Even now, it hardly seems real. I still see his face every day. Here, take a look."

He went to the desk and picked up a framed photo, which he handed to Alec.

"You see him sitting there?"

Alec nodded. From behind him, Damian looked on. A group of young men were seated at a table set for a formal dinner. The silverware and white plates gleamed in the light of the large candelabras. The photographer had taken the picture from the head of the table. The students were leaning forward and raising their glasses. Frank was the slender one in front, looking jovially into the lens. A young Dick Beerens sat beaming opposite him.

"Our college club," Dick murmured, gazing at the photo. He put it down with a cough. "Alec, last night when you called, you said you had found something at Frank's house and wanted my help. Can you tell me what it was you found?"

"Yes, I . . . that is, we think his death may have something to do with tulips. I know it sounds a little strange, but—"

"Frank? Hold on a second, Alec. Frank and tulips?" Dick's eyebrows shot toward his hairline. "What makes you think that?"

"We'd rather not say right now, if you don't mind. But there are indications that his death was somehow connected to the seventeenth-century tulip trade."

"So it has to do with this thing found at Frank's place?" Dick ventured. When Alec gave no reply, he shook his head. "Listen, boys, it's highly improbable that there's any link between Frank's death and the tulip business. Oh, maybe if we were living in the seventeenth century, but nowadays? Anyway, if he'd been thinking about the seventeenth century, I'm sure he would have mentioned it to me. Because when it comes to the Dutch Golden Age, sooner or later everyone comes to Dick Beerens, know what I mean?"

"That's why we thought of you. We thought maybe he had asked you something, or talked to you about it." Alec sounded hopeful.

"Well, we talked about my research now and then, but he never asked me for any particular information. What were you thinking he might have discussed with me?"

"We can't tell you everything now, but it does seem as if there's a connection. Still, we've no idea how or what, and we were hoping you could point us in the right direction."

"What exactly did you want to know about the period? There are so many places I could start. Just to narrow things down a bit, why don't you tell me what inspired this train of thought?"

"I see your point, but we'd rather not say too much at this stage."

"All right," Dick said with a sigh. "I respect your decision. There'll be no more awkward questions from me. But there is one thing I must say, on Frank's behalf, and as a friend. Please, just leave this to the police. I knew Frank well enough to know that he wouldn't want to see you involved." He emphasized his words with a nod. "You're sure there's nothing else you could let me in on? It would make things a lot easier for me."

When Alec shook his head, Dick patted him on the shoulder and said, "How about letting me tell you what I know about the tulip trade. Maybe that'll give you something to go on. Okay? Sit down, sit down."

They wove their way through the teetering stacks of books, which seemed to grow out of the floor like stalagmites. Crammed bookcases rose to the ceiling, and on top of the books were piles of loose pages, file folders, newspapers, and journals. They sat down on two folding chairs in front of Dick's desk, which was just as cluttered as the rest of the office. Next to the desk was a small refrigerator, and Dick stationed himself proudly behind it like a cafeteria manager.

"I ordered us some lunch."

On a serving tray on top of the fridge were a few sandwiches wrapped in cellophane. Here and there, a lettuce leaf was trying to escape the sweaty slices of cheese and curling cuts of meat.

Fantastic, a real Dutch-style working lunch, Damian thought, scanning the tray. All that's missing is the croquettes.

"The croquettes are on their way," Dick said, squeezing behind his desk. His little brown eyes darted over the desktop, and as he reached for his cigarettes, he reminded Damian of a hamster. His neck was so stubby that it seemed as if his head was mounted directly on his shoulders, and his thick mop of russet hair made his head look huge.

"Frank and the tulip trade," he muttered, and a deep furrow formed between his bushy eyebrows. He lit a cigarette, inhaled, and pensively blew smoke in the general direction of the fire alarm. The door opened and a girl in an apron stepped into the office.

"Ah, the croquettes." Dick balanced his cigarette on the edge of his desk and rubbed his hands together. "Thank you, thank you, put them down right here. Tuck in, gentlemen, tuck in," he said, as he reached for one himself and took a bite. "Okay," he said, leaving his mouth half open so the hot ragout filling would cool. "Let's get started."

Alkmaar

The fingers dug deep into his armpits. He felt the heels of his shoes sliding along the floor, catching slightly on the edge of each tile. Through
half-closed eyes, he looked down. His hands were tied together over his
stomach, rising and falling with each tug as he was dragged across the
floor. He could see the fingertips of the person dragging him, the thick,
irregular nails caked with blood. His blood. He tried to move his head,
and moaned.

All at once the stabbing pain under his arms stopped. He fell backward, his head slamming into the floor. From his throat came a wailing
sound. Slowly, his head slumped to one side, and he felt the cool stone
against his cheek. The rag was yanked out of his mouth. He took a deep
breath, running his tongue over his cracked lips.

"Cornelius? Are you still there?"

"Of course I'm here, Wouter," Cornelius answered. His voice was muted
by the candle wax in Wouter's ears, but Wouter could feel the hot breath
on the side of his face. Cornelius's words were cold and distant, but there
was something in his voice that gave Wouter hope. A faint, barely audi-
ble tremor. Did it signal fear? Or compassion?

"Cornelius," he panted, "untie me. I'll . . . I'll explain everything."

He kicked and thrashed, trying to sit up, but fell back to the floor with
a groan.

"It had to be done," he said. "There was no alternative. We all want to move forward, don't we? The church is trying to stop us. Are you listening, Cornelius? Do you hear what I'm saying? The church, Cornelius, the institution."

He slowly rolled onto his stomach and folded his legs underneath him. Using his fists for leverage, he pushed himself upright and straightened his back.

"We have to put up a fight. We can't simply resign ourselves to the situation. That would set us back years and years. Then there'd be no hope of scientific progress. Surely you see why? Once we can explain things for ourselves, we have no reason to believe in God. But they need us to keep believing, so they can keep us under control. Do you understand, Cornelius? Untie me and I'll explain. Come on."

He stretched his arms out in front of him and held up his bound hands.

"Please, Cornelius, help me. Don't do this, I beg you."

He heard shuffling behind him. Then came a blew to the back of his head, so hard that he heard his skull crack. Everything went dark.

SIXTEEN

"Tulips, windmills, cheese, and clogs." At each word, Dick pounded his desk with his hand. "They're all as Dutch as it gets, right? Wrong. Tulips have no place on that list. Where do most people think tulips come from?"

"Turkey," Alec said hesitantly.

"Right, that's what most people think. Well, most people are wrong, wrong, wrong. Santa Claus, now, he comes from Turkey. But the tulip, that symbol of our nation, started out much farther east, in China. That's its true origin."

Dick looked triumphantly at them.

"Yes, I can see the surprise on your faces. That's the same reaction I get when I tell this to my students. Isn't it the funniest thing? Chinese tourists coming all the way here to look at flowers from their own country. Airplanes full of them! Fabulous, isn't it?"

A bread crumb flew from his mouth, landing on his computer screen. He brushed it away with his sleeve.

"So, China. Western China, to be exact, to the north of the Himalayas. Wait."

He wriggled out from behind his desk and waddled over to one of the stacks of books. Carefully, he pulled a book from the pile and thumbed through it.

"Ah, here it is."

Resting the open atlas on his stomach, he pointed to a mountain range in China, near the Russian border.

"This, here, is one of the most inhospitable parts of the world." He circled it slowly with his finger. "Nothing grows there. No one lives there. Why would you? You'd have to be deranged. The summers are scorching and dry, and the winters last for months, with everything buried in snow. This is where Holland's pride originally comes from, the Tien Shan Mountains."

Dick withdrew his finger, leaving a stain on the map. How ironic, Damian thought. The birthplace of their country's beloved tulip, immortalized in the grease of a croquette, the quintessential Dutch snack.

"But," Dick went on, "even in the most uninhabitable regions, there are always microclimates, ecological niches with just a bit more sun or a bit more water. Yes, even in this forbidding place, there are valleys among the foothills with tracts of fertile land. And wherever there's fertile land, there is life, and wherever there's life, there are people."

He shut the atlas and slid it back into the stack of books in exactly the same place.

"It all started with the nomads of the steppes. They put their livestock out to pasture in those valleys, and so they were the first to notice the tulip. And more than just notice it—the flower captured their hearts. Imagine. There you are, trudging along with your herd. Winter is almost over, but it's still bitterly cold, and you're chilled to the bone. You clamber up and down the rocky slopes, hoping to find a patch of vegetation for your animals before nightfall. The sun's rays are still too weak to give any warmth. And then, suddenly, you can't believe your eyes. You rub them with your fists and look again. No mistake; it's true. Those slopes, there, in the distance, aren't dull brown or gray, but red, bright red!"

Dick dropped into his chair, leaning back and spreading his arms theatrically, a look of sheer joy and astonishment on his face.

"Can you picture it? A sea of color in the middle of that dismal, barren landscape. It must have been breathtaking. Utterly breathtaking."

Gazing off into the distance, he said, "Those flowers heralded the end of a cruel winter. As soon as the nomads saw them, they knew that summer was on the way, that the worst was behind them. And those were the flowers we call tulips."

He looked at them jubilantly.

"I had no idea that's where tulips came from," Alec said.

Dick nodded. "You're not the only one. Step by step, century by century, the tulip spread toward Turkey, along with nomadic tribes who decided to settle down. They came from the east, conquering the cities to the west and founding their own principalities."

Resting one elbow on his desk, Dick raised his index finger.

"These were no barbarians, mind you, but the heirs of an age-old culture and expert botanists, besides. They swept across the Balkans, taking the tulip with them. To them, it was not just beautiful and decorative, but sacred. They called it the *lâle*, using the same Arabic letters that make up Allah's name. Hardy yet elegant, the *lâle* was the symbol of eternity, of power and perfection, a hint of the hereafter, proof of the possibility of paradise on earth. It was also the symbol of beauty's submission to the Divine, for the flower humbly bows its head to Allah."

"A lovely image," Damian muttered.

"Lovely indeed. Through the years, the tulip has had a strange and marvelous history. It has brought happiness to many people but harm to others. Very grave harm. The tulip has inspired men to fight . . . and kill."

Alkmaar

Esteemed Sir,

In the early hours of July the 21st our plan went into effect. I am writing to inform you that we have completed the first step. As for Cornelius, you were right about him. He was easy to manipulate and did his job well. To ensure our success, I sent along one of my boys. Everything proceeded according to plan.

Meanwhile, Cornelius supposes himself innocent of any wrongdoing. He is confident that when he took Winckel's life he was defending his faith, and he feels certain that God will forgive him. And who can say otherwise? He is entirely ignorant of our plans for the tulip bulbs that will soon—very soon, with any luck—be offered for sale.

You know that this is just the first step. There is a great deal still to be done. All the signs seem favorable, yet one thing still vexes me. May the Lord in his wisdom provide that Winckel's children are not taken in by their appointed guardians. For if they are, it will be impossible for us to carry out the plan in its present form. Considering the importance of the task and my ties to the guardians, I shall make sure that all seven children are committed to my care.

I advise you to start preparing. Inform me when you are ready, and I shall set things in motion here.

You will receive descriptions of the tulips as soon as I have them in my possession. Then you can instruct the illustrators.

I believe the man who delivers this letter to be trustworthy. But if the seal has been broken, we shall have to find some other means of communication. Otherwise, this is the best way for us to remain in contact for now.

A.K.

SEVENTEEN

Dick gripped the edge of his desk with both hands, pulled himself upright, and leaned forward.

"Around fourteen fifty A.D., the Ottomans captured the city of Constantinople and renamed it Istanbul. The young sultan saw Istanbul as the heart of his new empire and embarked on a massive program of construction, building mosques, palaces, and private gardens. The people of the city followed his example, planting gardens of their own. Hanging gardens, kitchen gardens, flower gardens, you name it." A dreamy look crept over Dick's face. "A sight to behold. Like a second Eden."

"Ornamental gardens?" Damian said. "But the only gardens in Western Europe in those days were herb or vegetable gardens, weren't they? The only flowers Europeans grew were edible or medicinal."

"You're absolutely right. But our Ottoman friends were different. They planted gardens to enjoy the beauty of nature, the shade of a tree, the quiet of the afternoon, the fragrances. Over the years the tulip became their icon, the logo of the Ottoman Empire. And that's where Westerners first laid eyes on this magnificent flower."

Dick sank back into his seat and folded his hands over his stomach.

"We went there to forge ties with the greatest power in the Mediterranean world. And what we found in the gardens of Istanbul—their flowers—were unlike anything we'd ever seen before." He dug a cigarette out of the crumpled pack and lit it. "Dazzled by their shapes and colors, we brought them home with us. The truly mind-boggling thing about tulips was their variety, which was pretty much unequaled in those days. That helped to establish their reputation as superior to all other flowers. It also helped that they were easy to transport, tough as weeds, and suited to our cold, wet climate."

Dick swung forward and pitched his half-smoked cigarette into a plastic cup, where it hissed and died out in the last drops of coffee.

"Tulips were also popular because they conferred status. In the Renaissance, as modern science came into being, there was growing interest in botany. Gardens became status symbols, because they showed you had enough money to throw some away on useless fripperies. Think of how we buy SUVs today just for running errands. What are we, living in the wilderness? Practicing for the Paris–Dakar, maybe? Where are the Dutch mountains? We want to show the world we can afford a car like that. And people in the Renaissance were no different. But here in Holland, there was another side to the story: the rise of the sciences, the thirst for knowledge, and the dream of passing knowledge down to future generations. By cultivating tulips, we created new varieties: large, medium, or small, with rounded leaves or pointed ones, thick stems or thin, three petals, or four, or five . . . Unless we kept notes on how we produced all these varieties, the information would be lost forever. There was only one man equal to the task, and that was the great botanist Carolus Clusius, adviser to European rulers and noblemen and the kingpin of a huge network of plant lovers who shared bulbs, seeds, plants, and information."

Damian said, "I've read about him. Wasn't he the director of the botanical garden at Leiden University?"

"Quite right. He grew tulips from bulbs sent to him from all over the world. Then he studied the flowers and wrote about them. By this time, the tulip had become so popular that thieves kept breaking into Clusius's garden to raid his tulip beds. Oddly enough, this turned out to be a good thing, in a way. It brought valuable tulip bulbs to many parts of our country—quite illegally, mind you. Those were probably the predecessors of the bulbs that fetched such outrageous prices decades later. Of course, refugees also brought tulip bulbs to Holland."

"You mean the people fleeing Spanish rule and the Catholic church?" Alec asked.

Dick looked at him wryly and said, "So you managed to pick up something during your studies after all. Yes, many people who were persecuted for their religious beliefs headed north, to our free republic, where they were more than welcome. Sometimes cities even fought over them—figuratively speaking, I mean."

"Fighting to take in refugees—those were very different times," Alec mumbled.

"You can say that again. The thing is, many of those émigrés were wealthy, and more than a few were so grateful for the warm reception that they contributed generously to the construction of churches and city halls."

"So it wasn't just a question of tolerance?" Alec asked.

"Oh, I think tolerance had very little to do with it. We weren't that noble, never have been. But anyway, more and more kinds of tulips ended up here. And then along came something entirely unexpected."

Holland

The northeaster scoured the level landscape, whipping up silver shark fins in the ditches between the pastures and the fields. The rain lashed the ground and hardened into ice.

A fierce wind buffeted Alkmaar's city gate and swept the travelers inside. They came from all points of the compass, and some from distant lands. The journey was not without peril, for the icy roads leading to Alkmaar were treacherous. But they paid little notice, for the cold had numbed them and made them reckless.

The look in their eyes was adamant. Whatever happened, they would reach the city in time, because wealth and fortune awaited them on the morrow. Then the most valuable tulips in the world would be auctioned off in Alkmaar. And they would be there, no matter what the cost.

EIGHTEEN

Dick got up, pulled open the door of the fridge, and rummaged inside it. With a casual swing of his right leg, he pushed the door shut.

"How about a cola?" he said, throwing them each a can. He pried up the pull tab with a letter opener and took a long swig.

"So, tulips became a status symbol. But the Dutch republic wasn't like France, where tulips became the playthings of the aristocracy. In this country, merchants were the new elite. They had mansions built in the countryside, the bigger, the better. But they wanted even more, something that would really set them apart from their rivals. Their weapon of choice was not simply their gardens, but something much more specific: the size and content of their tulip beds. Of course, they lacked the skill to cultivate their own flowers, so they hired professional growers to do it for them. The demand for these new specialists grew steadily, and many soon opened their own bulb nurseries. They managed to snap up plots of poor, sandy soil at bargain prices, mainly in the region north of Amsterdam. The soil was unsuited to other plants but perfect for tulips, which took hold and even thrived there."

"And that was the origin of Holland's famous tulip fields," Alec said.

"Precisely."

"So the supply of tulips must have kept growing," Damian said.

"Yes, and the market changed. Ordinary tulips were no longer scarce, so prices plummeted, and they became affordable for people of modest means. The supply kept increasing, but demand increased too, because many more people could now afford to buy them. At the same time, wealthier buyers started focusing on the really rare and unusual varieties, what you might call the limited editions." Dick grinned broadly, tipped his head back, downed the last of the cola, and let out a burp.

"Excuse me, gentlemen." He wiped his mouth on his sleeve. "So here's the thing. The new breed of professional gardeners cultivated exceptional, novel varieties of tulips, producing just a few bulbs of each kind. The most expensive ones were called broken tulips, because of the beautiful, flamelike patterns on their petals. Some of them sold for thousands of guilders. Just a moment, I'll show you."

Steering with his feet, Dick propelled his chair toward the bookcase.

"Here, get an eyeful of this."

He rolled back over to Alec and Damian and laid the book on his lap. It was the catalog from an art exhibition at the Rijksmuseum in Amsterdam about the illustrators of tulip books.

"Here are some different tulip varieties. Look how exquisite they are, those colors, and those patterns. Incredible, isn't it?" As Dick paged through the catalog, showing Alec and Damian the prints, he missed the meaningful look that passed between them.

"Some of them are unique—this one, for instance." He pointed to a tulip with magnificent streaks of dark purple on its delicate white petals. "Tulips like that were hard to come by."

"And worth their weight in gold," Damian added.

"Yes, literally."

Dick maneuvered his chair back to the bookcase and returned the book to the shelf.

"More and more people saw that there was money in the tulip trade. Your very first investment, in just one or two bulbs, could fetch a tidy profit. That's when things went out of control. Everyone wanted more: more bulbs, more money, more trading."

"But there has to be a limit," Alec said.

Dick nodded. "And the limit was coming up fast."

NINETEEN

It was twelve thirty and the restaurant was packed with men in suits, the dark fabric absorbing the dim light. Their muted conversations were studded with peals of laughter. It was lunchtime in the City, London's business district.

Coetzer sat in the corner, his jacket slung over the back of his chair. Next to the remains of his lunch, the paper was open to the financial news. He fit in perfectly. Experience had taught him that no matter where he was, no matter who he was dealing with, blending in was a matter of life or death. Every detail had to be just right to ensure invisibility.

He pushed away his plate and folded up the paper. Just as the waiter was serving him his espresso, his phone rang. The waiter shook his head, put a finger to his lips, and pointed at a sign high on the wall: a cell phone with a thick red line through it. Coetzer nodded, making his way outside to take the call.

"Hello?"

"It's me. To be honest, I'd been expecting you to call me," the nasal voice said. "When that didn't happen, and I had to read in the paper what had become of Schoeller, and how you had handled the situation, I thought you might have pulled a vanishing act."

"Actually, I was just about to contact you, so that we could work out—"

"I presume you didn't find out anything, or else you would have phoned. Funny, I thought I was hiring a professional. If the aim had been to kill him, I could just as well have sent someone else. You were paid for your interrogation skills, not to smash a hole in a man's skull without even getting the information I asked for. I paid you half up front, but there's no way in—"

"One moment, please," Coetzer said. He walked about ten feet farther away from the restaurant, out of earshot of the customers who were standing around smoking. "It's not how I pictured it, either," he said quietly. "He would never have told me a thing, no matter what I did to him. He was tough. I don't have to work on someone for hours to figure that out."

"So you decided you might as well just do him in."

"What was I supposed to do?"

"Get him to tell you where it is, you moron. Find out where he hid it."

Only now that the man was losing his temper did Coetzer detect a slight accent. His client was not using his real name, any more than he was, but for some reason Coetzer had always assumed he was dealing with an Englishman. They were silent for a moment. Then the man said, "You failed."

Coetzer bit back his anger. A store of suppressed rage always came in handy for that essential burst of physical energy, like a shot of adrenaline.

"Some people never spill," he said.

"He was the nexus. Everything revolved around Schoeller. Now we are left with nothing. What do you propose to do about it?"

"There's still his nephew."

"What? The man who found him? You obviously haven't been reading the papers. By the time he got there, his uncle was already dead. Thanks to your brilliant work, Schoeller couldn't say a word to his nephew."

"That's not what I mean. His nephew was his only living relative, right? His sole heir? So he might have left him something."

Silence. "It's possible."

"Anyway, I'll look into it."

"You mean we'll soon have a second corpse on our hands?"

"That depends on what you ask me to do."

"Let there be no misunderstanding. I'm sure you realize that the payment we discussed will not be forthcoming. Investigating the nephew is part of the first job, so don't suppose I'm giving you a new one. This is what happens when you improvise. Get to work and make sure to keep me posted. Show a bit more sense this time and find out where the fuck Schoeller hid the bloody thing. Don't come back to me empty-handed, or you can kiss the rest of your money good-bye."

Coetzer snapped his telephone shut. He'd soon have the funds he needed to retire permanently to his farm near Cape Town, and he'd never have to take this kind of shit again. With a smile on his face, he strolled back into the restaurant.

Dawn walked into the video room.

"Jesus, Tim, what have you been eating?" Pinching her nose to keep out the garlic stench that filled the stuffy little room, she grabbed the chair next to him and pulled it as far away from him as possible.

He glanced at her in amusement. "Don't be such a drama queen. It can't be the worst odor you've run into in all your years on the job. Or are you trying to tell me a little garlic is worse than the smell of a corpse?"

"Depends what the corpse ate."

He turned to her, cocking his head. His glasses were covered with greasy fingerprints. As Dawn wondered how he could see anything, he leaned forward and breathed in her face. "Does it really?"

She wrinkled her nose. "Have you had time to look?"

In a corner above them were two monitors with frozen images of Schoeller's funeral.

"No, I just scanned through them to see if there was a break in the recording. But you've got the whole thing there."

"Good. So show me what you've got."

Tim pressed a couple of buttons. One screen showed the assembly hall at the cemetery and the other showed the lobby.

"Can you rewind to the beginning and turn on the sound?"

"Whoa, take it easy, what do you think I'm doing here?"

He punched a few more buttons and adjusted the controls. The hum of voices filled the room.

He rubbed his hands. "Okay, I'm ready. What are we looking for?"

"Don't know yet."

"You don't know yet?"

"That's right, I don't know yet. Just run the video."

The cameras had recorded the entire service, from the moment the guests arrived until they left after offering condolences to Alec. After two hours, the last guests walked out the door, followed soon after by Alec, Damian, and Emma.

Tim stopped the tape. "And?" He clasped his hands behind his head and leaned back. "Notice anything?"

Dawn shook her head. "No, nothing. It all looks normal to me."

"Wainwright doesn't actually think the murderer was there, does he? Come on, it's a myth that killers return to the scene of the crime or go to their victims' funerals. It's like he's forgotten the difference between fiction and reality. He must be watching too many cop shows."

Dawn raised her eyebrows. "Don't forget, he inspired a lot of those cop shows. Some of those stories are taken right from his career. If you only knew how many scriptwriters come to talk to him."

Tim shrugged. "Do you want the tapes, or should I take them to the archives?"

"Could you burn a DVD for me? I'd like to go through them again later."

Alkmaar

An icy blast of wind slammed the heavy door behind them. The girl who'd let them in was striding on ahead. In the middle of the entrance hall, she stopped and turned around. "If you wait here, I'll let the director know you've arrived."

Lauris Bartelmieszoon and Philip de Klerck stood, numb with cold, in the frigid entrance hall of the orphanage. Without exchanging a word, they removed their soaked hats and shook them out. Melting snow dripped from their cloaks onto the floor.

Lauris looked down, poked at a puddle of icy water with the toe of his shoe, and softly said, "How do you suppose they're doing?"

Philip turned his head and shrugged.

Lauris nodded and squeezed the brim of his hat. He was appalled that Wouter Winckel's children had ended up here. When Wouter had asked him and Philip to serve as guardians, this had not been what he had in mind at all. But they'd had little choice.

Hearing swift footsteps approaching, he tried to shake off his guilt. The door through which the girl had vanished was thrown open, and Adriaen Koorn, director of the Alkmaar Orphanage, entered the room.

"Gentlemen, you're here," he said, coming toward them. He was short, and his thin legs jutted out of his rotund body like stalks. His lower jaw jutted forward, placing his bottom row of small yellow teeth well in front of the top row. His skin was sallow, and his bulging eyes darted from side to side.

"Welcome," he said.

Lauris shook the man's hand, which was limp and sweaty. He wiped off his palm on his coat and instinctively stepped back.

"Follow me, please." Spinning around on his small feet, Koorn led them to the rear of the hall and opened the door.

The odor of peat hung thick in the air. Seated at the table in the center of the sparsely furnished meeting room was Willem Winckel, Wouter's eldest son. As soon as he caught sight of them, a smile lit his melancholy face, and he rose to his feet.

"Uncle Lauris, Uncle Philip, I'm so glad to see you!" he said as he embraced the two men.

"How are you, my boy? And the others? Is everyone all right?" Lauris asked, looking him straight in the eyes. The weather had been cold, and the orphans were not always in good health.

"Everyone's fine," Willem said.

"Of course everyone's fine." Koorn, who had moved to Willem's side, clapped the boy on the shoulder. "We take excellent care of our children, as you know. And after tomorrow's event, we'll be able to take even better care of them."

He rubbed his hands together with such an air of satisfaction that Lauris and Philip exchanged a knowing glance. They understood only too well that this auction was an opportunity for the director to bring in a great deal of money. The orphanage had to raise its own funds and relied on private donations, this they knew. Yet Koorn was being remarkably insensitive, especially considering that Willem was in the room. After all, it was the estate of the boy's father, Wouter Winckel, that they were there to discuss. Lauris felt embarrassed.

"Come," said Koorn, "take a seat. Let us begin."

They sat down around the table.

"Willem has asked me to explain how the auction will work. He tells me you've never been to one before, and he'd like me to describe the procedure, so that—as he puts it—you can make sure we follow all the rules. Of course, the entire process will take place under my close scrutiny, but you are the children's guardians and, as such, ultimately responsible for their well-being."

Irritated by the man's condescending tone, and troubled by his own conscience, Lauris said, "That's right, we're responsible, and what's more, we made a promise to Wouter Winckel that we intend to keep."

After Wouter's death, the orphanage director had persuaded the two guardians to let him take care of the children. All seven of them. Far too many for Lauris and Philip to handle. Philip was prepared to take the girls, and Lauris the boys, but the director had emphasized that in the orphanage all seven could stay together. "All they have left is each other," he said. After trying out the arrangement for a couple of months, the two guardians had decided to remove the children from the orphanage after all. But they thought better of it when Adriaen Koorn informed them that the auction was scheduled for February. After that, Wouter's children would have the means to live independently. Seven months had passed since they'd had that conversation.

"A promise?" Adriaen asked. Lauris saw the director's left eyelid twitch. His protruding Adam's apple bobbed uneasily.

"Yes," Lauris answered. "We promised that Mr. Winckel's children would want for nothing after his death, and that his estate would be divided among them fairly and honestly."

"Oh, is that the promise you mean?" Lauris detected a spark of anger in the bulging eyes. "Well, then, you can both rest easy now. Honesty and fairness are my watchwords, as anyone who knows me can confirm. Now, let me explain this whole business to you, so you can go back home with your minds at ease."

The sardonic undertone did not escape Lauris. He opened his mouth but felt a nudge at his elbow. Philip looked at Lauris, shook his head surreptitiously, and said, "If you'd be so kind . . ."

An hour later Philip and Lauris were walking out the front gate of the orphanage. In the shelter of the west wall of the church, they *wrapped their damp cloaks firmly around them and donned their hats.*

"Well? What do you make of this?" Philip asked.

"I don't trust him. We'll have to go to the auction and keep track of the bids for each lot. As Koorn said, Wouter's estate is now in the hands of the orphanage, and the children won't get their share till the proceeds have come in."

"How much did he say was going to the orphanage?"

"One-tenth."

"So the more they bring in, the more the orphanage gets."

"And that means they'll do everything they can to make the auction a success. That should benefit the children. Since it's obvious the director is already counting his guilders, I'm sure he's done a good job of advertising the event."

"You mean this should actually work out in everyone's best interest?"

Lauris nodded, but his expression was solemn. "Still, we'd better watch out, Philip. Willem asked us to come here for a reason. If he doesn't trust Adriaen Koorn, then neither do I."

They turned the corner. The wind lashed at their faces, and the whirling snow stung their flesh like a swarm of bees.

As Lauris and Philip made their way through the streets of Alkmaar, hunched against the wind, Adriaen Koorn hastened through the long, bare corridors to the north side of the orphanage. At the door to his apartments, he stopped and raised his fist to knock. Then, changing his mind, he turned the knob and entered.

The visitor was standing by the hearth, exactly where Adriaen had left him an hour ago, with his back turned to the door. He was still wearing his cloak, and the hood still covered his head. The man turned slowly to face him.

Adriaen unconsciously rubbed his upper arms. When he left to speak with the two guardians, it had been warm in the room, with a crackling fire in the hearth. The flames were still blazing, but now he felt a chill. It seemed as if all the heat was being sucked in by his guest.

"Forgive me," he said. "I didn't know it would take so long. If you'd given me some notice of your visit, I could've—"

"Have you got everything organized?" The voice from under the hood was muted and hoarse.

"Yes, as far as I'm concerned, we're ready."

The man thrust his hand into the folds of his cloak. When he withdrew it, he was holding a book. Adriaen stepped forward and took it from him.

"Is this it?"

"Yes."

"The descriptions were clear enough?" Adriaen asked, staring at the volume. Suddenly he jerked his head up apprehensively. His guest's icy gaze was boring into him. It clawed into his brain, so intense it almost hurt. Adriaen lowered his eyes.

"You have doubts?" the man asked.

"No, no, not at all." Adriaen's voice cracked.

"You have doubts."

The man tore the book from his hands and leafed through it with long, spindly fingers. Every few seconds, he brought his index finger to his mouth, licked the tip, and turned another page, disdainfully eyeing the bright watercolor illustrations. Then he shut the book and gave it back.

"What do you think? Will these pictures will rouse their interest?"

Adriaen nodded.

"Greed and folly are close companions." The man raised his head, looked at Adriaen, and said, "I've kept my side of the agreement. Alkmaar is teeming with buyers. The inns are all full, so the letters and pamphlets must have done their work."

For the past few days, Adriaen had looked on in astonishment as the traders poured into the city. He had expected a good turnout, but he never would have thought they'd flock to Alkmaar by the hundreds in such miserable weather. There wasn't an empty bed to be had in town; some of the locals had even given up their own in return for princely sums.

"I'll see you tomorrow morning at the New Archery Hall," the man said. He pulled his hood farther over his head and strode out.

No sooner was he gone than light and warmth returned to the room. With a sigh, Adriaen sank down onto the chair by the fire and stared at the book on his lap. The gold leaf on the cover caught the glow of the flames, dazzling him with its luster. Smiling, he caressed the soft red leather.

TWENTY

Dick gnawed his thumb. "The trouble really started when they extended the season. At first, bulbs were sold only in summer, because that was when they were harvested. But that wasn't enough for the tulip dealers. They wanted to make money all year-round. So what did they do? They started selling offsets—the shoots that sprouted from the bulb. Once the plant has flowered, you lift the mother bulb from the soil and remove the offsets. In time, they can mature into bulbs and produce offsets of their own. The problem is, it takes a couple of years for the offsets to become full-grown bulbs. But they were often sold well before that stage." Dick shook his head. "They should never have done it. When business transactions start to depend on trust, catastrophe is just around the corner."

"Are you saying people didn't really know what they were buying?" Alec asked.

"Correct. The seller would give the buyer a promissory note, a slip of paper describing what he had bought and when he could collect it."

"So they were speculating," Damian said.

"That's right. Trading was no longer seasonal. Instead, they could buy and sell all year. The dealers imagined that now they could really make their fortunes. And indeed, some of them did, but there was one problem, and it was a doozy."

Dick stood up, looking worried, and started pacing from one end of the musty office to the other.

"You see, there was no guarantee whatsoever that the offsets would be as hardy as the mother bulb, or that an offset from a prize bulb would produce exactly the same tulip. Yet in spite of these huge risks, the trade in offsets boomed. In fact, they were often traded before they were even removed from the mother bulb. Something else you must keep in mind," Dick went on, wagging his finger, "is that the weight of the bulbs was crucial. A heavy, mature bulb produces a lot more offsets than a lighter one. So bulbs were sold by weight, which was measured in aces. One ace was less than two-thousandths of an ounce. As you can imagine, the trade in promissory notes soon got entirely out of hand. Buyers couldn't be sure of anything. They had no way of checking the quality of a bulb or knowing what kind of flower it would eventually produce. They didn't even know if it existed, or was really in the dealer's possession."

"So in fact, they were paying a lot of money for scraps of paper that might turn out to be worthless, nothing but hot air," Alec said.

"It was a bubble," Damian added.

"A speculative bubble, precisely. The buyers were speculating on two things. First, the future price of the bulbs. They were hoping that the price would rise after they paid for the bulbs but before they collected them, so that they could sell at a profit. Second, they were betting that the weight of the bulb would increase while it was in the soil. A bulb weighing forty-eight aces could expand to two hundred aces in just a year's time. That would, of course, boost their profit. A three-hundred-percent return on investment in only twelve months. But the sellers were gambling too. In theory, buyers would make a down payment when they bought the promissory note, and agree in writing to pay a certain amount when they collected the bulb. But sellers could never be sure they would get the rest of their money."

Alec nodded, committing everything Dick said to memory. At the same time, he tried to find the connection to Frank. It could be lurking anywhere. But where? Up to now, Dick hadn't mentioned anything that seemed connected to Frank. The possibilities were starting to overwhelm him. Had Frank entrusted a large sum of money to the wrong person? Had he demanded repayment and instead paid with his life? How much did Alec really know about Frank's financial affairs? He'd never looked into how Frank had made his fortune. So far, Dick's story hadn't helped at all. They were wasting their time there. Alec sighed. Dick looked at him. "Does any of this seem relevant?"

"Not yet, but please go on. I'll have to let it all sink in."

Dick gave a slight nod. "Okay, so in sixteen thirty-five and thirty-six, this speculative trading sent bulb prices soaring. That attracted a new group of buyers, who were more interested in guilders than in gardening. They came from all walks of life and sold everything they had—their cattle, their looms, their kilns, their anvils—just to get into the game."

Damian said, "I once read that those stories about humble craftsmen investing all their money in tulips were just tall tales."

"It probably varied from place to place. Still, in the centers of the tulip trade, like Alkmaar, Haarlem, and Amsterdam, there's good reason to think that all sorts of people were looking for a piece of the action."

"But if they sold the tools they needed to practice their trades, then they had nothing left to fall back on."

"That's right, Damian. That was the problem. The boom reached its height in the final months of sixteen thirty-six. By then, people were paying insane amounts. As the market attracted new buyers, demand kept growing, so prices kept rising. It simply couldn't go on."

Dick went back to his chair and sat down, looking glum. "The year sixteen thirty-seven was a financial disaster for the tulip trade. A huge auction took place in Alkmaar. That was the beginning of the end. It changed everything. The bubble burst, leaving thousands of people penniless."

Alkmaar

The gales of the day before had cleared the air, and the wet streets of Alkmaar glistened in the morning sun. Most of the ice had melted, leaving only a thin crust on the shady patches along the road to the New Archery Hall, the guild hall of the city's longbowmen. Its gable was finely etched against the bright blue sky. The gold weather vane on the spire, an archer poised to shoot, pivoted slowly on its axis, uncertain which way the wind was blowing.

Far below, a group of men were waiting at the door. When it opened, they pushed their way inside and hurried to the small room at the far end of the corridor, where they were admitted two at a time.

Adriaen Koorn was pleased. The auction hall was full, and there was still a line of people waiting. The first bidders had shown up at seven o'clock that morning and been taken to view the tulip book commissioned months ago from a local artist.

Yes, Adriaen thought, since last July we've accomplished many things. The artist had produced 168 watercolors of the flowers in Winckel's collection. As instructed, he had devoted special attention to the 124 tulips, since they were bound to fetch the highest prices. To publicize the auction, they had written to Holland's best-known flower merchants and distributed pamphlets through their network of contacts throughout the republic.

All these preparations had taken time, but as it turned out, time had worked in their favor. Winckel had died the previous July, and now it was February. In the intervening months, the prices of most varieties of tulips had doubled. The orphanage's share of the expected proceeds came to far more than he had originally anticipated. Adriaen rubbed his hands together. Yes, he had plenty to be pleased about.

Willem Winckel felt sick to his stomach. The sun was beating down through the windows, and vapor was rising from the dense, damp crowd. It was warm and stuffy, and the stench of onions and alcohol hung heavy in the room.

He ran his hand over his face. The foul air forcing its way into his nostrils and throat was not the only thing making him nauseous. Another sickly odor filled the room. Every corner, every chink in the woodwork, every mote of dust was permeated with greed, like a haze only he could see, growing thicker with each new bidder who came through the door.

There was another reason for his queasy feeling. As he had lain in bed the night before, unable to fall asleep, the thought had struck him that his family was entirely dependent on other people's avarice. They had no choice but to encourage their greed and to hope it kept growing in the hours that followed. Only after the sale could he promise his brothers and sisters a secure future. The future his father had worked for all his life.

He knew it wasn't just their freedom that his father had wanted to secure. Wouter Winckel's dream had been another kind of freedom, a kind they'd often discussed in the months before his death: human freedom, freedom of speech and action. Wouter's words still rang in Willem's ears: "However much you may possess, freedom is beyond price. It is better to live in poverty and be free than to live in prosperity and be shackled by other people's prohibitions."

Willem surveyed the room. The bidders seemed to him like grave robbers, frantic to lay their hands on his father's tulips. They were huddled together in their black cloaks, their eyes glued to the sale list in their hands. The list was more than a simple enumeration of the tulips in the

estate of the innkeeper Wouter Bartelmieszoon Winckel. It was a har-
binger of hope, prosperity, and immeasurable riches, because the tulips
in question were the most valuable in all the Dutch republic. They included the rare and precious Admirael van Enckhuysen, two Viceroys,
an Admirael van der Eijck, an Admirael Liefkens, a Bruyn Purper, a
Paragon Schilder, and dozens of other coveted varieties.

Willem stole a glance at his younger brothers and sisters, sitting beside
him in the front row. He felt certain the auction would raise at least
enough for a house and someone to manage the household. One thing
was certain: they had to get out of the orphanage as soon as possible. He
needed to be able to move freely. Standing beside the grave, he had solemnly sworn that his father's death would not be in vain. He, Willem
Winckel, would take up his father's work.

Startled by the sound of the doors slamming shut, he peered over his
shoulder. All the men in the room still had their eyes on the list, except
one. The stranger sat bolt upright on his chair, staring fixedly ahead of
him. His neck was so long and thin that it was hard to believe it could
support his head. He held a Bible close to his heart, and his lips were
moving. Suddenly, without a blink, his eyes stared straight into Willem's.

At the first tap of the hammer, all the men in the room turned as one
to the auctioneer. Their eyes swept past Willem, all but those of the man
with the Bible, which held him in an unrelenting gaze. Willem felt his
blood run cold in his veins. He tore himself away and turned his attention to the front of the room.

TWENTY-ONE

Alec looked up.

"Did you say sixteen thirty-seven?"

"That's right. Why do you ask?"

"No reason," Alec said, shooting a look at Damian. "I didn't know if I had heard you right."

His mind raced with possibilities. When Frank had pointed to the date, had he meant that he'd fallen prey to some similar scheme? Or was something else going on, something Alec hardly dared contemplate? Had Frank been the evil genius behind some plot to bilk people out of their money? And had it cost him his life? It just couldn't be true.

Alec rose and wandered over to the window, staring pensively outside. He'd had enough. He was exhausted, and nothing they'd learned seemed relevant at all. How long would this guessing game go on? He turned around.

"I hate to say it, Dick, but this isn't getting us anywhere. China, Turkey, sultans, flowers, bulbs, aces, auctions. I'm totally lost. All this information and nothing we can really use."

Alec felt his anger getting the better of him, but he couldn't hold back. "What does any of this have to do with Frank? Can either of you tell me that? Not a damn thing. What the hell does the tulip trade, or the whole fucking seventeenth century, have to do with a man who had both feet firmly on the ground, a man who lived in this world, in the present, in the now? Not a goddamn thing. You know what? Let's just drop it, we'll never work it out. We should leave the whole thing to the police."

"It'll be all right, Alec. I'm sure we'll figure out what Frank was trying to tell you," Damian said.

"Nothing is going to be all right, Damian. I've lost Frank, the only family I had. Look at me now, what a loser. After all he did for me, I can't do a thing in return."

Dick patted Alec on the shoulder. "What makes you think Frank had anything to do with all this? Or that he was trying to tell you something? If you told me that, maybe I could do more to help you."

Dick followed Alec's gaze as he threw Damian a questioning look. Seeing Damian shake his head, Dick returned to his chair with a sigh. "I must say I'm disappointed you won't confide in me."

"It's not that, Dick. It's just that I . . . well, to tell you the truth, I talked to Frank right before he died."

Dick's mouth dropped open. "You talked to him?"

"Yes, just for a moment. He was in a lot of pain and . . . well, I made him a promise I intend to keep."

Dick nodded. "In that case, I understand. Look, why don't I just finish my story. You never know, right?"

Alec nodded and sat down on the windowsill.

"The bulbs at the auction in Alkmaar were put up for sale by the orphanage. They were part of an inheritance left to seven children who had ended up there. The bulbs were sold on behalf of the orphanage, so the orphanage received a share of the proceeds. That's how it worked in those days. After two hours of frantic bidding, the sale came to an end. The auctioneer was drenched with sweat, and the entire collection had been sold. The proceeds were huge. Do you have any idea how much money they made? No, of course not, how could you. Hold on, where did I put that thing?"

Dick leaned over, rummaged in a desk drawer, and produced a

course reader. He thumbed through it rapidly and, stopping at a page in the middle, said, "Wait till you hear these figures."

The auctioneer began by formally announcing what was for sale. When Willem heard the name of Wouter Winckel, his heart filled with pride. This was all his father's doing. Without knowing the first thing about the tulip trade, Wouter had thrown himself into it, studying the market and keeping track of its movements. He knew exactly when a tulip was undervalued or overvalued and it was time to make his move.

Willem had heard the rumors. People in Alkmaar were saying that Wouter had been murdered for his bulbs but the thieves had been unable to find them. Willem knew better. He knew the true motive for his father's killing, and with the proceeds of this auction, he could take revenge on the murderers. The money was vital, not just for him and his siblings, but for the entire world. He had to keep that in mind. He couldn't let himself be distracted by the greed that pervaded the hall. In the end, it would all be to his benefit.

The bidding began. The first bulb to go under the hammer was a red-and-white Boterman. Weighing in at 563 aces, it sold for 263 guilders. The second was a Scipio, which weighed only 82 aces but fetched the handsome sum of 400 guilders. Willem was stunned. How could this be? The next was a Paragon van Delft, one of his father's favorites. The winning bid was 605 guilders.

When the auctioneer announced the Bruyn Purper, a hush fell over the room. This was a lot that many people had been waiting for, because the flower, with its shades of purple and brown, was quite exceptional. The bidding went on so long that Willem almost believed it would never end. When the hammer finally fell, the selling price was 2,025 guilders. Willem glanced at the orphanage director, who was sitting beside the auctioneer's podium with a rapturous smile on his face.

After an hour, the auctioneer announced a short recess. The tension in the room was suddenly broken as everyone started talking at once.

Some were in good spirits and congratulated each other on their pur-
chases, while others looked morose. Willem rose from his chair when he
noticed the orphanage director approaching him.

"It's all going very well, just as we expected. Isn't it marvelous? We'll
remember this day for a long time to come." You bet we will, Willem
thought, and he nodded politely.

After the recess, it was time for the two Viceroys, one weighing 658
aces and the other 410. Willem had seen the stunning illustration in the
tulip book: two flowers side by side with flamed midnight-blue petals. To
his astonishment, the first sold for 4,200 guilders and the second for 3,000.
But the biggest surprise was the Admirael Liefkens, a variety known for
its sinuous lines of color. The tiny, lightweight bulb went to a dealer so
desperate to get his hands on the rare specimen that he bid 1,015 guilders.

Two hours after the bidders had poured into the room, the auction
was over. Something inconceivable had taken place. Never before in the
history of the tulip trade had an auction brought in so much money.

Dick shoved his reading glasses up onto his forehead. "Can you imagine the suspense in that auction hall? One bulb after another, selling
at record prices."

He lifted his eyebrows, and his glasses fell back onto the bridge of
his nose. Then he returned his attention to the course reader.

"It's all right here in the historical record. See for yourself."

He handed Damian the reader, open to a reproduction of the list of
prices. The page was divided into two columns, giving the weight and
selling price of each bulb in minute handwriting.

"Unbelievable," Alec said.

"Unbelievable is the word. This is where it all went wrong," Dick
continued. "Because the bids were so high, the auctioneer kept raising
the starting prices. The bidders went into a frenzy. The higher the
prices, the more they wanted those bulbs."

"What were the total proceeds?" Damian asked.

"The auction raised ninety thousand guilders all together. It says so right here." Dick pointed to the page. "On the right-hand side, all the way at the bottom."

"My God. If you convert that to modern currency, it's more than six million euros," Damian said.

"At least. Incredible, isn't it, all for a handful of bulbs. The orphans walked away with almost twelve thousand guilders each. And the orphanage ended up with nine thousand guilders. But anyway, the children had nothing to complain about. In two hours' time, they made a fortune."

Dick walked over to Alec and Damian, standing in front of them with his hands clasped behind his back. "A few days later, the tulip trade took a nosedive. The experts still don't know exactly why it all happened so fast—practically from one day to the next—but that list had a lot to do with it, that much I know. It was one of the reasons the bubble finally burst."

"This list?" Damian looked at him in surprise. "How so?"

"Right after an auction, it was standard practice to draw up an inventory of what had been sold and at what price. That was how dealers kept track of the value of different bulbs. A few days after the Alkmaar auction, this list started passing from hand to hand. The story of the huge proceeds spread like wildfire, all over the republic. Everyone in the trade was ecstatic. The list led them to believe that the value of their bulbs had soared."

Dick slowly shook his head and grimaced.

"But it didn't work out that way. The figures on the sales list became the new standard. That drove up the average selling price, and soon the country was in the grip of a feverish obsession. Some bulbs were sold and resold ten times a day, at higher prices every time. A few people sensed the limit had been reached and got out of the market as fast as they could, before it was too late. A couple of days later, at an auction in Haarlem, it became clear just how disastrous the Alkmaar auction had been. The asking prices in Haarlem were so high that hardly any bulbs were sold. That news spread quickly too. In just a few days, everyone knew."

"So they all wanted to get rid of their bulbs before the market collapsed," Alec noted.

"Exactly. And of course, it didn't work. They couldn't sell those bulbs for love or money. Within a few days, the whole tulip trade was gone, vanished, kapoof." Dick squinted pensively. "Yes, sixteen thirty-seven was the year of reckoning for tulip speculators. Fortunes were lost, vast fortunes. It was a terrible time. The impact was catastrophic."

After his visitors had shut the door behind them, Dick sat for a while, gazing out into space. He rested his elbows on the table and buried his face in his hands.

"It's all my fault," he said softly, and he lifted his eyes to the ceiling. "Oh, Frank. If I'd known it would turn out like this, I would never have got you involved." With trembling fingers, he lit a cigarette. "I'll put everything right again. I will personally see to it."

TWENTY-TWO

Tara stood in the doorway of the dimly lit room looking at her step-father, who sat hunched over his desk, not looking up. He probably didn't even hear me come into the house, she thought.

The commanding figure her mother had married so many years ago had recently faded into a mere shadow of his former self. He had always been loud and boisterous, the kind of man you couldn't ignore. Now he sat huddled in his chair, his head bowed over his paperwork.

She unbuttoned her coat and looked around at the lighter patches of wallpaper where valuable paintings had once hung. The bookcase was half empty. Apparently he'd sold part of his book collection as well.

She'd already noticed that a lot of his things had disappeared since the last time she'd been there, a couple of months earlier. Coming into the house, she'd seen the empty space in the hall where the grand-father clock had always stood. Now, looking around the room, she realized that the large nineteenth-century globe was gone from its corner. She put down her travel bag and went to his side.

"Simon?"

A shiver ran through his body. As he lifted his head to face her, he gave a feeble and uncertain smile. His eyes were dull and his gray beard, which had always been close trimmed, looked as if it had been neglected for weeks.

"Oh, Tara, it's you. How're you doing, sweetheart?"

"Not too great, actually. Were you sleeping?'

"I guess I dozed off."

She kissed him on the forehead, and the odor of unwashed hair filled her nostrils. He'd probably come straight out of bed to his chair, putting on the same clothes he'd worn the day before. Or maybe he hadn't been to bed at all. She sat down on his desk and folded her arms.

"What am I supposed to do now?"

"I don't know, love. I don't know."

"Simon? Do you know where it is?"

He looked at her sadly. "If Frank had told me that, you'd have known long ago. Don't worry about your research, darling, there's no danger. Everything will be all right. Let me take care of it."

She leaned in and took him by the shoulders. Through his sweater, she could feel his jutting bones.

"What do you mean, everything will be all right? Don't treat me like a child. We're in a real mess." She let go. "What now? Where do we go from here? What are we going to do? You know how much is at stake for me. There's got to be a Plan B, right? Didn't you and Frank ever consider the possibility that something like this would happen?"

Simon looked at his stepdaughter, wondering how she'd become so self-centered. Was she really oblivious to his financial troubles? All she ever thought about was herself. For years, he had brought her up and cared for her. Was it his fault she had turned out this way? So cold and ruthless?

He gave a deep sigh. "I see you brought your bag. Planning to stay?"

She nodded. "I don't feel safe on my own, after what happened to Frank. I . . . I'm afraid he might have let something slip about me. I didn't know what to do, and I thought I might be safer at your place."

"Frank didn't tell them a thing."

"How can you be so sure?"

He reached out and turned on the desk lamp. "Because I knew the man. Besides, why would he mention your name? You don't know any-thing, do you?"

She shook her head. "I wish I did, then at least I could do some-thing. But now . . ."

Tara went to the window and peered outside. Leaves blanketed the gravel drive. She shivered. When she turned, Simon was standing beside her. He reached over and stroked her cheek. She jerked back her head as if she'd been stung by a wasp. He withdrew his hand and looked at her sadly. Then, all of sudden, his eyes narrowed, and he took a step back. "Do you have a hunch, then?"

"About what?"

"About where Frank might have hidden it?"

"If I did, I wouldn't have to ask you, would I? What kind of a ques-tion is that? Is it any of your business, at this stage? I don't think so."

Simon cleared his throat. "No, forget I mentioned it. You're right, I was out of line. We should have done things differently. We should have realized from the outset that this might happen and taken pre-cautions. Frank was not a young man. He might just as easily have died of natural causes, or in an accident."

"Are you sure he never planned for this scenario?" she said hope-fully. "Maybe he left some notes somewhere. How about in his will? I mean . . . it can't just end this way, can it? Simon?"

"If he wrote anything down, Alec would probably know."

"That's an idea, I could talk to Alec." Then she glanced around. "What have you done with all your things?"

"Sold them."

"Has it really come to that?"

He lowered his eyes in embarrassment. "I'd rather not talk about it. I'll get by."

Tara nodded. She had more important things on her mind—anyway, more important than her stepfather's financial woes.

TWENTY-THREE

Alec and Damian walked along the Singel in silence. Though it was still early afternoon, it seemed as if twilight was already settling over the canal. In the tall seventeenth-century houses, most of the windows were lit. Two tourists rode by on bright yellow rental bikes with the seats too low, pedaling awkwardly onto the bridge that arched over the Singel. Halfway up the slope, they climbed off and walked the bikes to the top, where they got back on and raced down the other side. An oncoming driver managed to swerve just in time, honking his horn furiously as he hit the brakes.

"I have to pass by the shop and see what we're taking to the antiques fair. After that I'll drive you to the airport. Do you want to come with me, or would you rather get back to the house?" Damian asked.

"No, I'll tag along." Alec thrust his hands deep into his pockets. "What do you make of Dick's story? Have we learned anything at all?"

'Well, we know a lot more about what was going on in sixteen thirty-seven."

Alec turned to Damian. "Do you really think Frank's murder has something to do with the seventeenth-century tulip trade?"

"I can't think why else he would have pointed to that date. It's the only solid information we have to go on."

"Yes, but what did he have in mind? An auction? The stock market? It couldn't have been the tulip trade, there's no way."

Damian nodded. "Well, I've been mulling over other possibilities, like seventeenth-century art. Could there be a connection there?"

"You mean something to do with one of his antiques? One of his paintings? He had a landscape by Jan van Goyen from around that time. I don't know exactly when it was painted. I should check if it was in sixteen thirty-seven."

"Hey, that's true, I'd forgotten all about that painting." Damian stopped in his tracks, his eyes gleaming. "Jan van Goyen. Remember how he died? He was filthy rich—his paintings brought in enough to pay the bills, but he made his fortune investing in property and—"

"—tulips," Alec chimed in. "Christ, you're right, that's how he went bankrupt. When he died, he had nothing but debt. The painting must still be at Cadogan Place. Tibbens would have noticed if it was missing. I'll check it out when I get back to London."

They fell silent again and continued down the Singel until, suddenly, Alec grabbed Damian's arm and gave a sharp squeeze. With a mesmerized stare, he pointed toward the last short stretch of the canal, across the square. Damian followed the line of Alec's finger toward the flower market and looked at him blankly.

"Follow me." Alec ran across the street. At the first flower stall, he ducked beneath the awning and headed straight for one of the racks. Plastic bags filled with tulip bulbs were hanging from metal rods. Over the heads of two Japanese tourists, he snatched one of the bags and dangled it in front of Damian's face.

The strip of cardboard stapled to the plastic was decorated with a fiery red tulip. In the background, long rows of flower beds receded toward a point on the horizon. Beside the tulip was a fluorescent price sticker: €4.50.

Flushed with excitement, Alec looked at Damian, who took the bag, unsure how to respond.

"Bulbs," Alec said.

"Yes, I can see that."

"Don't you get it? We let that stupid date throw us off the scent."

Damian looked at the bag in his hands, which contained five dark brown, onion-shaped bulbs. Dirt trickled through the perforated plastic into his palm.

"Come on, Damian, use your brain. Don't you remember? The bulb fraud a couple of years back."

Damian's head shot up. "Christ, that's right. It was in the paper again just recently. There was a fund or something that invested in tulips."

Alec nodded, took back the bulbs, and returned them to the rack. "It made the papers even in England. I don't remember exactly what the story was, but I know it was some kind of scam. People invested millions and never saw their money again."

Damian pulled out his cell phone and dialed.

"Emma, will you do me a favor? Can you find anything on the Internet about a recent tulip fraud? It would've been in . . ." He glanced at Alec.

"Two thousand three or four."

"Did you get that? Right, in Holland. What did you say? No, I'll be back later, we're on our way to the shop now. Then I have to pick up the car and take Alec to the airport. Okay, I will. See you later."

He put away his phone. "I wonder what she'll find."

"The next step is to find out whether there's any connection to Frank, and if so, what. I sure hope he wasn't—"

"What? You don't think Frank was involved, do you? Or at least, not like that . . . I mean, Frank wasn't a con artist, was he?"

"God forbid. But as awful as it is, we can't rule out the possibility. Don't you agree?"

"He would never do a thing like that."

"No, not the Frank we knew. But how well did we really know him? He never said a word about that tulip book, not even to Dick, otherwise it would have come up. That's weird, right? It's a collector's item, one of a kind, something to be proud of." Alec shook his head dejectedly. "We thought we knew him, Damian, but I'm starting to have my doubts. I blame myself too. I'll always feel guilty about the way I treated Frank. All I thought about were my own needs. I couldn't have cared less what was on his mind. What's worse, it didn't even occur to me. I didn't think to ask how he was doing, really ask. Do you know what I mean?"

TWENTY-FOUR

The glass doors of London City Airport slid shut behind him. Alec made his way to the taxi stand and got in the first taxi.

Forty-five minutes later, he was standing on the steps at Cadogan Place. It dawned on him that this house, where he had spent most of his childhood, would never be the same to him again. He wanted to be rid of it, as soon as possible. That shouldn't be too difficult, he thought: a beautiful building, in a desirable location, just a ten-minute walk from Harrods.

A piece of yellow plastic clung to the doorpost—a leftover scrap of crime-scene tape. Alec pulled it off and stared at it, then crumpled it into a wad. He turned the key in the lock and opened the door.

"Tibbens," he called out. "Are you there?"

"Alec! I'm over here, in the study."

Alec crossed the entrance hall and entered the room. The wall to the right was empty. The large mirror that had always hung over the mantelpiece was leaning against the wall to his left, next to the paintings, which Tibbens had taken down. Along the baseboard, the floor was covered with a sheet. Tibbens was standing on a stepladder, with a dripping paint roller in one hand.

"I couldn't get rid of it," he said. "I wanted to finish up before you got back, so you wouldn't have to see it again." He sniffed.

"I understand," Alec said.

Tibbens put down the roller and carefully climbed down the step-ladder. Alec saw that his face was dotted with minute flecks of paint. He looked even more melancholy than usual. His eyelids, the corners of his mouth, and the deep grooves along his nose and chin were all sagging. In just a few days, he had aged dramatically. His close-cropped hair looked grayer, and his face was pale with exhaustion.

"How're you doing?"

"Not too bad, I suppose. I just can't get used to him being gone. It's as if he could walk in at any moment to ask me a question, or show me something. And whenever my phone rings I think it's him. You know what I mean?"

Alec understood only too well. For more than twenty years, Tibbens had been Frank's right-hand man. He didn't live in the house, but he was there seven days a week, from early in the morning till late at night. He had been Frank's cook, butler, chauffeur, and assistant, taking care of all his employer's needs, making sure he wanted for nothing. The two men had cared deeply about each other.

"Come with me."

Alec took Tibbens by the elbow and led him through the hall to the living room, where it was as if nothing had changed. The yellow walls made the room seem filled with sunlight. Three sofas, heaped with cushions, were grouped around the hearth. On a thick rug in the middle of the room stood a coffee table piled with books and magazines.

Tibbens sat down, and Alec went over to the wall where Frank had hung a few paintings from his collection. The only modern work was a group portrait. The man and woman were beaming. The little boy between them was not. He was clinging to his mother's legs and burying his head against her body.

Each time he saw the painting, Alec felt he had known, even as a child, that something terrible was about to happen, that this was the last photo that would ever be taken of his family. Frank had commissioned the painting of the photograph many years ago.

Alec remembered almost nothing about that time in his life and didn't know if the few memories he had were real or his own fabrications, concocted from childhood photos and stories Frank had told him. He scanned the wall until he found what he was looking for. Taking the small painting in his hands, he carefully removed it from its hook.

The clouds over the Dutch dunes hung heavy in the air. On the horizon, the sails of three ships billowed in the wind. A small boat made its way along the coast. The two oarsmen strained forward, barely equal to the stiff breeze. In the foreground were three men. Two of them sat face-to-face, and the third lay on his stomach in the sand, facing the others, the soles of his feet turned toward the viewer. To the left there was a farmhouse, shaded by the thick foliage of a stand of trees. Near the house, a woman in a bright blue skirt was milking a cow.

"What are you doing?" Tibbens asked.

"I want to check something."

He turned over the painting and read the yellowing label pasted to the wood on the back.

> *Jan van Goyen*
> *Dutch, 1596–1656*
> Dune Landscape, *1634*
> *Oil on panel*

Useless, Alec thought. He'd been hoping that something would be hidden behind the painting. A letter from Frank, explaining everything, or at least giving a clue—something, anyway. He put the painting back in place and sat down opposite Tibbens.

"I could have told you what was on that label," Tibbens said. "I mean, if you want to know how much it's worth, if that's what you're after, then—"

Alec held up his hand. "No, no. I'm sorry if I gave that impression. I just wanted to know when it had been painted, that's all. Just curious." Then he leaned forward and said, "I have to ask you a couple of questions. I'd like you to answer me honestly."

"Of course, why wouldn't I?"

"Well, you might think I'm better off not knowing."

"What are you talking about?"

"When I was at Scotland Yard, they asked me whether Frank had ever had casual encounters. What they meant was, did he ever pick up men, on the street or God knows where, and bring them home?"

"He didn't do that sort of thing. No two ways about it," Tibbens snapped. He stared down at the carpet, shuffling his feet. With the toe of his shoe, he brushed the thick pile to one side.

"You said you'd be honest with me."

"I'm not trying to protect you. I just don't want his name to be dragged through the mud."

"You don't have to protect Frank anymore. Besides, who'll ever know? I won't tell a soul."

Tibbens looked at Alec. He was pressing his right fist against his lips, and his eyebrows were drawn together.

"Tibbens, don't you trust me?"

He moved his hand away from his face. "All right, then, so be it. A long time ago, in his younger years, he did that sort of thing on occasion. But it's nobody else's business. It wasn't against the law."

Alec wasn't surprised. Many years earlier, he had come home in the middle of the night and run into a young man who was just slipping out of Frank's bedroom. They had nodded at each other, without saying a word. Alec had never asked Frank about it. It was none of his business.

"The last time he brought anyone home," Tibbens went on, "was at least ten years ago, maybe longer. He lost interest. Those days were over. That couldn't have had anything to do with it. The police asked me the same question. They wanted the names of everyone he knew, everyone he'd ever called on the phone or written to."

"What did you tell them?"

"Why, I told them what I knew—that is, what I had a mind to tell them. No need for them to know everything. I didn't say a thing about the young men. You know how it is. Before you know it the newspapers and magazines would be full of rumors and gossip about his life. Where do you think those journalists get their information? They've got their contacts at Scotland Yard. Frank's life was his own. It's private, and it's staying in here," he said, pointing at his head. "And somewhere else too."

Tibbens rose and left the room. Just as Alec was about to go after him, he reappeared with a box in his hands.

"This is for you: his private correspondence, part of it, anyway. The rest is in those other boxes." Tibbens put down the box and jerked his thumb toward the hall. "I put them over there for you."

"What am I supposed to do with them?"

"Don't ask me. 'If anything happens to me, give the letters to Alec.' That's all he ever said. A while back, he asked me to store it all at my place. Every month he'd give me a new stack, and I'd put it with the rest. Well, it's yours now."

"What about the police?"

"They didn't ask, and I saw no reason to mention it."

Alec glanced at the box. It was filled with papers, right up to the top. "I felt the same way," he said. "I didn't tell the police everything I knew. I promised him I wouldn't."

"Promised? How's that? When did you talk to him?"

"When I found him here."

Tibbens stared at him in disbelief. "You don't mean he actually spoke to you?"

"Yes, he did. At least, he asked me something."

"What? What did he ask you?" Tibbens had risen to his feet and was wringing his hands.

"I'll tell you later, when the investigation is over and they've caught the killer. I can't say right now."

"But maybe I can help." His voice trembled. "I knew the man better than he knew himself. I could read him like a book."

"I know, and there is a way you can help. Did you ever notice anything strange? Did you ever wonder whether Frank was keeping something from you?"

"Such as?"

"I'm sorry, I don't really know what I'm looking for. How was he doing financially? Did he have any debts that you know of?"

"I couldn't say. If he did, I wasn't aware of it. I suppose his solicitor will tell us more about that today, when we see him. Hmm, something strange, you said?" He pondered the question. "No, I don't think so. There is one thing, mind, but I don't know how much it matters. He went away for a long weekend twice a year."

"There's nothing strange about that, is there?"

"No, of course not, but he went on his own. You know I always accompanied him, right? I once asked him what he was planning to do, but he wouldn't tell me. 'Just a short break,' he said. But you know and I know that your uncle had no interest in short breaks. Every trip he took had a purpose." Tibbens nodded. "Aye, he was always a bit secretive about those weekends. I even wondered if he was having an affair, but for goodness' sake, he could've just told me that."

"Did he always go to the same place?"

"Yes, always Lake Como."

"So what's the big secret? We all went there together more times than I can count. Why wouldn't he take you with him? How many times did this happen?"

"A dozen or more, I'd say."

"So it started around two thousand two?"

"That's right. It probably doesn't mean a thing. Maybe he really did want some time off."

"Strange," Alec said.

"Aye. Right, are you coming along?" Tibbens glanced at his watch and got up. "The solicitor's expecting us in half an hour."

"One more thing. Do you know if Frank was investing in tulips, or if he had any connection to the tulip business?"

"The tulip business? Whatever gave you that idea?"

Alkmaar

Willem elbowed his way through the crowd, pushing aside all who stood in his way. Fresh air, he thought, I need air, I can't breathe.

Finally, after what seemed like an eternity, he was standing in the doorway of the New Archery Hall. Taking a deep breath, he felt the icy air hit his lungs. He coughed, then looked around furtively and headed briskly down the street. At the first side alley, he spun around the corner and leaned against the wall. His breath made an odd wheezing noise, like a chick peeping for its mother. He turned to the wall and pressed his forehead against the stones. The cold seeped into his skin, bringing him the relief he longed for. His nausea slowly subsided. He laid his hands flat against the wall, lifted his head skyward, and said softly, "It's all taken care of. We'll be fine now. There's no need for you to worry."

Willem knew his father hadn't believed in heaven or life after death. Neither did he, but still. He had to deal with it somehow. This was the only way he could think of. Then, suddenly, he let out a cry.

"Easy, young fellow, easy. What's the matter?" Cornelius looked anxiously at Willem, removing his hand from the boy's shoulder.

"Oh, it's you, sir. Pardon me, I was startled."

"No, no, it's my fault. I should have let you be instead of alarming you like that. Will you join me?"

Willem meekly accompanied Cornelius back in the direction of the auction house. "I told him he doesn't have to worry about us," he murmured.

"Yes, I heard you praying," Cornelius said. He reached out and patted Willem on the back. "Very good, my boy, very good. He'll be your strength and your shield in the difficult days ahead. As long as you trust in Him, everything will turn out all right."

Willem would have liked to say all sorts of things. That it wasn't God he'd been talking to, but his father. That he didn't need God, because he believed in himself, in love, in the power of nature, and in humankind. That God didn't even exist, at least not the way most people imagined, and that his father's work would have demonstrated that. And he wanted to tell Cornelius that he, Willem Winckel, would carry on that work. But he said nothing.

TWENTY-FIVE

Damian kissed Emma's head. He put his hands on her shoulders and looked at the computer screen in front of her. She was scrolling down a page on a newspaper's website. Emma turned toward him and placed her hand on his.

"Have you figured it out?" she asked.

"What? Frank's secret?"

"No, what you're taking to the antiques fair, for the stand."

"Oh, that, yes. We'll do an English library this time."

"Sounds nice. And how about Dick? Did he have anything interesting to say?"

"Oh, he gave us plenty of information, but not too much that we can use. He took us through the whole history of the tulip trade, its rise and fall. But I still can't see the connection to Frank."

She pointed to the printouts stacked beside her monitor.

"You and Alec were right. There was a tulip scam, in two thousand three. The investors lost millions, and the newspapers called it the Great Bulb Fraud."

He pulled up a chair and sat down next to her.

"So you two think Frank might have had something to do with it?"

"Maybe. In sixteen thirty-seven, the year that Frank pointed to, the tulip market collapsed, and investors in bulbs lost all their money."

"You think Frank was trying to tell Alec that he was involved in the fraud?"

"It's one possibility."

"The thing is, though, how can we know for sure? There's almost nothing about the people who lost their money—at least, I can't find much. I do know there were a lot of them."

"How many?"

"Well, this article says that about two hundred private investors were involved. I can imagine they don't want their names all over the papers. I'd feel the same way. Imagine the humiliation."

"Is it really as bad as all that?"

"It's pretty bad," she said, shuffling through the stack of paper and finally pulling out a page. "Here, all in all they lost thirty-two million euros."

Damian whistled softly. "Thirty-two million? Where did all that money go?"

"That's what everyone would like to know. It just vanished. They'd put it into something called the Tulip Investment Fund. It's still not clear what went wrong, exactly, or who was conning who. What I can tell you is that the money was supposed to finance the development of new tulip varieties. Apparently that costs a fortune, and growers are always looking for backers to invest in new projects. I guess if you can grow a better tulip, the world will beat a path to your door."

"So what kind of money did the investors expect to make?"

"The brochure hinted at a possible twenty-five-percent return in just one year."

"Sounds too good to be true."

"And it was. Now everyone is pointing fingers at everyone else. The tulip fund insists that it gave the money to the growers, and they embezzled it. They actually had buyers lined up for the tulips. Tulips that didn't even exist yet."

History repeats itself, Damian thought.

"Unbelievable, right? They were buying something that existed only on paper. Nothing had actually been grown. Anyway, the fund managers are blaming the growers, but the growers blame the fund. They say the managers put the funds in a foreign account. Another suspect is the bank that lent investors the money to buy shares. The investors say the bank should have warned them about the risks. Apparently it's impossible to develop a new variety of tulip in less than a year. So all the talk of a twenty-five-percent return within twelve months was optimistic, to say the least. In the end, the investors didn't get one cent of their money back."

"Now the question is whether Frank was involved," Damian said. "Maybe he invested in this fund and lost everything."

"You think he may have borrowed money?"

"Maybe. It's the kind of thing that could get a person in very hot water."

"Damian," Emma said cautiously, "you know there's another possibility."

"What's that?"

She wobbled uneasily in her chair. "It could have been the other way around."

"What's that supposed to mean?"

"Well, Frank could have been one of the people who made off with that money. That could be the connection."

Damian stood up, pushing his chair back. He gazed down at Emma with a frown.

"I can't believe it. First him, and now you."

"Him?'

"Yeah. Alec suggested the same thing. I don't understand you two. How could you suspect Frank of something like that? How could you think that of him?"

"All I'm saying is, we can't just rule out the possibility. Apparently Alec feels the same way, despite the pain it must cause him. After all, it's his uncle we're talking about."

"Don't forget, I knew Frank too, almost all my life. You know what we went through together, how close we were. And later, there was that whole awful business with Alec, when he went to the clinic, remember? Frank and I, lugging him in like a sack of potatoes? And afterward, when we had to keep an eye on him? Frank had to watch every move that Alec made. In that kind of situation, you really find out what a person's made of, I can tell you that much."

Emma looked up at him in outrage. "You don't have to tell me anything. I knew him for as long as you did, or have you forgotten?" Her voice broke into a sob. "I loved Frank."

She took a deep breath and said, "But that's not what matters now, Damian, that's not the point. What we need—"

He snorted. "Of course it matters. How can you just turn against someone you knew so well?"

"Look, a long friendship isn't the same thing as a close friendship."

"Any other platitudes you'd like to share?"

Emma gave no answer and kept her eyes fixed on the screen, scrolling down the page, her hand trembling on the mouse.

Damian swiveled her chair to face him, and holding on to its arms, he leaned forward. Staring into her eyes, he said, "Hold on a second. Who is this really about? Are we talking about Frank? Or are you talking about yourself? Well?"

She looked away, and he let go of the chair with a curse. Suddenly she understood that he'd always known, and seen that there was nothing he could do. Still, he had chosen her, even though she'd cheated on him with his best friend. She felt like kicking herself. How blind she'd been, to go chasing after something she could never have. Was that why she'd wanted to win Alec's love? Because she knew she never could? Was it the challenge that excited her? Or was it simply that she wanted him? She knew perfectly well that she and Alec weren't a good match. They would drive each other insane. So there was no chance of a real relationship, just a romantic thrill. I must be crazy, she thought.

Emma turned to Damian and opened her mouth to speak, but he had already stormed out of the room.

TWENTY-SIX

Tara dragged herself up the stairs, feeling drained and hollow. All the energy she had poured into her work over the past months seemed to have fizzled out. The unimaginable had happened.

Looking back, the stupid thing was that she'd always had the feeling something would go wrong. She had started to worry the moment Frank told her she wouldn't have the bulb until the very last minute, when everything else was in place. Not that she was afraid Frank would back out. No, he was focused on his goal, just as she was. It wasn't the same goal, but that didn't matter.

Where had Frank hidden the bulb? A few months before she had asked him that very question, but he refused to tell her anything. "It's safer this way," he said. "It's best if I'm the only one who knows."

"But what if something happens to you?" she asked.

"Oh, then the bulb will turn up eventually."

But look at them now: no Frank and no bulb. She hoped he'd at least had the sense to keep it in a safe, under lock and key.

She went into the bathroom and turned on the faucets in the tub. She could still remember it as if it were yesterday: Simon and Frank explaining their idea and waiting expectantly for her response. With a shriek of delight, she had thrown her arms around them and hugged them tight, her heart racing.

At that moment, everything had fallen into place. Every choice she'd ever made, every decision, all her priorities—they all made sense. So did the sacrifices: the boyfriends she'd never had, the invitations she'd turned down, the vacations she hadn't taken. It had all been worth it.

Until now. Now she was starting to have her doubts, and that was the last thing she needed. She got undressed and stepped into the hot water. As her head slid beneath the surface, tiny bubbles tickled her ears. She pushed back her hair and closed her eyes.

She wasn't the only one changed by all this. Simon was different too. From the moment their plan began to unfold, bad luck had seemed to hound him. He got into financial difficulties, and his health started to decline. But, she could tell, that wasn't all that was eating away at him. He'd had money troubles in the past and taken them in his stride. Sooner or later, he'd always found a solution. This time, things were different. He couldn't seem to climb out of the hole—a hole that he had probably dug himself.

Instead of relaxing, Tara's brain was working at top speed. She got out of the tub and wrapped herself in a towel.

Maybe Simon was right, and Alec had the information she needed. She would have to find out fast, before it was too late.

TWENTY-SEVEN

Down below it was gray and drizzly. Up here the sun was blazing on Alec's face. He closed his eyes and savored the warm rays.

Damian had sent his private jet to bring Alec to Amsterdam. It had been ready for departure when Alec arrived at London City Airport, and the two pilots had escorted him across the damp asphalt to the streamlined aircraft. Alec had nestled into the leather lounge chair, and ten minutes later they were flying straight through the low-hanging clouds and into the sunshine. He could hear the pilots conversing quietly in the cockpit.

No sooner had he opened his eyes than he squeezed them shut again. The sky was so blue it hurt. He leaned back and thought over the meeting with the solicitor.

As they entered the office, they'd seen Frank's will lying on the long mahogany table. After the solicitor had read it aloud, Tibbens and Alec turned to each other in surprise.

"Not what you were expecting?" the solicitor asked Alec.

"It's just that I didn't know he felt so strongly about it. It wouldn't have surprised me if he'd left his money to the RSPCA. But to science?"

"I was thinking the exact same thing," Tibbens said. "I never knew science to be one of his interests."

When Alec asked whether Frank might ever have invested in tulips, the solicitor told him that Frank had given up risky investments long ago. He'd decided to play it safe, sold all his shares, and put his entire fortune into a high-interest bank account.

Alec sat up straight and checked the monitor in front of him. Still a few more minutes before they landed. He stretched his legs and stared at the toes of his shoes. Frank and science? He just didn't get it. The solicitor had promised to send him a list of all the organizations Frank had left money to. Maybe there was some connection to his own past problems. Could they be researching cures for drug addiction? Or was the money going to clinics like the one he'd been in?

He thought back to the night that Damian had discovered him in the bathroom during one of those wild parties, his nose deep in the cocaine that their host had laid out. A few days later Alec admitted he'd been doing coke a couple of times a day—"for inspiration," he had said.

Frank and Damian had put all their energy into persuading him to go into rehab. Six months later they'd picked him up from the clinic. He'd stayed clean ever since. Frank had been so grateful to the clinic that it wouldn't have surprised Alec if he'd left them a generous donation.

The pilot turned around and shouted that they were about to land. Alec fastened his seat belt and looked outside. The sun had disappeared; they were passing through the clouds. Droplets crept like bugs across his windowpane. He swallowed to relieve the pressure in his ears. When they emerged from the cloud bank, he saw Amsterdam spread out below. Curving rows of streetlamps traced the canals around the city's heart, circles of light contracting toward the center like layers of onionskin. He always enjoyed this unique view, the magnificent old city lying at his feet.

Why shouldn't I move to Holland? he wondered as he gazed at the dots of light. But no, it was probably better for him to stay in England.

Whenever he saw her—no, whenever he saw them together—his guilt resurfaced. Talking to Damian on the phone was one thing, but seeing him, having to look him in the eyes . . .

They'd fallen out of touch over the past few years, but Frank's death had changed everything and brought them closer again. Alec knew he should confess, tell Damian he had betrayed him by sleeping with Emma, that one night, three years ago. Now his relationship with Emma was strained and guilt ridden. The awkwardness they felt in each other's presence was glaringly obvious. Damian must have noticed, though he'd never mentioned it.

With a soft thud, the wheels hit the landing strip. The pilot applied the brakes, and the streamlined aircraft slowly taxied to where the other private airplanes were parked in a neat row.

Damian was waiting in the small concourse. "What've you got in that thing?" he asked, looking at the large suitcase Alec was pulling along behind him.

"Frank's correspondence."

"Correspondence?"

"Yeah. I don't know what's in them. I haven't looked yet. Frank asked Tibbens to save some of his letters and such, I don't know why. So I brought it all with me. I think we should go through the whole pile. After all, Frank must have had a reason for giving it to Tibbens. There's got to be some kind of clue there somewhere."

"Well, let's hope so."

In the car, Damian explained what Emma had found out about the tulip fraud. After mulling it over, Alec said, "What if Frank was involved in that scandal?"

"Involved how? Would he have been one of the good guys, the investors who got taken for a ride, or—"

"—was he the one who made off with the cash? Is that what you're getting at?"

"Yeah, maybe. Yeah."

Alec stared pensively ahead of him. "How much did you say was missing?"

"Thirty-two million."

"If Frank embezzled it, it's gone now, funneled into some other account. He doesn't have it. I've seen the will, and his entire estate doesn't add up to that."

Damian couldn't help feeling relieved, but he also knew the money could have been used for something else. Frank would've been crazy to hold on to it. Maybe he'd set up a dummy corporation and sent it all to the Caymans. There were so many ways to make money disappear.

"No," Alec said, shaking his head. "It doesn't make sense. It's just not like Frank. You know what he put in his will? Half of his estate is going to science."

"Huh? I never knew Frank was interested in science."

"Right, neither did I. I can't get my head around it."

"How much did he leave?"

"Twenty million pounds."

"No small potatoes, then."

"The solicitor said Frank had changed his will a few years ago."

"But why science?"

"That's what I have to figure out. By the way, I asked Tibbens whether he thought Frank had been hiding something. The only thing he could think of was that from two thousand two onward Frank went on weekend trips twice a year. Tibbens didn't know why, or who with."

"But he did know where Frank went?"

"Yeah. Lake Como."

Damian raised his eyebrows. "That hotel where he always used to take us?"

Alec nodded.

TWENTY-EIGHT

Coetzer stood on the pavement, looking up. Behind him, the Thames rolled swiftly past. His jacket was flapping wildly, as if the wind were trying to carry him away. If he could just hold out a little longer, he could go home, back to the warmth of South Africa. Shivering, he pulled his jacket tight around him and crossed the street.

All he'd had to do to find Alec Schoeller was check the phone book. Even without a house number, Coetzer would have known which apartment to go to. Every brick building in the row had tiny windows on the upper floor, except for this one, where they'd been replaced with a picture window running the length of the façade.

He went to the front door and pressed the top bell. Inside he could hear a faint buzz. He pressed his ear to the door. Nothing. He rang the bell again. No one. Just as he was reaching into his pocket for his tools, he heard someone coming to the door.

The woman was wearing a light blue bathrobe with worn threads of terry cloth dangling from the sleeves. Her bright blue eye shadow had collected in the folds of her eyelids, and clumps of mascara hung from her lashes. The lapdog tucked under her arm glared at Coetzer and growled fiercely.

"You're here for Mr. Schoeller, I presume?"

She swept back a lock of hair that had strayed from her beehive hairdo. Lipstick filled the lines at the corners of her mouth. She chose her words carefully to mask her thick Cockney accent.

"Yes, I am. Is he in?"

"Not momentarily, you've just missed him. Whom shall I say was calling?"

"Oh, rotten luck. I'm here to pick up a painting for the gallery. Didn't he mention it to you, then?"

"No, I'm afraid Mr. Schoeller didn't say anything to me. I'm awfully sorry, but I can't help you. You'd better come back another day, when he's at 'o—that is . . . when he's available. Good day."

Coetzer just managed to wedge his foot in the door. As he wrapped his hand around the doorpost, he felt the hot breath of the dog, which yapped and went for his thumb. Bloody hairball.

"Just a moment," he said. "I'll give him a ring."

She slowly opened the door a little farther.

"He was going to leave the painting right there for me, so all I have to do is pick it up. Wait a moment, I'll call him now."

As he punched the number, she looked him up and down, clutching the dog to her chest like a hot-water bottle.

"Alec, hi, it's Jack," Coetzer said, as he listened to his voice mail. "Yeah, I'm at the house. Slipped your mind, did it? Well, happens to the best of us. Listen, mate, we need that painting today. What? Yeah, she's right here with me. Okay, fine, I'm sure she won't mind. Right, later, bye."

Just as she reached for the phone, he slipped it into his jacket pocket.

"I would have liked to speak to him myself," she said crossly. "I can't have just anybody tramping in and out."

"Oh, sorry about that, he was in a rush. But anyway, you heard it, I'm supposed to go ahead and get the painting now. He said I should ask you to let me in, if you'd be so kind."

"I've got the key. I always take care of his cat when he's away."

"How long will he be gone for?"

"A week or so. He left this afternoon to visit friends in Holland. Isn't it just terrible what happened to his uncle?"

"Terrible thing, that."

"The man was killed, did you hear that? Brutally murdered, his head practically hacked off. They say he was robbed too, they stripped the house bare. You're not safe anywhere these days, not even in your own home. It doesn't bear thinking about."

"Heard about that, terrible, just terrible." The irony in his voice escaped her.

"But fortunately, I have Shakespeare, don't I, widdle-tiddlums?"

She gave the dog a kiss, leaving a large orange blotch on its furry head. When she looked up, Coetzer saw a couple of dog hairs clinging to her lips. Filthy hag.

"Well, you'd better come in then. I'll show you upstairs."

"Oh, that's very kind of you, but there's no need. I know my way around the place."

She contemplated the steep staircase.

"Very well, then."

From the pocket of her bathrobe she produced a ring of keys, picking out one with a grimy pink ribbon attached to it.

"Bring it back before you leave, all right? Just knock on the door over there," she said, pointing. "No mess, if you please, I've just tidied up so Mr. Schoeller can come home to a nice clean flat. Lord, what a pigsty. Leaves his clothes lying any old place, and that fridge of his—"

"I'll just be a moment," Coetzer broke in. "As soon as I've got the painting I'll be off."

He climbed the stairs, opened the door, and felt something brush against his calf. Instinctively, he pulled his leg aside. The cat meowed and sat down a few feet from the door, its yellow eyes taking his measure. Coetzer walked over to the animal, kicking it as he passed. With a yowl, it fled the entranceway, racing ahead of him into the living room.

The walls were white and bare, all except one, which was decorated with a large abstract painting. On the deep-pile beige carpet were two chairs with billowing leather cushions in angular chrome frames. Against one wall was a buffet holding a sound system and stacks of CDs. At the far end of the room was a dining table covered with small piles of newspapers and letters, next to a large delft serving dish full of pens, receipts, paper clips, loose keys, and miscellaneous clutter. In the middle of the room was a staircase. Coetzer made his way up, with the cat at his heels.

The upper room smelled strongly of paint. Canvases were propped against the walls, on one of which there hung a large unfinished painting. All that had been done was the light blue background. The table in the middle of the studio was covered with brushes, half-empty tubes, and cans of paint. It was clear that this area was off-limits to Alec Schoeller's helpful neighbor.

Coetzer began in the far left corner, meticulously combing the entire room. When he was done, he went over to the canvases stacked against the wall and examined them one by one. The last one was so small that he had to stoop to reach it. He picked it up and wiped off the dust. She was reclining on a sofa, her arms resting over her head. Her green eyes looked out at Coetzer so tenderly that he began to feel ill. He flipped the painting over. On the back was a name in pencil: "Emma." Suddenly he knew where he had seen her before—in the photograph on Frank Schoeller's piano, wearing a wedding dress. But the man at her side bore no resemblance to Alec.

He tucked the painting under his arm and went back down the stairs. In the living room, he went through the same process, picking up everything and turning it over. Then he sat down at the table and pulled one of the stacks of paper toward him. As he was going through the newspapers and letters one by one, he heard a shout.

"You still up there?"

Bloody bitch. Het got up and went to the door.

"Yes, I'm still here, is anything wrong?"

"Are you having trouble finding it?" she shouted up the stairs. "You've been in there for ages. You're not making a mess, are you?"

"Still looking. It's not as easy as I thought."

"Need a hand, then?"

"Don't trouble yourself. I'm sure I'll find it."

Hearing the door bang shut below, he went back to the table. On top of the smallest stack was a newspaper folded open to an article about Frank's murder. In the margins, Alec had made some doodles, one of which looked like a snail shell. In the middle of the spiral he had written a date—1637—followed by a thick black question mark. He had put so much pressure on the pen that the newspaper was almost torn. Beneath it was the word "tulips," with another question mark.

Coetzer knew enough. He picked up the painting and went downstairs. In the hall below, he knocked on the neighbor's door, which opened right away.

"Ah, I see you've found it," she said, looking at the painting he held under his arm. The dog tried to slip out of the apartment, but with skill borne of experience, she slid her leg over, trapping the animal between the doorpost and her fleshy calf. Coetzer glanced down. Her slippered feet looked surprisingly young, and on the band across her toes, little feathers were swaying gently.

When he gave her the key, she said, "Let's have a look, then." Her hand shot toward the painting and snatched it from under his arm.

"This one?" She stared in surprise. "Is this what you came to fetch? He did this years ago. I remember the exact day he—"

Cunt. "That's right, but now we've found a buyer at last. Could I have it back, please? I'm in a bit of a hurry."

"A buyer? Strange, I thought he only sold those paintings of squares and such. Don't care for them myself, but never mind. Hard to believe people will pay good money for a few streaks of paint like that. Now, if it was a nice portrait, like this one here, or a lovely vase of fl—"

"Sorry, but I really must be going. Thank you kindly. Good-bye."

He turned and strode out of the house.

"I'll let him know you dropped in!" she called after him.

TWENTY-NINE

The hallway was filled with the tantalizing aroma of fresh bread, garlic, and sautéed onions.

Alec smiled. "Mrs. Sartori?"

Damian nodded, and Alec went into the kitchen. She stood with her broad back toward him, stirring a pan at the stove. As he entered, she turned. Tomato sauce dripped from the spoon onto the floor. With a joyful whoop, she set the spoon on the counter, wiped her hands on the dishcloth draped over her shoulder, and rushed over to Alec with open arms.

"Alec, *caro*, how are you?"

She wrapped her arms around him and hugged him tightly. Then she grasped his arms and looked up into his eyes.

"Think of it this way, Alessandro. It's like we say in Italy: You'll meet again someday, in a better world than this."

He choked back his emotion. "You're right, I'll keep that in mind."

"All right, then. Let's eat. Food is good for the soul, you know. It heals all wounds."

"Where's Emma?"

"She's out having dinner with a friend. I guess she thinks she'll eat better there than she does here. Well, if they want to throw away their money, who's stopping them? Not me. Sit down, sit down."

One end of the long table was laid with a white tablecloth and set for two. Mrs. Sartori prodded Alec out ahead of her and pushed him into a chair.

"Now, where is Damian? Hold on, I'll call him. Daaaamian! *Mangi-are! Pronto!*" Her voice boomed through the house.

An hour and a half later, they lifted the heavy suitcase and spilled its contents onto the kitchen table.

"Let's see," Damian said, carefully spreading out the pile.

The whole tabletop was covered with letters, invitations, cards, clippings, handwritten notes, and printed e-mails. They each took a stack and began leafing through them. For a while, the only sound in the kitchen was the soft scrape and rustle of paper.

"What a chore. It's utter chaos," Damian said. "Have you come across anything interesting yet?"

"No, it's a mess. Maybe we should sort everything by date first—or even just by year."

"Yes, that might help. At least we know what we're looking for. Anything about tulips or the seventeenth century . . ."

". . . or those trips to Como. Those are the only leads we have so far, right?"

"I think so."

They went on working in silence until Damian said, "It looks like he started collecting this stuff for you in two thousand two. I haven't seen anything older than that."

"Hey, Damian." Alec brandished a sheaf of paper. "Look at all these letters he sent asking for information. Why would he have saved all these?"

"I can't see any pattern," Damian replied, flipping through them. "Universities, pharmaceutical companies, botanical institutes, laboratories, DNA research, everything under the sun."

"Right. Brochures, registration forms, research reports, you name it."

"We'll set them aside and go over them again later."

After a while Alec said, "You know what seems strange to me? Those postcards. Have you run into any yet?"

"Yeah, I just saw one. It was signed 'Simon.' That was a friend of Frank's, right? Simon Versteegen?"

"Yeah, they went back a long way. I think they did business sometimes, so they probably had plenty of reasons to write each other, but still, there's something weird about those cards. Why would Simon send Frank cryptic little messages like that? Besides, they're the only postcards Frank saved for me."

They picked through the stacks of paper, fishing out ten postcards in all.

"You're right about those messages," Damian said. "They're weird. This one says, 'Up another ten.' And this one says, 'Doubled.'"

"They're all about figures." Alec stared at the card in his hand, brooding.

"And what are we supposed to make of *this*?" Damian asked, after Alec had laid all the cards side by side with the pictures facing up.

"The theme seems pretty obvious. He didn't just pull these off the rack at random. Here's one with lots of scientific instruments. A chronometer, a sextant, and a telescope. And here's Leonardo da Vinci's sketch of a flying machine." As Alec described the cards, he tapped each one with his index finger. "A portrait of Galileo Galilei." He flipped over the card and looked at Damian. "You know when this was painted? Sixteen thirty-six. You see? They're all connected to the seventeenth century."

"You're right."

Damian studied the pictures with a frown. Then he reached out and pulled one toward him.

"Do you see what I see?"

Alec nodded.

Eight men dressed in black were gathered around a table. Light shone on their broad white collars. A beam slanting down from the upper left corner illuminated the naked body lying on the table. The skin was pale, almost transparent, in contrast to the soles of the man's feet, which looked unwashed. A loincloth was draped loosely over his genitals.

Three of the men were leaning in to examine the body. The two behind them gazed directly out at the viewer. One held a piece of paper covered with writing too small to read. They seemed somewhat disturbed, as if the person looking at the painting had burst into the room without warning. One of the two men at the bottom left glanced at the viewer out of the corner of his eye. The man behind him looked straight ahead, toward the central figure of the painting, the only one wearing a hat—a large, black one with a wide brim. He sat bolt upright in his chair, his mouth open slightly. He was gesturing with his left hand and holding a forceps in his right, which he was using to keep open the incised skin of the dead man's forearm. All the muscles and tendons were exposed from the elbow to the tips of the fingers.

"Finally, something to go on." Damian stared excitedly at the postcard.

Alec nodded. *"The Anatomy Lesson of Dr. Nicolaes Tulp."*

Alkmaar

The three men who had sat in different parts of the room, bidding on every lot, met at the entrance to the New Archery Hall. Squinting in the glare of the winter sun, they huddled together and exchanged glances without saying a word.

The door behind them opened and the tall man stepped out, still clutching the Bible to his chest, his finger marking a page. He looked at them and nodded. Visibly relieved, they nodded back. Then, without so much as a greeting, they turned and left, dispersing into the street.

He was satisfied. They had arrived with empty purses and were returning home with empty hands, but he felt richer than ever. They had completed their mission successfully. He was sure of it.

Never before had tulip bulbs fetched such high prices. During the auction, it had been hard for him to contain himself. How had it come to this? Wealth and finery was all they cared about, all that gave their lives meaning. He had seen it around him, spreading like the plague. The weaver who lived around the corner had sold his loom and used the money to buy tulip bulbs. And the blacksmith who shod his horse had closed his business and started investing in tulips.

He hoped it would soon be over and they would all go back to their proper station in life, to the tasks God had ordained. Then true Christianity would return to the republic, which over the past years had slowly transformed into an abyss of greed, egotism, and blasphemy. If his plan worked as he prayed it would, the masses would pour back into the house of God, driven by their fear of the future. Then he would help them restore meaning to their empty, miserable lives.

For now, he would simply watch and wait. Great changes were coming for all of them, that much was certain.

THIRTY

"What could these messages mean?" Alec asked. "What were Simon and Frank up to? I know they were friends. Simon came to visit now and then, but I certainly wouldn't call him a regular guest. He had a stepdaughter about my age. I can imagine he and Frank might have talked to each other about child rearing, that kind of thing. They were both going it alone."

"When did they meet?"

"When they were students, I think, like Frank and Dick. But why was Simon sending him those cards every year? Simon's the one we have to talk to."

Alec stood up abruptly. "I just realized something, Damian. How stupid of me not to think of it before. The whole time, I've been wondering where it was I saw Simon's name recently. God, I could kick myself. I remember thinking there was something funny about it. Hold on, I'll be right back."

He leaped up, raced out of the kitchen, and returned a moment later, holding a book.

"The condolence register," he said, a little out of breath. "Here, look . . . wait, damn it . . . where was it?"

He leafed through the pages at a furious pace.

"I thought it was a weird message. Oh, here it is, look what he wrote."

Damian looked at the hurried scrawl, which stood in stark contrast to the other, neatly penned, expressions of sympathy.

Alec,

The death of a loved one is always bewildering. Maybe I can help you understand.

Yours, Simon Versteegen

Under the message was a telephone number.

"He wants to tell you something."

"That's for sure," Alec said, clapping the register shut.

Alec sat at the kitchen table, tapping his nails against his full wine-glass. His gaze wandered over the objects in front of him. Damian had kindled a fire before he went upstairs, and the gold leaf of the tulip book gleamed in the light of the flames. Next to the book lay the post-cards. Alec fanned them out.

"What were you trying to tell me, Frank?"

He picked up the tulip book, then changed his mind and put it down again. He pushed himself away from the table and stretched.

"Aren't those illustrations just amazing?"

Emma draped her jacket over a chair and kissed him on the cheek. She sat down and pulled the book toward her. Gently, she stroked the cover. He looked at her hand, remembering how she'd touched him the same way. He could feel her caresses down his back again, remembered the look in her eyes when he turned to face her. Cut it out, Alec, he thought to himself. You've had too much to drink.

She looked up. "Yesterday I took a good look at this book. I'm starting to wonder whether it really holds the clue we're looking for."

"Would you like some wine?"

"I'd love some."

As he got up to fetch a glass, she said, "Maybe we were wrong, and Frank meant something completely different."

"I'm coming around to that point of view myself."

She picked up the glass, took a sip, and said, "Here's what we'll do. We'll go through the whole book once more, but this time we'll do it right. One page at a time. Who knows. Maybe we missed something."

"Go through it again? Now?"

"Yeah, right from the beginning. Now, where are those gloves?"

"Here, use this." He grabbed a dishcloth and handed it to her.

Alec looked over Emma's shoulder as she slowly turned the pages. Every illustration was superb. The tulips were rendered in minute detail. One of the leaves of the tulip in front of them was sagging under the weight of a snail that crept toward the tip. On one of the petals in the next illustration, the artist had painted a fly, so lifelike that you'd think it might take wing at any moment. The tulips were magnificent, executed with such devotion that each new page made Emma and Alec more deeply aware not only of their beauty but also of the power that dwelled in their simplicity. Not a petal too many, the outlines crisp and clear. They were exuberant in a way, but also modest, as if they were unaware of their own splendor. It was the combination of their simple forms—the bloom, the slender stem, the tapering leaves—with the brilliant colors of their petals that made these flowers so special.

Alec was starting to appreciate why so many people had fallen under their spell, and how a bouquet of real tulips could cost more in the seventeenth century than the still lifes that now filled the walls of museums. Yes, he believed that if he'd been alive then, he too might been swept up in the tulip craze.

"If you notice anything unusual, just say so."

He nodded, and she went on leafing slowly through the book. After she had turned the final page, she placed one hand flat on the endpaper and the other on the back cover. Just as she was about to close the book, she said, "That's strange."

"What?"

"This part feels uneven. Like there's something there. Here, feel this."

She took his hand and laid it on the inside of the cover. He ran it over the paper intently, with her hand pressed gently against his.

"Yeah, it's uneven."

"That's what I thought."

She lifted the book, running her eyes over its contours.

"Here, look at this, there's a kind of bulge, right?"

Alec leaned in, his cheek almost brushing hers.

"You're right," he said excitedly. "There's something inside."

"But what?"

"There's only one way to find out."

Startled by Damian's voice, Emma let go of the book, which fell to the table. Damian rushed forward, cursing. "Em, how could you be so clumsy? I told you to be careful with that book!" He picked it up and examined it closely.

"Oh, sorry, I, um . . . did we wake you?" Alec stammered.

"No, I was still up. What were you saying?" he asked gruffly. "Something about a bulge?"

"Yes," Emma said, "there."

Damian ran his hand gently over the endpaper. "You're right; I can feel it too. It's uneven."

"Pull it open." Alec was leaning over the table, staring at the book.

"Pull it open?" Damian looked at him in astonishment. "Are you out of your mind? This is a museum piece. I'm not about to start mucking with it. No, we're going to do this properly."

"What do you mean, properly? Do you think I care how much that book is worth? To hell with doing it properly. I want to know what's in there, now."

"Just calm down, okay? You're acting like a spoiled child. When will you learn to stop acting on impulse? Count to ten and think for once, instead of just rushing in." His gaze fell on the empty bottle. Picking it up, he said, "This doesn't help, of course. I see you've been living it up again."

Damian slammed the bottle down on the table. Emma opened her mouth, but before she could speak Alec said, "So that's it? That's what you're all worked up about? Or is this about something else? Well? Do you think I should follow your example? Is that it? The incomparable Damian Vanlint will show us all just how it should be done. Mr. Vanlint, that paragon of perfection, who always looks before he leaps! Well, look at yourself for once. It takes you months to make a decision. Think it through, weigh the alternatives, blah blah blah. You're acting like an old fart."

"And you're acting like a fired-up teenager. Control yourself for once."

"Control myself? Why should I? I've lost the person I loved most in the world, remember? Don't you get it?"

"I'm keenly aware of that, and in case you've forgotten, I loved Frank too. But I'm not using that as an excuse to lose my head or hurt the people who matter most to me. Unlike you. You're using Frank's death to—"

Alec pushed his chair back and strode around the table. He stopped right in front of Damian. "Easy for you to talk. Your life's a bed of roses, you've got it made, you just let it all wash over you," he said, gesturing in Emma's direction. "Not all of us have such luck."

"If I've got it made, as you put it, it's because I work hard, instead of wallowing in my own misery."

Emma slammed her hand down on the tabletop. "Stop it, please, both of you. That's enough."

"More than enough," Alec said, putting his hand out. "Give it here, it belongs to me."

"Alec, listen," Damian said in a steady voice. "We'll talk about this more tomorrow, okay? I know professionals who could open this up without damaging it. Why shouldn't we ask for their help? What's the problem? Do you really think a few hours are going to make a difference?"

Alec stared at him.

"Alec, he's right," Emma said. "I mean, suppose it's nothing, suppose there's nothing there, and we ruin something tremendously valuable, just because we wanted to find out right away. We can't do anything now anyway. What's wrong with waiting till tomorrow?"

Alec lowered his arm. "Maybe you're right. Sorry, I think we're both just worn out."

"Worn out, right," Damian snapped. "I'm going to bed."

He walked out the door with the book tucked under his arm.

THIRTY-ONE

Dawn handed Wainwright his mug and sat down on the corner of his desk. As she warmed her hands on her own cup, she looked at him. His eyes looked puffy and half closed. She knew he got up every morning at six A.M. so he could make it to the office in time, just like most people who worked in the center of London. Since property was unaffordable for mere mortals, it was nothing special to spend four hours a day commuting. She thanked her lucky stars that she lived with her aunt, whose rental apartment was not too far away.

"Well?" He leaned back, with his hands clasped behind his head.

"I think you're right, about Alec holding back, I mean. But that's not to say he's guilty of murder. By the way, did you ask him if he took a book from the shelf?"

"Yes. He says he didn't, but he's lying. There's no doubt in my mind he took it with him."

She put down her mug. "So it wasn't the killer?"

"No, it couldn't have been. The blood on the palms of Frank Schoeller's hands had already dried by the time the book was removed. It must have happened later, after the murder. Look."

He handed her a stack of color photos. She looked at the first print. Schoeller's head was lolling to one side. His eyes were shut, and the expression on his face was peaceful. The left shoulder of his pajama top was stained crimson with blood from his head wound. The palms of his hands were facing up, and a rectangular outline was clearly visible.

"What else do you know about Alec? Wife? Family? Friends? Any surprises?"

"No wife, and no girlfriend either, as far as I know."

Wainwright raised an eyebrow and nodded encouragingly.

"Forget it, sir. You should see the women he dates. Top models, actresses—I haven't a ghost of a chance."

"Dawn, you know true beauty—"

"—lies within. No argument from me, sir. What they never mention is, if you don't like the packaging, you don't stick around to find out what's inside. Anyway, Frank Schoeller was the only family Alec had."

"What about Damian Vanlint?"

"He's Alec's best friend. They've known each other for years. Oh, that reminds me, I wanted to show you something. Wait here, I'll get it."

She left the office and returned a moment later with a folder in her hand.

"Shall I give you the short version, sir?"

"Let's have it, then."

"Damian Floris Vanlint. Born on September fourth, nineteen seventy, in Amsterdam. His father is the property magnate Florian Vanlint. Worth a fortune."

"The father's still alive?"

She nodded.

"Parents divorced. Mother remarried a couple years later. She lives in Italy. Damian went off to boarding school in England at the age of fifteen."

"Yes, that's where the two of them met, wasn't it?"

"Right. Damian Vanlint also met his wife there: Emma Caen, born and raised in France. At the age of twenty-one, Vanlint inherited part of the family fortune."

"What kind of money are we talking about?"

"Big money, sir. There's a Dutch magazine that publishes an annual list of the five hundred richest people. For the past few years, Damian Vanlint has bounced around between two hundred and two twenty."

"And how much money does it take to qualify for this list?"

"Hold on, I've got the figure." She flipped through the file. "Okay, here's the latest edition. Look, here it is."

She gave the magazine to Wainwright. Tucked between two pages was an English translation of the paragraph about Damian. Wainwright fished it out:

#218. Antiques dealer. €98 million.

As the heir to his family's financial empire, Damian Vanlint is more than likely to remain in the top 500 for the rest of his days. Every year he sends this magazine a letter asking not to be included in our list, but our first loyalty is to our readers. Vanlint spends his days trading antiques, and his swelling assets attest to his acumen. But after work, he is also a sought-after guest at parties and soirées that most of this country's so-called celebrities can only dream of. Now all he has to do is produce an heir to the Vanlint throne, with a little help from his lovely wife.

"Well, well, ninety-eight million euros. Sounds like he's not just frittering it away, either."

"No, sir, quite the opposite, in fact. He made a few large investments to set himself up in the antiques business and now owns two shops in Amsterdam's art and antiques district, just a stone's throw from the Rijksmuseum. He lives in a large historic house overlooking the city's most exclusive canal and has other properties somewhere in the north of the country and in the Seychelles."

"And does this golden boy perchance have feet of clay?"

"He's only human, sir, if that's what you mean." Dawn pulled some press clippings out of her file. "See for yourself."

Though most of the articles were in Dutch, Wainwright could tell by the typefaces and the poor-quality photos that they came from gossip magazines. A few English clippings caught his eye.

"'Damian Vanlint flees love nest!'" Wainwright declaimed. "Oh, here's another one: 'Vanlint dumps heiress.' So our Mr. Vanlint is a heartbreaker. Scrappy too, I see."

He held up a blurry picture of Damian punching a photographer while using his other hand to pull the man's camera off his neck.

"The police filed a report on the incident, but they decided to go easy on him, because he was constantly being hounded by paparazzi."

"Why's that?"

"Because he was dating Lindsay Bancroft."

"Daughter of the hotel magnate?"

"That's the one."

"By the way, have you looked at those tapes yet?"

She nodded curtly. "Nothing."

"Then we have a few problems." He ticked them off on his fingers. "One, Schoeller won't tell us what he's got. Two, I have no idea what book he made off with. Three, Tibbens is no help at all. Four, we have no fingerprints. And five, we have no suspect." He presented his closed fist. "What does that leave us with?"

"Nothing, sir."

"I want you to look at those tapes again." He raised a finger. "This time through my eyes, the eyes of the master."

THIRTY-TWO

She knew Wainwright well enough to know she couldn't come back empty-handed. But if there was nothing to see, there was nothing to tell. Simple as that. She flung her legs over the arm of the chair and pressed the button on the remote control. The monitor flickered to life.

Two hours later, Dawn still hadn't seen anything unusual. She sighed and paused the video, deciding to watch the end later. First, she had to find something to eat. After getting a cup of noodle soup at the cafeteria, she returned to watch the end of the recording. The last of the guests trickled out, and a man came into the assembly hall, heading for the spot where the coffin had lain. He picked up Frank's photo with both hands, removed it from the stand, and leaned it against the wall. As he started adjusting the first row of chairs, Dawn picked up her chopsticks. Keeping one eye on the screen as the funeral director straightened up the room, she carefully pulled the lid off her soup. Steam rose from the cup, and she waved it away from her face. She dipped her chopsticks into the broth, brought her lips to the Styrofoam rim, and tried to take a sip. A scalding noodle landed on her chin. With a curse, she put down the cup and dabbed at the burning spot. As she bent to pick up the cup again, she saw something move out of the corner of her eye.

She rolled her chair closer to the screen. On the far left, she could just catch a glimpse of the lobby.

"Shit."

She hit Pause and the picture froze. A man was standing beside the condolence register. She pressed Play. He picked up the pen, and as he leaned forward to write, she got a good look at him. Freezing the frame again, she studied his profile.

"What's he doing there? Everyone else left ages ago," she muttered.

She slid the DVD of the arriving guests into the player. A second monitor came on.

The camera was mounted above the table where all the mourners came to announce themselves. The young woman at the table checked them off the long list she had in front of her. Not only did they have images of everyone at the funeral, but they had also turned on the microphone and could attach a name to each face.

Dawn's eyes flitted constantly from left to right, from the frozen image of the man to the moving images on the other screen. Then suddenly she shot forward and hit Stop.

"Gotcha!"

He walked with a slight stoop and seemed overcome by sorrow. When he was asked his name, he spoke so softly that she could barely hear him.

She stopped the DVD, pressed Rewind, and turned the volume all the way up.

"Versteegen, Simon Versteegen."

She pushed the button, and as the prints came sliding out, she pressed Play. Then she picked up her soup and leaned back. This time, she watched every move that Versteegen made. During the ceremony he had been seated in the middle of the assembly hall, looking down at the floor the whole time as if deep in prayer. Only when Alec took the podium did he raise his head. Throughout Alec's speech, Simon's eyes were fixed on him. Dawn watched Simon stand in line to offer Alec his condolences, talk to a few of the other mourners, and shake hands. Then he wrote something in the condolence register and left the building. But at that point, the lobby was still filled with people.

Dawn shut off all the equipment and tapped the prints with her chopsticks. "So why did you come back? That's what I'd like to know."

London

JUNE 13, 1663

Dear Mr. Winckel,

I was most grateful to receive your letter and to hear of your decision to make a very generous donation to our Society. Imagine my astonishment when I read how much you intend to give. As you know, we are financially dependent on private benefactors, and you are doubtless aware how much this contribution will mean to us.

You wrote that your late father had made numerous donations in support of natural science during his lifetime. I am deeply honoured that you have chosen to entrust us with the inheritance you received from him and have prudently managed for so many years.

Forgive me for saying so, but when I heard how your father had earned his fortune, I could not help but think that at least some good had come out of the tulip trade. Apparently, not everyone was ruined when the market collapsed. Your father must have had remarkable business acumen and known just when to sell his bulbs.

I can assure you that the money will be in safe hands with us, and that we will put it to good use. Despite all our efforts over the past decades, our studies are still at an early stage. There are countless questions yet to be answered, and countless others we have not even asked.

Thanks to your munificent gift, we can carry on our quest to solve the strange and wonderful riddles of nature. Your countryman, Christiaan Huygens, an esteemed member of our Society, expressed his delight when he heard the news and promised he would visit your home to thank you personally on behalf of all our members.

We received still more good news a month ago, when our King granted us the privilege of calling ourselves the Royal Society. Twenty years ago a group of scholars came together to discuss their ideas. Little could they have known that two decades later this enterprise would be a respected scholarly institute established by Royal Charter.

We are deeply gratified by the trust you have placed in us, and we shall not disappoint you. It is our great pleasure to offer you honourary membership of our Society.

Your faithful servant,
Sir Robert Moray
President
The Royal Society of London for the Improvement of Natural
    Knowledge
London, 1663

THIRTY-THREE

Simon felt terrible. It was as if his body were rejecting the mess he'd gotten himself into, like an organ after a failed transplant. The pain increased with every step he took and everything he did. It had twisted his mind, and now it was torturing his body.

He pulled the curtains closed to keep out the daylight, and then he got into bed. With one hand, he twisted off the top of the brown plastic bottle. Pills rolled into his hand. He swallowed two of them, closed his eyes, and lowered his head into his pillow. He could feel the hairs on his arms rising. A shudder went through his body. He pulled up the cover and concentrated, trying to picture it: the pills reached his stomach, were swamped in gastric acid, and dissolved into molecules that entered his bloodstream. He tried to take slow, regular breaths. He heard the echo of his breathing in the room and, a few moments later, fell fast asleep.

Alec snapped his cell phone shut. Simon Versteegen hadn't wanted to say anything on the phone. After they'd agreed to meet that afternoon, Simon had given him his address and hung up, without even saying good-bye.

Alec looked outside. The weather was the same as the day before, as if there had been no night. He went over to the kitchen table. Beside the sorted stacks of paper was a heap of correspondence they still had to sift through. He had just settled down to the task when the front door slammed shut and he heard Damian's footsteps in the hallway.

After last night's shouting match, Alec dreaded the prospect of facing Damian. The wine had certainly influenced his behavior, but that was no excuse. Besides, he recalled every word of the conversation, so how drunk could he have been?

"I see you're hard at work. Want some coffee?"

Alec nodded. Damian went to the espresso machine and placed two cups under the spouts.

"You were out early," Alec said.

"They picked up the stuff for the antiques show this morning. I wanted to make sure they loaded everything safely. It wouldn't be the first time things went into the van in perfect condition and came out damaged."

He put Alec's espresso down on the table and said, "I made a few phone calls about the tulip book. We have an appointment at the auction house this morning, with Jacob Wolters. He appraises rare books for a living and knows how to handle them."

"Perfect. What time are we supposed to be there? I arranged to see Simon this afternoon."

"Where?"

"He lives in The Hague."

"No problem, Wolters is expecting us in half an hour." Then he looked Alec in the eyes. "Don't you agree that it was better to wait? Those few hours didn't make any difference."

Alec couldn't conceal the irritation in his voice. "I'm glad you're so sure it didn't make any difference. I guess you know more than I do." Seeing Damian's face fall, he said, "Sorry, I don't want to get started again. Sometimes I just . . ."

Damian sighed. "No, you're right. I know I'm impossible sometimes."

"You ought to have more confidence in me. I can take care of myself, I've been doing it for years. You know that."

"I know, but I was worried that Frank's death would be too much for you, that you would fall back into your old ways."

Alec shook his head. "I admit it's been hard, but I'm still clean. And if I can get through this . . ."

". . . you can get through anything." Damian clapped him on the shoulder. "I'll say no more about it."

THIRTY-FOUR

Alec's eyes scanned the yellow brick building, a fine example of the Amsterdam school architecture of the 1920s. On the left and right, two bay windows bulged like fat cigars. The brickwork between them formed a decorative pattern of verticals and horizontals, like strips of wallpaper pasted to the façade.

Damian pushed open the heavy front door. They entered the hall and went up to the reception desk, which was decorated with posters from past auctions. The low table next to it was piled with old catalogs, all of them chained to the legs. To dispel any lingering doubt, each one bore a label in thick black marker: DISPLAY COPY! The receptionist's eyes lit up when she saw Damian. "Good morning, Mr. Vanlint. How are you today?"

"Fine, thank you. We have an appointment."

"That's right, with Mr. Wolters. He told us you were coming. Go right ahead, Mr. Vanlint, you know the way."

Their footsteps clattered on the black tiles and reverberated down the long corridor. The art nouveau ceiling lamps shed a feeble light, and Alec noticed that the musty smell of old paper, which had infiltrated even the lobby, was growing stronger as they walked on. The door at the end of the hallway was ajar.

"*Entrez*, come in," a young man's voice rang out. Mr. Wolters came up to them and extended his hand. "Good morning, Mr. Vanlint, it's good to see you again."

After Damian had introduced him to Alec, the three men sat down around a table so large that they could have used it for billiards. Above it a row of green glass lamps hung from a copper rod, filling the room with a weak, spectral glow. They were surrounded by shelves of antiquarian books, as if the walls were upholstered in leather. The gold lettering on the books gleamed against the dark spines. There were shelves between and above the two high windows overlooking the courtyard, and even in the space above the door.

"Now, Mr. Vanlint, what have you brought me? I've been burning with curiosity ever since you called."

To rest his elbows on the tabletop, Jacob Wolters had to sit up straight. His delicate features and pointed chin gave him an almost elfin appearance, and his hands looked out of all proportion to the rest of his body as he laced his long, elegant fingers beneath his chin.

Damian slid the book over to Wolters, who reached into his pants pocket, retrieving a glove. He pulled the book toward him. Nodding slowly, he said, "Very fine indeed. Superb binding, seventeenth century." Then, with a guarded look, he asked, "Is there anything you feel I should know, Mr. Vanlint?"

Damian opened his mouth to speak, but Wolters held up his hand and said. "Before you answer, there's something I must tell you. The thing is, I've seen this book before."

"What?" Alec's eyebrows shot up.

"You see, we sold it at auction a couple of years ago. Right here in Amsterdam," he said, peering at Alec out of the corner of his eye. "How did it happen to come into your hands?"

"Do you remember who bought it?"

"Certainly. It was Mr. Schoeller." He turned to Alec. "I suppose he was a relative of yours? When you introduced yourself, I thought of him right away."

Alec nodded. "He was my uncle."

"Oh, dear, I'm very sorry about your loss. I'd heard he recently passed away. What a tragedy." Wolters shook his head in disbelief. "Yes, his death came as a great shock to us all. He was a valued customer, and we were always glad to see him. A very knowledgeable man, a true connoisseur."

Wolters opened the book and stared at the bloodstained title page. "Oh, my God, is that . . ."

"Yes," Alec said.

"How horrible," Wolters said softly. He cleared his throat and continued. "This book is a florilegium, from the Latin, meaning 'gathering of flowers.' Albums of this type were made when the tulip trade was at its height. Some are collections of loose illustrations, while others are bound volumes like this one. If I'm not mistaken, there are only forty-three of these books in the entire world." He shook his head. "What a terrible thing. Of all the books your uncle owned, how sad that it happened to this one."

"I'm sorry we had to confront you with this," Alec said, "but there was no way around it. Anyway, what do you mean, how sad that it happened to this one?"

Wolters looked up. "Please, don't misunderstand me. What I'm trying to say is that this book meant a great deal to your uncle. He had to have it, no matter what the price. I must confess, I was puzzled. I knew he was passionate about seventeenth-century art, but I'd never realized he was interested in rare books. When we notified our regular customers that this book was up for sale, he called the very next day. He paid very handsomely for it too."

Alec looked at Wolters thoughtfully.

"But I understand you need my help. What can I do for you?"

"There's something strange about the back cover," Alec said. "Run your hand along the endpaper and you'll feel it."

Wolters shut the book and lifted the back cover. Turning his gaze to the ceiling, he passed his hand over the endpaper so gently that his palm barely touched it.

"Hmm, I assume you mean the bulge. That's certainly unusual."

"We think there's something in there," Damian said. "I didn't want to risk opening it myself."

"A wise decision. This is a very rare and valuable book. I'll see what I can do."

Wolters stood up, went to the door, and adjusted the dimmer. Alec and Damian squinted in the glare of the lights. Wolters opened a drawer, took out a loupe, and placed it in his left eye. Then he leaned in to examine the endpaper, making his way along the edge so slowly that his head hardly seemed to move. The only sound in the room was the hum of the hygrometer. After a few minutes, Wolters straightened his back and removed the loupe.

"There's definitely something in there, and I can see it wasn't put there by a professional. The edges are coming loose in some places. That'll make things easier for us. I'll begin with just one opening, at the top. Perhaps that'll be sufficient, and it's less likely to cause damage."

They looked on nervously as he slid the razor-sharp blade of a scalpellike instrument between the endpaper and the cover and began, bit by bit, to slit the edge open.

"What in the world could Mr. Schoeller have put in here?" he muttered as he bent over his work.

"To tell the truth, we don't really know if he was the one who put something in there," Alec said. "Maybe it was somebody else."

"Well. Let's take a look."

Wolters slid tweezers deep inside the opening he had made. A moment later, he carefully pulled them out.

THIRTY-FIVE

In October and November, flights out of London City Airport were often canceled due to fog. Coetzer had spent five hours in the small, crowded departure hall. When he decided he'd had enough, he went up to the check-in desk and convinced the booking agent that his wife in Holland was about to give birth. With great difficulty, she booked him on a flight out of Gatwick.

Eight hours later, he was at Amsterdam's Schiphol airport, standing in line at passport control. He knew where Alec had gone. All he had to do was find out where this friend of his lived.

The odor of the woman in front of him made him nauseous. She was standing too close, and he couldn't move back; there was someone else behind him, almost touching him, invading his space. He stepped to one side. The stinking bitch had a child, who was staring at him like an idiot. He snarled, and the boy turned back to his mother in fright. *Insolent, filthy little worm.*

"Sir?" The passport officer looked at him inquiringly.

Coetzer presented his passport to the young man. The officer typed in a code on his computer.

"Are you here for business or pleasure?"

"For pleasure. I'm visiting friends."

"Enjoy your stay."

He made his way through the busy concourse to the car rental desk.

Coetzer slowly turned into the narrow driveway. The bright headlights lit up the front of the building. The yellow walls looked freshly painted, without a trace of graffiti. He reached for the bag on the backseat and stepped out of the car.

"Welcome to our hotel, sir. Do you have a reservation?"

"Yes," he said gruffly, handing his car keys to the valet.

"Do you have any luggage, sir?"

"No, just the bag." He waved the man away. "I'll take care of it." He strode into the hotel and to the reception disk.

"Good evening, Mr. . . ."

"Lancaster," he said, placing his passport on the counter.

"Ah, Mr. Lancaster. Welcome. Have you stayed with us before?"

"No," he said impatiently, "but I'll be fine, don't worry. I don't need anyone to show me the way."

"Very well, sir," the receptionist said, unruffled. "You're staying for one night, is that correct?"

"I might stay longer. I'll get back to you."

"That's fine, sir, but would you please let us know as soon as possible? We have very few vacancies at the moment." He returned the passport. "Could I have your credit card? And would you do me a big favor and fill in this form? Thanks so much."

Coetzer grumbled and handed over his credit card.

"Have a very pleasant stay, Mr. Lancaster. Your room is on the second floor. You can take the stairs if you want, of course, and the elevator is over there."

Coetzer retreated to a quiet corner of the lounge and tapped a number into his cell phone. "Yes, it's me, I'm in The Hague. Did you find that address? Okay, and the house number? Got it."

As he walked down the recently renovated corridor to his room, a smile played on his lips. Oh, the irony. Could it really be a coincidence?

Right before his eyes were two rows of enormous tulips, extending from the wainscoting almost to the ceiling, their green leaves curling coyly toward their slender stems. The most beautiful tulip varieties the world had ever known were painted on the walls of his hotel.

THIRTY-SIX

Clamped in the jaws of the tweezers was a piece of paper.

"What have we here?"

Wolters walked over to the light box at the end of the table. He switched it on and laid the paper carefully on the glass plate.

It was about six inches long and four inches wide. The edges were worn in places, and the faded writing was almost illegible.

"What on earth is that?" Alec asked, frowning at the capital letters in old-fashioned script.

"I have no idea," Wolters said.

He took the tweezers and prodded the paper into the center of the glass pane. "My guess is that it's old, perhaps as old as the book. But what is this all about?"

They stared at the letters.

```
YYHK  PNKY  DQHT  MBPI  ALNL  PWUH
XLOQ  KIGY  MMPU  MSDP  TWBF
WZTM  TCYA  AUFV  PZXN  ZCYB
WILM  TTKE  KMSZ  XNXO  YBXL
LBPQ  HAPI  VMCS  XGAM  GANA  FAIUL
```

"Thanks a lot, Frank," Alec said. "A coded message. That's just what we need."

"Yes, but what kind of code is it?" Damian looked at Wolters, who slowly shook his head.

"Don't ask me, that's not my field. I've seen old codes before, but I really don't know the first thing about them. It looks like a job for our cryptologist. First I'll see whether it's authentic, then she can get to work. I hope she'll be able to decipher it for us. Do I have your permission to pass this on to her? I'll get in touch with you as soon as we've figured it out."

"Do you think that'll be this afternoon?" Alec asked.

"I'll do my best. The question is whether she has time, and whether she can crack the code, of course. We'll have to wait and see."

THIRTY-SEVEN

"I feel like we keep taking one step forward and two steps back," Alec said, as Damian pulled out of the parking lot.

"I agree, we still haven't gotten anywhere. I'm pinning my hopes on Simon. Has he said why he wanted to talk to you?"

"No, he hung up so fast I didn't even get to say good-bye."

"Does he know I'm coming with you?"

"No, he'll see that for himself. I tried to tell him, but he kept cutting me off."

"Did you talk to Simon at the funeral?"

"Not really. He must have shaken my hand at some point, but I don't even know that for sure. It was all such a blur. Anyway, the last time I saw him was at least twelve years ago."

"Frank saw a lot of him, right?"

"Yeah, but they always met in Holland."

"Or at Lake Como."

"Apparently."

Damian merged onto the highway, joining a long, slow procession of cars.

From the Aston Martin, they looked out at the stately building, which was whitewashed and overrun with ivy. Vines circled the pillars by the entrance and trailed down from the canopy like jungle plants.

"I don't think he's home," Damian said, peering at the windows by the front door. They were dark, as were the ones on the upper floor.

"Yeah, that's strange. But look, the gate's open. I'll ring the bell, just to be sure." Alec got out of the car. "If nobody's home, I'll leave a note, and if anyone answers, I'll come and get you."

"Sure. I'll wait over there." Damian pointed to the nearest parking space, some distance away.

Alec walked up the drive to the front door. Just as he put out his finger to ring the bell, the door swung open. Before he had time to react, a hand reached out and grabbed his sleeve, pulling him into the house.

Inside, it was pitch-black. All Alec's senses were on the alert. He crouched and held out his arms, preparing to fend off an attacker. Feeling a hand on his shoulder, he whirled around, grabbed the wrist, and squeezed it hard.

He heard a cry of pain and released his grip in surprise. He was standing so close to her that he could feel her ragged breath against his face.

"Were you followed? Did they see you?" she whispered.

"Followed?" he asked. "See me? What are you talking about? I'm here to talk to—"

"I know who you're here for," she said. Her words were broken by a sob, and her hand tugged sharply at his jacket. "Did you watch out on the way here, and when you came to the door? Did you take a good look around?"

"Of course not. Why would I do that?"

"Come with me." She grabbed his sleeve again and pulled him farther into the hall.

"Wait a second, what—?"

She turned to him. "You have to help me."

He could hear that she was crying, and now that his eyes were adjusting to the dark, he could see her face glistening with tears.

"Come upstairs with me. I have to show you something."

He took her by the shoulders. "Stop. Hold on. What's going on here? Who are you? Listen. I didn't come alone, I brought a friend. He's—"

She froze. "What?"

"He's waiting in the car, just down the street."

"Does he know?"

"Know what? I have no idea what you're talking about."

"Later, all right? Follow me now, please, there's no time to lose. I have to show you something, then you'll understand."

"No. I'm not moving until you tell me who you are."

She sighed. "I'm Tara, Simon's stepdaughter, remember? Now, are you coming or not?"

She ran upstairs, and he followed her. Halfway up, she stopped and turned to him, towering above him.

"I've been staying here for a few days. This afternoon I went out, just for a couple of hours. Simon always takes an afternoon nap, so when I got back and the house was silent, I thought he was still asleep. But at five o'clock I went upstairs to wake him." She paused. Then she said softly, "I'm so glad it's you. When you came to the door I thought . . . I don't know what to do. You have to help me."

She grabbed the collar of his coat and pulled him after her. Taken by surprise, he stumbled, but caught hold of the bannister just in time.

"Tara, be careful."

She took his face in her hands, pulled him close, and pressed her lips to his ear: "Maybe this is your chance to do something meaningful for the first time in your sheltered little life."

Before he could respond, she let go, so abruptly he almost fell over backward. Cursing, he clutched the railing as she turned around and made her way upstairs.

In the hallway, she stopped at one of the closed doors. As soon as he caught up with her, she turned the knob and entered the room.

The curtains were closed. There was a strange odor in the room that Alec couldn't identify. He sniffed and looked at the shadowy contours of the bed that Tara was standing next to. She leaned forward slightly and turned on the bed lamp.

Alec stared open-mouthed at the bed. From where he was standing, all he could make out was a bloody mass. Tara was looking at the body, drawing labored breaths. He slowly stepped over to her.

The man was lying on his back. His arms were at his sides with the palms facing up in a gesture of surrender. His face had been smashed with such force that it seemed to spill out onto the pillow. At first glance, the rest of his body looked undamaged. Alec's gaze swept over it, then stopped short. To the left and right of the hips, there were two footprints on the bedsheet. Someone had stood over the man to deliver the fatal blow. Alec looked up. The ceiling was spattered with blood, and the wall behind the headboard was streaked with red. He turned to Tara, who had draped her arm over the head of the bed and buried her face in her sleeve.

"Simon?" he asked quietly.

She nodded. "That's how I found him."

She reached out her hand and stroked the bloodstained scalp. A tear fell from the corner of her eye. "At first I could hardly bear to look. But I stayed with him. I couldn't just leave him."

She wiped her eyes, smearing Simon's blood onto her cheek. Suddenly her whole body started to tremble.

Alec stroked her back. "Take it easy, now, come on."

The trembling gradually subsided and she started to breathe more regularly.

"Thanks. I'm okay now," she said. Then she pointed to the wall behind the head of the bed. "Did you notice that?"

It was as if a child had dipped three fingers into a jar of finger paint. When Alec realized what it was, his breath caught. He looked at Tara. She nodded and said, "You see what it is?"

"A tulip." Alec's voice wavered. "What was his connection to tulips?" When she shrugged, he said, "Tara, he asked me to get in touch with him. Do you have any idea what was going on, or why he needed to talk to me so urgently? It had something to do with Frank's death, I'm almost sure of it."

Tara nodded. "Right, my condolences."

She said the words flatly. Alec couldn't help thinking that even Wainwright had put more feeling into them.

She went on, "It sounds like you don't know a thing about it."

"About what?"

Without responding, she turned to walk out of the room. But before she reached the door, Alec grabbed her arm and spun her toward him.

"A thing about *what,* Tara?"

She looked cold and remote. But an instant later, there was fear in her eyes.

"Take me with you. We have to get out of here."

"Not until you tell me what's going on."

His grip made her wince with pain. She wrenched her arm free. "I'll tell you after we get out of this place. Come on! First they killed Frank, and now Simon. Do you really believe we're safe here?"

She turned and ran out of the room. Alec raced after her. Downstairs, she yanked her jacket off the coatrack and snatched up a travel bag. Warily, she opened the front door and peered outside. Then she reached back and took Alec's hand, pulling him after her.

"Where's the car?" she asked when they reached the front gate.

"Over there, on the left."

They ran toward it. Tara pulled the door open and clambered in.

"We have to get out of here, fast."

Damian looked at her in astonishment, staring at the red streak of blood on her cheek.

"Hurry up, start the car. Let's get out of here."

"Alec? Where's Simon? Did you talk to him?"

Alec climbed into the backseat. "She's right, Damian. We should go. Simon is dead."

Damian turned around. "What the hell are you talking about?"

"Just drive!" Tara shouted.

Damian turned toward her. Her hands were clenched in her lap. She was breathing heavily and looking around anxiously. He started the car.

Alkmaar

1665

He could hear something in the distance. Someone was calling. Was that his name?

Slowly, he opened his eyes. Light pierced his head like a knife, and he closed them again. He heard mumbling. There was someone walking in the room. He could sense the light growing dim, and the sharp pain in his head gradually eased. He felt hot, so hot. He ran his tongue over his cracked lips.

"Water."

Was that him? Was that his own voice he heard? High and soft, like a woman's? In his mind, his voice sounded very different, clear and strong.

A hand slid under his neck and lifted his head. He felt a cold, hard object pressed to his lips. Liquid ran into his mouth and dribbled over his chin. Someone wiped it away with a cloth.

He tried to say something. He could tell he was moving his lips and tensing his vocal cords, but the only sound that emerged was a faint groan. A cool hand stroked his forehead.

"Quiet now, take it easy. Everything's all right."

All right? He couldn't even talk. Nothing could be farther from all right. Who was this idiot? He opened his eyes a little. Someone was standing over him. He strained to see. Little by little, the room came into focus. When he saw who it was, he relaxed and managed to lift his hand in greeting.

"It's me, Father. The whole family's here."

Then it started coming back to him. The agonizing pain in his left arm, like a dagger thrusting toward his heart. His body, toppling to the ground outside his house. He'd been conscious but utterly helpless. He couldn't do anything, couldn't move a muscle or speak a word. All he could do was look and listen. He heard voices. People cried out, and someone started tugging at him. He felt warmth spread through his lower body and smelled his urine. His eyes filled with tears, not of pain but of shame. To think that people were looking on as he relieved himself. He could remember nothing more.

Now, Willem Winckel looked into the face of his eldest son. He wanted to smile at him, reassure him, but he couldn't. He was growing weaker by the moment and could feel the life ebbing out of him.

Maybe everything really is all right, he thought. The work my father began has borne fruit.

In total secrecy, Willem had continued that work and had managed to keep it secret from his family all these years. That whole time, he'd been afraid. Yes, looking back, he saw that he'd lived in fear most of his life. A fear he could share with no one.

His heart swelled with pride when he looked at his son, Wouter, who resembled his grandfather Wouter Winckel so much it was almost frightening. It was as if, along with the name, the boy had inherited his grandfather's traits. The young man had the same build, the same bright blue eyes full of hope and life. His personality too was eerily familiar.

Willem turned his attention to the blurry forms behind Wouter, gradually bringing them into sharper focus. There were his four daughters, standing by the wall with their arms around each other. They looked at him with fear and sadness.

He gestured to his son, who brought his ear to Willem's mouth. Willem felt the boy's hair brush his face, as soft as down. It smelled like fresh air, like forest.

"I want to have a word with you, alone." His voice cracked and wavered. "Let me take leave of the girls first. It's time."

Wouter beckoned to his sisters. One by one, they kissed their father on the cheek and left the room, sobbing.

Wouter sat on the edge of the bed and looked at his father with a frown. "What is it, Father?"

"There's something I've been meaning to give you for some time. Fortunately, it's not too late. Would you fetch my pouch?"

"Here it is," Wouter said, picking it up from the chair beside the bed.

"Oh, good, I was afraid for a moment—open it up."

Wouter painstakingly loosened the tight knot in the leather cord. Willem patted the mattress, and Wouter emptied the pouch onto the bed. Willem fumbled through the coins until he found what he sought. Taking it in his hand, he said, "This is the key to our safe. You'll find something there that once belonged to your grandfather, something he left to us. Your uncles and aunts entrusted it to me. Now it's yours. I hope in time you will give it to your eldest son. Let it be handed down to all future generations, from eldest son to eldest son. And each time it is passed on, let the story of my father, your grandfather, Wouter Winckel, be told."

He began to cough. Wouter took the cup, tipped his father's head again, and gave him a sip of water.

"Easy now, Father. I know what Grandfather did, what he accomplished."

"Hush, Wouter," said Willem, short of breath. "Hush. Hear me out. Everyone in the family must learn that he was killed because he believed that freedom of thought—the freedom we all possess, which no one can take away—must lead to freedom of action and expression. Our descendants must never forget that freedom is mankind's greatest treasure." He pressed the key into his son's hand.

"But, Father, what . . . ?"

"You'll see." He shut his eyes.

Wouter stood up. "Father?"

Willem struggled to open his eyes again. "One more thing. Be careful, and use it only for good. You will be sorely tempted, and that could destroy you. If there comes a time when you fear you cannot resist, think of me, and of your grandfather."

He let out a long breath and closed his eyes.

THIRTY-EIGHT

"Where do you want to go?" Damian turned to Tara, his eyes meeting Alec's in the rearview mirror.

"Let's start by getting out of here," Tara said anxiously. "And make sure no one tails us."

"Tails us?"

"Just keep your eyes open."

"Okay, fine." Damian accelerated and drove away. Suddenly he was dazzled by a pair of light-blue xenon headlights coming up behind him. Tara turned around. The glaring light blinded her. She squinted and ducked down.

"Just drive to . . ." she said, panicked. "I don't know, drive any-where. I don't care, as long as we get out of here."

"Amsterdam?" Damian suggested.

"Yeah, Amsterdam, but first try to lose the car behind us. Here!" she shouted. "Turn left here!"

Just in the nick of time, Damian veered to the left, steering the Aston Martin into a narrow side street. A moment later, the metallic lights were blazing behind them again.

Tara looked in the side mirror. "Try to shake him off, we have to lose him."

"Who the hell is it?" Damian asked. "What's going on?"

"Just do it!"

He hit the gas and the car surged forward. The lights behind him dwindled and finally disappeared. Then he slammed on the brakes so hard that Tara nearly flew headfirst into the windshield.

"What are you doing?" she shouted, as Damian put the car into reverse. In one smooth motion, he pulled into a parking bay and dimmed his lights.

"Don't do that! Come on, don't be crazy. We've got to keep going!"

Damian reached over and pushed her down. "Duck!"

The car slid past. After a few seconds they looked up. The red taillights took a long time to vanish. Once they'd disappeared, Damian started the car and sped out of the parking space. At the end of the street, he made a sharp turn to the right and then an immediate left into a side street. Suddenly the headlights were glaring into his rearview mirror, their light casting a reflection over his eyes like a clear blue mask.

"Hold on tight."

He floored the gas and turned right, hurtling through a red light and into a busy intersection. Cars swerved left and right, honking their horns. Wrenching the wheel to the right, he drove full speed into a one-way street. Then he jammed his foot hard on the brakes and turned left, up a small driveway.

He switched off the engine. The small space was filled with the sound of their labored breath. When they heard a car approaching, they slowly turned their heads. The headlights cast two white stripes on the asphalt. The car rolled past. A minute later, Damian lowered his window and listened closely.

"I think we've lost him," he said softly. "Let's wait here a while longer to make sure. Alec, what happened to Simon?"

Alec described how they had found Simon. Then he said, "Tara, he'd asked me to come by. Do you know why he needed to talk to me so urgently? And what is all this, anyway? Who's following us?"

She looked at him, her lower lip quivering.

Alec put his hand on her shoulder. He could feel her muscles contract, like a wild animal unused to being touched.

"Well?"

To his alarm, she buried her head in her neck, balled her fists, and howled.

THIRTY-NINE

Detective Felix Nieveld maneuvered his car past the crowd that had gathered by the gate and pulled into the driveway. He got out and greeted the driver of the coroner's van, who was leaning against his vehicle with his arms crossed.

"Where is it?" Nieveld asked the officer in the doorway.

"Upstairs."

"Is Verkerk there?"

The officer nodded.

Nieveld put on his white coverall and pulled up the hood. As he climbed the stairs, he heard Verkerk's voice booming from one of the upstairs rooms. He stopped in the doorway and surveyed the room. Two crime-scene investigators were at work, and Verkerk was standing by the bed. Nieveld's eyes widened in surprise as he joined his partner.

"Boy, he's in bad shape. Do we know who it is yet?"

"The name's Simon Versteegen."

"Who found him?"

"His housekeeper. She leaves around lunchtime and comes back in the evening to cook for him. She's downstairs. We didn't learn a thing from her. She was hysterical when we got here."

"I can imagine. What was the murder weapon?"

"We haven't found anything. Here, see these prints? The killer stood over him and struck him at least twice. Look at this."

Nieveld followed Verkerk's finger up to the ceiling. The spattered blood formed a long streak, like the tail of a comet.

"And how about that?" Nieveld pointed to the wall. "What is it?"

"Search me," Verkerk said. "The letter U on a stick?"

Nieveld leaned forward to take a closer look. He rubbed his chin, pondering. "Look at these two diagonal lines here, rising from the top of this vertical one. You know what this reminds me of? A tulip."

"A tulip? Oh yeah, I see what you mean. You think it's some kind of signature?"

"I wouldn't call it that, unless we find the same thing at another crime scene," Nieveld said.

"A serial killer? In Holland?"

"Yeah, it doesn't seem too likely, does it?"

FORTY

Tara stood looking out the window. The illuminated arches of the bridge over the canal met their reflections in the water, forming two large circles of light, the upper half sharp and clear, the lower half blurred. Two cyclists passed the house, weaving skillfully between the bollards to let a car pass. A shiver ran through Tara, and she pulled the shawl that Emma had lent her tighter around her shoulders.

"Here," Emma said, setting down a tray of appetizers. Damian followed her, holding a bottle of wine, and poured everyone a glass.

Tara turned to Emma. "Can we close the curtains?"

"Of course."

"Thanks. I'll feel a little safer."

Alec sat down on the couch and turned to Tara. She looked tense, clutching her glass with both hands.

"I think you've got some explaining to do."

She nodded. "This all seems so unreal."

"Do you have any idea who might have done it?"

She cleared her throat. "Well, it might have been someone who lent him money. Every time I went to visit, a few more things were gone." She looked at them. "You can't imagine how much he had collected. He used to be absolutely loaded, but for the past couple of years he's been in a downward spiral. All his money, furniture, paintings, jewelry, even family heirlooms—it's all gone, everything he owned."

With a bitter laugh, she said, "Isn't it absurd, the way things turn out? He was always determined to make more money. That was what got him rich, and it was also what drove him so deep into debt."

She sat down and folded her arms. "When the trouble first started, he couldn't believe it. He said he knew the risks, but this was a sure thing. It couldn't go wrong."

"What couldn't go wrong, exactly?" Alec asked.

"I don't know the details. I guess he put all his money in some investment and lost it. He was probably playing the stock market. He'd been trading stock for years, so he must have thought he knew what he was doing." She shook her head.

"Was it a fund that invested in tulips, by any chance?" Alec asked. He frowned anxiously. "Was Frank involved too? Was he another one of the investors?"

"How should I know?" she said tartly. "Are you telling me Frank was investing in tulips?"

"I'm asking because of that mark on Simon's wall."

Emma stared at Alec, mystified, and he told her about the drawing above Simon's bed.

"I don't have a clue what that's about," Tara said. "Listen, I think Simon had borrowed money and couldn't pay it back. Simple as that. He was always getting involved in risky schemes."

"So you think he was killed by the people he borrowed from? But what would be the point of killing him?" Emma asked. "They'd never see their money again."

"I think it was too late for that. This was Simon's punishment. I'm afraid he's after me now."

"The person who lent him the money, you mean? Is that who was following us?" Damian asked.

"Who else would it be? Simon never did anything wrong, except for trying to make a quick profit. The trouble is, I've got nothing to give him, nothing at all."

"Do you think that's why Simon wanted to talk to me?" Alec asked. "Did he need money? Did Frank know what a mess Simon was in?"

Tara turned to him. "I didn't know Simon wanted to talk to you, so I don't know what he had in mind. I saw you coming up the path and remembered who you were. Otherwise I would never have opened the door."

Alec cursed under his breath. They were still groping in the dark. All their efforts had left them none the wiser. Frank and Simon must have invested in that fund, it was the only explanation. Or had Simon tried to borrow money from Frank? And then what? Both murders seemed to have something to do with to tulips. That couldn't be a co-incidence. He had to find out whether Frank had been involved in the fund.

"Listen, Tara. As I was saying, there was a fund that invested in tulips. Something went wrong, and now hundreds of people have lost a lot of money. Could Simon have had anything to do with that?"

She gave him a guilty look. "I really don't know."

"Still, it's clear they were doing something that involved tulips. Here, look at these." Alec went to the chest of drawers and took out the postcards. He spread them out on the coffee table. "Simon sent all of these to Frank, two a year, starting in two thousand two."

"All the pictures have something to do with the seventeenth century," Damian added. "You see? A sextant, a portrait of Huygens, and a chronometer."

"And this is the most important one of all." Alec pointed to the card with the Rembrandt painting.

Tara looked up. "What makes you think that one's the most important?"

"It seems pretty obvious, when you think of the title. *The Anatomy Lesson of Dr. Nicolaes Tulp*. Tulp—tulip. Get it?"

"I know what the painting is called, Alec. I just don't think these cards have anything to do with tulips. Simon was probably referring to that fund of theirs."

Alkmaar

1665

The bed had been made. The room no longer smelled of death. There was nothing to suggest that this had ever been Willem Winckel's bedroom, let alone that Wouter's father had languished here on his sickbed for weeks.

Wouter put down the candlestick, went to the foot of the bed, gripped it firmly, and began to push. Screeching and groaning, the bed scraped across the floor. Wouter paused to stretch, then drew a deep breath and resumed pushing, until he finally uncovered a small trapdoor. He placed the candlestick on the floor next to it, sank to his knees, and pushed the key into the lock.

He was surprised how easily he could turn the rusty key. The lock sprang open with a click. He wrapped his hands around the metal ring and pulled the trapdoor open.

For a moment, he thought the shallow space below was empty. He lowered the candle into the opening. Its light revealed something in the far corner, wrapped in brown cloth. Wouter leaned down and pulled it out.

When he opened the cloth, the candlelight glinted on the silver casket. The lid was decorated with dozens of tulips, their stems elegantly intertwined to form an oval frame around one central flower, which was engraved with such precision and detail that the flickering flame seemed to bring it to life.

He slowly lifted the lid. Inside was a red velvet bag tied with a black cord. He undid the cord and reached into the bag. The first thing he pulled out was a small leather pouch. Putting it down beside him, he reached into the velvet bag again. Something brushed against his fingertips. He caught hold of it and pulled it out. A slip of paper. He sat down on the floor, placed the candlestick between his legs, and unfolded the note.

He had to read it three times before it sank in and he began to believe it. Then he laid it aside and stared at the pouch. Now he understood what his dying father had meant when he spoke of the temptation that Wouter would have to resist. But Wouter was not worried about himself. His concern was to hide his father's treasure somewhere safe as soon as possible. Not in a box under the floorboards. He had to think of a place where no one would find it. It had a purpose, and he knew what that purpose was.

FORTY-ONE

"Fund? What fund?" Alec asked.

Tara went to the window and pulled aside the curtains. A boat filled with tourists floated down the canal. As it passed, all the passengers looked up at her.

She turned around. "The one Frank and Simon set up a couple of years ago. They called it the Science Capital Fund, or just the Fund for short. Didn't Frank ever mention it to you?"

Alec shook his head.

"Well, Simon told me about it," she said. "They were raising money to support scientific research."

"That accounts for all that information Frank had collected," Damian said to Alec. "And it helps to explain why he left all that money to science."

"But if it wasn't a secret, why didn't he ever say anything about it to me? And why were they sending each other cryptic messages?"

"Maybe Frank was trying to protect you," Tara replied. "They were involved in some risky business."

"Raising money for scientific research doesn't sound all that dangerous to me," Alec said.

"What made it risky was the Fund's mission. Frank and Simon believed that the more money they put into science, the more evidence scientists could gather that humans are the product of evolution, and that our world wasn't created by God but by natural processes. To find that evidence, scientists would have to do research. And research costs money."

"I don't understand. Frank never gave any indication that he cared so much about evolution, or that he had a problem with religion."

"It wasn't religion they had a problem with. It was the rise of fundamentalism in all the world's religions, along with growing intolerance for nonconformists and nonbelievers, that they were determined to fight. As you might imagine, some people were opposed to their activities."

Tara sat down and leaned in close to them.

"With all their connections, they raised huge sums, tens of millions a year. And every year they managed to bring in more."

"What did they think all that money would buy them?" Emma asked.

"Something everyone says money can't buy. Freedom."

A silence fell. Then Alec said, "Freedom isn't for sale."

"Frank and Simon believed that freedom of thought and freedom of action, two of our country's most cherished values, were under threat." Tara stared intently at the others. "Don't you see? Every day, all over the world, our fundamental freedoms are crumbling away. It's happening little by little, step by step, but it *is* happening."

"So they wanted to win back our freedom by wiping out religion? That sounds pretty shortsighted," Damian said.

"Their aim wasn't to wipe out religion. They believed in the universal right to worship whatever god you choose. But they felt it was time to stand up for the atheists. They were worried that someday they would be persecuted, that it was their turn now."

Alec ran his hand over his face. So the thirty-two million euros that had disappeared in the bulb fraud would have been very useful to the Fund. What if Frank had thrown integrity to the winds for the sake of his dream and embezzled that money? The tulip book, the money they needed to carry out their plans—it was all falling into place.

"Tara, let me explain." He glanced furtively at Damian, who gave him a withering look. "When I found Frank, he was holding a book."

FORTY-TWO

Tara looked around the room. She felt like a guest at a five-star hotel. Facing the bed was a small table with a television and a compact sound system. By the window, which looked out over the beautiful garden behind the house, there was a desk with a computer. She sank down onto the bed and laid one arm over her eyes. So it was true after all, she thought.

As soon as she'd seen Alec walking to the door, she'd realized Simon must have asked him to come. Her stepfather must have thought that Frank had passed on information to Alec, and as it turned out, he had been right. Earlier that evening, when Alec had told her about the coded message in the tulip book, it had been hard for her to keep silent. She'd wanted to cry out that she knew what the message would say. It would point them to the bulb of the Semper Augustus, the most valuable tulip in seventeenth-century Europe, the most exquisite tulip of all time. Even now, some people claimed that it had never really existed. They saw it as the holy grail of tulips, the embodiment of flawless beauty, an abstraction that no one could ever possess.

She knew better. The Semper Augustus was real. Frank had found it and selected her to bring the flower back to life. But he had hidden the bulb until they were ready to use it, and now nobody knew where to find it. Frank had been after the money that the new Semper Augustus would raise for the Fund, but Tara couldn't care less about that. The only thing that mattered to her was the fame, the recognition that the experiment would bring her.

Two floors below, Damian looked at the papers stacked on the floor of the living room. On top of each stack was a sheet of paper with a year written on it.

"Emma, right?"

Alec nodded. "You know what she's like," he said and set to work.

Looking at his friend, Damian realized how much he didn't know. He'd always thought Emma would raise the subject, and he had wanted to give her the chance to confess. But as the years went by, he felt less and less confident that she would. He could remember the scene as if it were yesterday. He'd returned home one night, earlier than usual, from a trip to France to buy antiques. Alec had arrived in Amsterdam the day before and was staying with them. In the front hall, Damian had called their names, but no one answered. Halfway up the stairs, it occurred to him that they'd probably gone to a restaurant for dinner and were still out on the town somewhere. But when he called out again to double-check, Emma came rushing downstairs. As soon as he saw her, he knew. A thousand things seemed to give it away: her flushed face, her tousled hair, and most of all, the nervous look as her eyes met his. She kissed him and lowered her head.

"Em?"

Without a word, she turned away and went back upstairs. Since that night, they had never discussed it.

Damian took another look at Alec, who was rifling through the papers. Ever since their school days, everyone had said how different the two boys were—Damian calm and deliberate while Alec was brash and impulsive. Sometimes he felt that he had adapted to those expectations, that his personality had been shaped by others and now was set in stone. But these days, Damian's caution was working against him, and his instincts felt sharper than ever. Frank's death seemed to have jolted him awake.

Unless he talked to Emma about that evening, he would never know for sure. But did he really want to know? It wouldn't change the way he felt about her, or would it? And if it would, was he willing to take the risk? He could choose to share the rest of his life with a woman who was dreaming of another man. Damian's parents had set a bad example—his father had grappled with exactly the same dilemma. In the end, he had decided to confront his wife, and they had separated soon after.

For the first time in his life, Damian was truly scared. Scared that when the bomb went off, it would destroy the precarious balance that he and Emma had found and sweep away everything that mattered to him. But was the status quo really so wonderful? Or was he so obsessed with perfection that he went around pretending everything was perfect and under control? If so, he was only fooling himself, and it was time to stop.

"Alec," he said, "I . . . um . . . I want to ask you something. I . . ."

"Damian, she's holding something back."

"Emma?"

Alec looked startled. "No, not Emma. What gave you that idea? I'm talking about Tara."

"Oh, right. What do you mean?"

"Before Emma showed Tara to her room, she pulled this out of Frank's papers. She told me she'd thought of it as soon as she heard Tara's last name. Here, take a look, it was sent in two thousand five."

From: frank@schoeller.com
To: t.quispel@alab.com
Re: to be continued

Just a quick update: I'm still working hard to scrape the money together. Don't worry, though, I'm sure we'll find it somewhere.

I realize you're eager to get started, but you'll have to be patient. Please continue with the preparations, so we can get faster results later. As you know, time is of the essence.

Warm regards,
Frank

Damian looked up. "I had no idea Tara and Frank were in touch in the first place, let alone that they were working together so closely."

"No, neither did I."

"What do you think they needed the money for?"

"I don't know. It sounds as though she needed it fast. Damian, suppose she was losing patience, for whatever reason, and decided to put pressure on Frank?"

"You think she was responsible for Frank's death? How would she stand to benefit?"

"And who would you say *did* stand to benefit?"

"Well, he left all that money to science. But Tara just explained to us why he did that. How does she fit into the story?"

"I don't know," Alec said. "Let's have another look at that e-mail."

He read it one more time, carefully, and said, "Tara's domain name—alab—do you have any idea what it stands for?"

A minute later they were seated at the computer together, staring at the screen.

"Are you thinking what I'm thinking?"

Damian nodded. "She must be involved somehow. This can't be a coincidence."

Alec read aloud: "'The Ancient DNA Laboratory specializes in isolating genetic material from extinct organisms, fossils, and ancient skeletal remains.'" He pointed at the screen, "Click on Organization."

They saw it right away. Heading the list of sponsors was the Science Capital Fund.

"Bingo." Alec printed out the Web page and tucked it into his pocket.

"The question is what she's not telling us. And why she never mentioned her connection to Frank."

"It pisses me off," Damian said. "She's lying straight to our faces."

"But maybe this is the breakthrough we've been hoping for," Alec said. "We'll find out soon enough. She'd better have an awfully good reason for not telling us about it."

Damian nodded.

"So what was it you wanted to ask me?" Alec said.

"Oh. Uh . . . nothing. Forget about it."

As Damian was getting into bed, Emma opened her eyes.

"Sorry, sweetheart, I didn't mean to wake you."

"I wasn't sleeping yet, just lying awake thinking."

"About what?"

"About us, and how happy I am to be with you."

Damian turned to face her and brushed a lock of hair out of her face. "Really?" When she gave him a puzzled look, he said, "I know what happened, Em, between you and Alec."

Her eyes filled with tears and her lower lip started to tremble. "I'm so sorry," she whispered, "but I had no choice, it had to happen sometime. Do you understand?"

Damian sat up. Now that he had heard it from her mouth, he was more shocked than he had anticipated.

"To be honest, I don't. How many times did it happen?"

Emma threw off the covers and rose to her knees on the bed. Holding out her hands, she said, "Just once. I swear, Damian, it was just that one time."

He looked at her. "And now?"

"What do you mean?"

"What do you think I mean? What are your feelings for him now?"

"I'm crazy about Alec, you know I am. I always have been. But I married you."

Damian climbed out of bed and looked her straight in the face. "The question is, why? Because Alec wasn't ready? Because he had to sow his wild oats? Is that it?"

Emma slid off the bed, wrapping her arms around his waist and gazing up at him. "It's simple, Damian. I married you because I love you. Obviously I should have brought this up earlier, instead of waiting for you to mention it. Alec and I thought you knew—"

"And you were right."

"—so we figured you understood that it would never happen again. Damian, maybe I shouldn't say this to you, but Alec and I should have slept together a lot sooner. Then we could have put it behind us, and this would never have happened while we were married."

He spun away from her and headed for the bathroom. He pulled the door shut and leaned his forehead against the cool wood. He thought about slamming his fist into the door but stopped and let his arm fall to his side. He'd thought he had accepted the situation, come to terms with it, but Emma's words felt like a slap in the face.

Was this what he wanted? To share his life with someone who'd betrayed his trust? His stomach cramped with pain and nausea. He went to the sink and turned on the faucet. The cold water burned against his face.

FORTY-THREE

"And?" Wainwright asked, as Dawn walked into his office. "Did you find anything else on those tapes yesterday?"

"Good morning to you too, sir. Yes, I found something. I just don't know whether it means anything."

"Go on."

"I printed it." She put the stills on his desk. "Here, have a look."

After a few seconds, Wainwright said, "I see a man writing in the condolence book. What about it?"

"Do you see anyone else in the picture?"

Wainwright shook his head.

"Now take a look at this one."

She laid a second photo over the first.

"Okay, there's a crowd of people in this one," Wainwright said. "So he was there twice."

"Exactly. He wrote in the book once, then came back and wrote in it again when everyone else was long gone."

"And do we have this condolence register?"

Dawn shook her head. "I assume Alec Schoeller has it."

"Bugger, we should have taken it with us. Who is this man, anyway?"

"His name is Simon Versteegen," she said, doing her best to imitate the guttural g that Simon had used when he gave his name at the funeral.

"Never heard of him. Williams, why don't you get in touch with your friends in the Dutch police? Ask if they know anything about him. Don't make too much of it—it's probably nothing, but it's all we have to go on. Who knows, maybe we'll get lucky and find our first real lead."

"We know he had been holding a book with gold leaf."

"Did you happen to look at his bookshelves while we were there? There was gold leaf on more than half of those books, either along the edges or on the binding. That's no use to us."

Dawn flipped through her Rolodex and picked up the phone.

At that very moment, on the other side of the North Sea, Ben van Dongen was pulling the rubber band off his lunch box. He lifted the lid and moaned, "Oh no, not again," at the sight of the Nutella sandwiches and mandarin orange. His little boy would soon be making the same face at the sight of his father's liverwurst on brown bread. Ben picked up one of the sandwiches and took a deep breath. Just as he was about to take his first sugary bite, the telephone rang. He licked the stray Nutella off his fingers and picked it up.

"Van Dongen."

"Hi, Ben, this is Dawn Williams at Scotland Yard."

Two years ago they had met at an international conference on crime fighting. They'd hit it off right away and spent most of the two-day event in each other's company. Since then, they had exchanged a few e-mails, but it had been several months since the last message.

"Dawn, how are you? Great to hear from you. It's been awhile. How's life in rainy England?"

"I'm fine, thanks. How are things with you?"

"Can't complain. Are you still working for Wainwright?"

"That's right."

"He's a good man—difficult sometimes, but sharp, very sharp. I read an article about him recently, when you caught the serial killer. Good job, by the way."

"Thank you."

"But I suppose you're not just calling to catch up. Is there anything I can do for you? Are you still working on the Schoeller case?"

"Yes, actually that's what I'm calling about. The investigation is still in progress, and I have a question for you. There's a Dutchman we're looking into, and we're wondering if you've ever heard of him."

"What's the name?"

"Simon Versteegen. Does it ring any bells?"

The line went silent. She was on to something, she could tell. She put Ben on speaker and reached for a pen and paper.

"Simon Versteegen. Yes, I know the name. Why do you ask?" In the background, she could hear him rattling away on his keyboard.

Come on, Ben, don't hold out on me now, Dawn thought. "He was at Schoeller's funeral."

"So they knew each other?" He sounded excited.

"Ben?"

"Yes?"

"Would you be so kind as to tell me what's going on? Where did you hear his name? Have you talked to him?"

"Uh, no, not exactly. They found him at his home yesterday, murdered. I just got the report."

"Yes," Dawn hissed under her breath. Then she asked, "Did you find him? Did you see him?"

"No, it wasn't in my district. So you're telling me Schoeller and Versteegen knew each other? If you'll send me the report on Schoeller, then I can—"

"Whoa, Ben, not so fast. You scratch my back, I scratch yours. How was Versteegen killed?'

"Hold on a sec, I'll open the file. Let me see, where was it? Okay. His head was smashed in."

"Was he tortured?"

"Tortured? I don't know, I'll have to ask. Wait, I'll just skim through the report . . ."

After a few seconds he said, "I don't see anything about torture here, though the killer really did a job on his cranium. But anyway, this isn't the final version."

"I want to see it."

"You want to see what?"

"The body, the photos of the crime scene, everything."

"Wow, that's a tall order. I'll have to talk to the rest of the squad—it'll take some time."

"The two murders are related, Ben. I'm sure of it. This can't be a coincidence. If we want to solve the crime, we have to find the connection between the two men. To start with, I need to know exactly how Versteegen was killed, and I mean *exactly*."

"Hmm."

"How about this. I'll take the next flight over and bring our report with me. In the meantime, you can make whatever arrangements you need to make so that I can look at your information. And remember, I need to see the body too. Is that a deal? I'll call you back as soon as I know my arrival time."

Before Ben could start protesting, Dawn hung up. Ben sighed, scrolled through the numbers in his cell phone, and pressed a button.

"Hague Police Department, Nieveld speaking."

"Good morning, Felix, this is Ben. Everything okay there? Good. Listen, I'm going to need your help."

FORTY-FOUR

Damian slid a cup under the espresso spigot. He had woken up at five thirty, his conversation with Emma still echoing in his mind, making it impossible for him to get back to sleep.

Her admission that she had slept with Alec had rattled Damian much more than he'd expected. He'd been sitting in his study for three hours already, looking through auction catalogs for interesting antiques. That had kept him busy for a while. As he stood in the kitchen, his cell phone rang, and he quickly returned to his study to pick it up.

"Hello, Mr. Vanlint, this is Jacob Wolters."

"Good morning, Mr. Wolters. You're at work early today."

"Yes, I wanted to get back to you as soon as possible about the progress we've made."

"You figured out the code?"

"Well, no, not exactly. We have managed to confirm that the manuscript is authentic. The paper and the handwriting both date from the seventeenth century, no doubt about it. I also showed it to our cryptographer. The good news is that we now know for sure what type of code we're dealing with."

"That certainly sounds like good news. What type is it?"

"It's a Vigenère cipher. Of course, that's also the bad news."

An awkward silence followed.

"Sorry, is that supposed to mean something to me? Why is it bad news?" Damian asked.

"Ah, right, I thought you might have heard of it. It's a fairly well-known encryption method, invented about four hundred years ago by Giovanni Batista Belaso. For a long time it was absolutely unbreakable, but these days we know how it works. It's a fairly straightforward system."

"And . . . ?"

"The problem is, Mr. Vanlint, the message can be deciphered only with the help of a key, a code word, and we don't know what that word is."

Damian's heart sank. Alec was right. Every time they thought they'd come a little closer, they found themselves right back where they'd started. Every flash of insight revealed a new problem.

Noticing Alec in the doorway, Damian motioned to him to come closer. Pointing at the cell phone, he mouthed, "Wolters." Then he put the phone on speaker and wrote "Vigenère cipher" on a slip of paper that he pushed toward Alec.

"So without that word, there's no way to crack the code?" As Damian spoke to Wolters, he looked up at Alec and shook his head.

"No way whatsoever. The Vigenère cipher uses polyalphabetic substitution. That means you use a *tabula recta*—a square table of alphabets—to replace the letters. It's a kind of table—each row is a complete alphabet, but the alphabet keeps shifting forward, one letter at a time."

"Oh, I think I've seen that kind of thing," Damian said. "So the first row goes from A to Z, the second from B to A, then C to B, and so on."

"Exactly, you go on like that till the table is complete. The next step is to pick a code word. First you write your message—for example, "I don't eat chicken." Then you remove all the punctuation and the spaces between the words. What's left is a string of letters, called the plaintext. Underneath the plaintext, you write your code word, repeating it as many times as necessary, until you reach the end of the string. Suppose your code word is 'car.' Then you write those three letters, C-A-R, over and over, underneath the plaintext."

"So if the message is 'I don't eat chicken,' let's see . . . you put the C under the I, the A under the D, the R under the O, the C under the N, and so forth. Is that the idea?"

"That's right. The next step is to take each letter combination, like the first I in the plaintext plus the C in 'car,' and replace it with a single letter from the grid."

Meanwhile, Alec had started up the computer. He tapped Damian on the shoulder and swung the monitor around to face him.

THE VIGENÈRE CIPHER: USING THE TABULA RECTA
FIND THE LETTER FROM THE PLAINTEXT
IN THE VERTICAL ALPHABET
FIND THE LETTER FROM YOUR CODE WORD
IN THE HORIZONTAL ALPHABET
THE INTERSECTION OF THE ROW AND COLUMN
IS THE LETTER FOR YOUR CODE MESSAGE

A B C D E F G H I J K L M N O P Q R S T U V W X Y Z

B C D E F G H I J K L M N O P Q R S T U V W X Y Z A

C D E F G H I J K L M N O P Q R S T U V W X Y Z A B

D E F G H I J K L M N O P Q R S T U V W X Y Z A B C

E F G H I J K L M N O P Q R S T U V W X Y Z A B C D

F G H I J K L M N O P Q R S T U V W X Y Z A B C D E

G H I J K L M N O P Q R S T U V W X Y Z A B C D E F

H I J K L M N O P Q R S T U V W X Y Z A B C D E F G

I J K L M N O P Q R S T U V W X Y Z A B C D E F G H

J K L M N O P Q R S T U V W X Y Z A B C D E F G H I

K L M N O P Q R S T U V W X Y Z A B C D E F G H I J

L M N O P Q R S T U V W X Y Z A B C D E F G H I J K

M N O P Q R S T U V W X Y Z A B C D E F G H I J K L

N O P Q R S T U V W X Y Z A B C D E F G H I J K L M

O P Q R S T U V W X Y Z A B C D E F G H I J K L M N

P Q R S T U V W X Y Z A B C D E F G H I J K L M N O

Q R S T U V W X Y Z A B C D E F G H I J K L M N O P

```
R S T U V W X Y Z A B C D E F G H I J K L M N O P Q
S T U V W X Y Z A B C D E F G H I J K L M N O P Q R
T U V W X Y Z A B C D E F G H I J K L M N O P Q R S
U V W X Y Z A B C D E F G H I J K L M N O P Q R S T
V W X Y Z A B C D E F G H I J K L M N O P Q R S T U
W X Y Z A B C D E F G H I J K L M N O P Q R S T U V
X Y Z A B C D E F G H I J K L M N O P Q R S T U V W
Y Z A B C D E F G H I J K L M N O P Q R S T U V W X
Z A B C D E F G H I J K L M N O P Q R S T U V W X Y
```

"I know this must be disappointing, Mr. Vanlint, but there's nothing we can do. As soon as you think you've found the code word, let me know, and we can decipher the message in no time."

"Well, it was very kind of you to go to so much trouble. We'll take it from here and get back to you soon."

"Oh, one more thing before you hang up. It's about the tulip book. I know it may be a sore subject right now, but I would advise your friend to have it restored. It's well worth the trouble, I promise you that."

"Yes, I know it's a valuable book."

"It's not just that. This particular tulip book has a rather unusual story attached to it. It's one of the last ones ever made, for the sale of the tulip collection that had belonged to Wouter Bartelmieszoon Winckel."

"What was that name again?"

"Wouter Winckel, a renowned seventeenth-century tulip trader. He ran a tavern in Alkmaar but was better known for his unparalleled collection of tulip bulbs. When he died his children ended up in an orphanage . . ."

". . . and after his tulips were sold, the bubble burst," Damian said softly, glancing at Alec.

"Ah, so you're familiar with the auction. Then you know what absurd prices were paid there, and you must understand that this book has special value."

"What else can you tell me about Wouter Winckel?"

"Not much, except that he probably died of the plague. There was an outbreak around that time."

"Hmm."

"You could pay a visit to the municipal archives in Alkmaar. They're almost certain to have more information about him there. I know the archivist well—we've often worked together. His name is Harold van Benthum. Mention me when you call him, and I'm sure he'll do everything he can for you."

After hanging up, Damian said, "So what we need now is a code word."

"As if we didn't have enough to worry about. Thanks a lot, Frank." Alec slumped into a chair. "If he had made up a code word himself, we might have been able to guess what it was. He could have used my name, or yours, or Emma's. No, I know, he would have used 'Bruno.' That was his old dog, remember? Or 'Madeleine,' that was his mother's name. Or 'tulip,' of course. What could be more obvious? But somebody else picked the code word, back in the seventeenth century."

Damian rapped his fingers on his desk. "So we need some kind of seventeenth-century word. But how do we find it? It would have been nice if Frank had said something to you about it, instead of just pointing at that date."

Alec leaped out of his chair, staring at Damian. "What did you say?"

"It would have been nice if Frank—"

Alec came over to him, leaned on the desk, smiled, and said, "You're a genius. That's exactly what Frank did."

"What are you—"

"When he pointed to the book. At first, I thought he was saying 'tulip,' but that wasn't it."

"What was he saying?"

"'Tulipa.'"

"Tulipa. Are you sure?"

Alec nodded. Damian was startled by the sound of his phone ringing again.

"Damian, my boy, this is Dick." Dick's voice was almost unrecognizable. He sounded tired and subdued. "I have to talk to you, but please, come alone, without Alec. Do you have time now?"

"Sure, I can be there in fifteen minutes."

"No, no, not at the office. Let's meet at that big café on the Spui."

"Okay, I'll see you there. Oh, maybe you can help us with something. Have you ever heard of a man named Wouter Winckel? A seventeenth-century tulip dealer from Alkmaar?"

He heard a sharp intake of breath. Then Dick hung up. Damian stared at his cell phone, bewildered.

"That was Dick. He wants to meet, right now."

"Great, let's go," Alec said, turning to leave the room.

"No, Alec, he wanted to talk to me alone. I don't know why, but he was very clear."

"That's odd. Did he say anything about Wouter Winckel?"

"No, he just hung up. I think it would be a good idea to take Wolters's advice and go to Alkmaar to see what other information about Winckel we can dig up."

"While you're talking to Dick, Alec and I can go to Alkmaar. Right, Alec?" Emma said, as she came into the room.

"Sure," Alec said, "but what'll we do with Tara?"

Damian stood up. "She can stay here. After what we went through in the car yesterday, it might be better for her to lie low for a while. Besides, we don't want to tell her any more than we need to. We can leave her a note. I'll stop by the auction house and tell Wolters to try 'tulipa.' Then he can get to work right away. Who knows, maybe things are finally going our way, and 'tulipa' really is the code word."

Tara smiled. As silently as she could, she slipped back down the corridor.

FORTY-FIVE

Dawn didn't care much for modern architecture, but there was something about the building that intrigued her. As they drove through the security gate, she craned her neck and peered through the windshield. Yes, it had a certain appeal. She had read about it. The Netherlands Forensic Institute was a high-tech marvel. Not just the building, with its layers of glass and steel, but also its labs, which were known for their cutting edge equipment and advanced techniques. She recalled that the new institute had cost tens of millions to build.

"Not bad, huh?" Ben said.

"Yeah," she replied, flashing him a smile. "Not bad at all."

They parked the car and headed toward the entrance. The glass doors slid silently open and they stepped into the futuristic lobby.

"He's coming to pick us up," Ben said to Dawn, after he'd signed them in and handed her a visitor's pass. As they walked over to the waiting area, they heard footsteps approaching.

"Oh, here he is now. Dawn, let me introduce you, this is Kees van Loon."

Kees looked at her with curiosity. He was a large man, more than six feet tall, his blond hair stiff with gel. He extended his hand.

"Good morning. I am Kees. Welcome. I am not speaking English very well, but I will try. Will you go with me, please?"

They followed him down a long corridor and around a corner. Kees stopped at a door. He slid his pass through the reader and pushed the door open. They found themselves in a preparation area. On the other side of a large window Dawn saw a steel table with a body bag.

"There are the suits," Kees said, pointing to a pile of plastic packages. Once they were covered from head to toe, he led them into the room. There was a powerful odor of disinfectant, but the smell of the corpse was stronger. Dawn ran her hand over her surgical mask.

"You never get used to it," Ben said.

She nodded in agreement. When Kees unzipped the body bag, she had to fight the urge to back away.

Ben turned to her. "Sorry, I guess I should have warned you. It's not a pretty sight."

That's the understatement of the century, Dawn thought. Ben had said something about the condition of the body on the phone, but she hadn't expected this. His face was gone. What remained was a pulpy mass of gore like a squashed blood orange.

Kees pulled over the operating lamp with a practiced gesture and shone it onto the spot where Versteegen's face had once been.

"The killer has used enormous force," Kees said. "A blunt object, we are thinking maybe a big hammer, you know, a . . . Ben, what do you call it in English, a—"

"—sledgehammer," Ben replied.

Dawn nodded. "Are there any other injuries?"

"No, just the opposite. Someone stroked his head. Here, on the scalp, you see a couple of fingerprints, yes? Here. We have no idea who has made them. It was not a big person, maybe a small man, maybe a woman. You know of the footprints on the mattress?"

"Yes, Ben told me."

"They were from a man, a big man. So this is something strange. Maybe the murderer was not alone, or maybe someone else found Mr. Versteegen before the housekeeper."

"The housekeeper told me that Versteegen's stepdaughter had been staying with him," Ben said to Dawn. "We haven't managed to track her down yet."

"Did you happen to find any gold leaf on his body?" she asked hopefully. Except for the crushed skull, there was nothing to indicate this was the same killer. No lacerations on the chest, no missing nails. Yet she knew it was the same man, she could feel it.

"Gold on his body?" Kees asked.

"Gold leaf, the kind they use to decorate old books."

"No, nothing like that. Why are you asking?"

"Ben probably told you I'm looking for a connection between this case and the murder of Frank Schoeller. They knew each other. On Schoeller's hands, we found flakes of gold leaf."

"And you think it came from a book?"

"That's right."

"If you cannot find the answer, send us a sample," Kees said, and he zipped up the bag.

FORTY-SIX

In the car, Emma felt uneasy about being so close to Alec. Why on earth had she suggested that the two of them go to Alkmaar together? What had she been thinking? She wanted to kick herself. After last night's conversation with Damian, this was the dumbest thing she could have done. She turned to Alec, who was sitting calmly beside her, his hands lying loosely in his lap.

She took a deep breath. "Damian knows."

He went rigid. "How long has he known?"

"Since the day it happened, I think. He suddenly started talking about it last night."

"So what did he say?"

"I've just told you that. He said he knew," she snapped.

"He didn't say anything to me about it." Alec looked at her. "Emma, what's done is done, there's no going back now. I didn't know you would regret it so much."

Her stomach clenched and her face grew hot. Images of the night they had spent together flashed through her mind. The tension between them had been building for years. The way she saw it, that moment of release had been inevitable.

"I don't regret it one bit, Alec. It's just that I feel so guilty."

Alec nodded. So often he'd wanted to tell Damian, but every time, the fear of ruining their friendship had stopped him. Now he could no longer pretend it had never happened. He had no choice but to talk to Damian about it. That was what he should have done right away, the morning after. He should have gone to Damian. He should have said something. But he had lacked the courage.

"I'll talk to him," Alec said.

In the reading room at the municipal archives, they each filled in a visitor's card. When Alec had called Harold van Benthum and mentioned Wolters's name, the archivist had grown excited and offered to do some preliminary research for them. At the information desk, they asked if they could see Mr. Van Benthum, and the man on the other side put out his hand.

"Ah, it's you. I'm Harold, pleased to meet you. You told me Jacob Wolters sent you here?"

"That's right," Alec said.

"Give him my best wishes when you see him. Now, please come with me," he said, emerging from behind the desk. "I've already pulled a few things off the shelves for you."

He led them through the reading room into the hallway and ushered them into his office. "You can work here if you like. There are fewer distractions."

The small room was organized efficiently. Along the right wall was a desk with a computer. The desktop was bare except for a mouse pad. Next to it was a poster of the Grand Canyon. Against the left wall were two narrow tables, one covered with neat stacks of file folders. On the other table were three thin folders, and beside it were two chairs. Harold went over to the table and tapped the folders with one finger.

"This is what I've been able to find so far. I'll keep looking, but in the meantime you can go through these."

"It's so kind of you to go to all this trouble for us," Emma said.

Harold stroked his beard. "No trouble at all. These days a lot of people here like to give the impression they're in a rush. Usually the opposite is true. Have a seat. I'd say it's time for a cup of coffee."

He opened a thermos and filled two cups decorated with the Alkmaar city coat of arms.

"Right, I'll be back in a little while." In the doorway, he turned back to face them. "I can hardly believe you own the tulip book they made for the sale of Winckel's collection. I can certainly imagine you'd like to know more about him." He grinned and said, "If you ever feel inclined to lend the book, I'm sure the city museum would be very interested."

"I'll keep it in mind," Alec said.

They each opened a folder and went to work. After a few minutes, Alec said, "Here's something intriguing. This article is about the history of Doelenstraat, a street in Alkmaar's historic center. Wouter Winckel's inn used to be there. It says he was a respected businessman, an innkeeper, and a tulip dealer. His tavern was called the Old Archery Hall."

"Is it still around?"

"No, it was demolished in the twenties to make room for a school. It does say something about another building with almost the same name: the New Archery Hall. The city museum was housed there until the year two thousand. Hold on, there's a reference to another article. Oh, here it is."

He skimmed through it and said, "That's funny. This other building—the New Archery Hall—happens to be the place where his tulip collection was auctioned off."

Emma stirred her coffee. "Remind me how much they made?"

"Ninety thousand guilders," Harold said, somewhat short of breath, as he walked into the room with a couple of documents under one arm. He put them down and said, "It was an unbelievable sum. In fact, when I first saw the figure a few years back, it seemed so unbelievable that I did a little research of my own."

"And? Did you come up with anything interesting?" Alec asked.

"Well, I couldn't figure out why the auction brought in such huge proceeds. I guess it must have been market forces at work. That was probably also why the bubble burst right after the auction—a combination of factors. But I'll tell you what I did discover."

Harold pulled up a chair and sat down.

"Apparently, just before the Alkmaar tulip auction, someone made a deal with the director of the orphanage. A few days earlier, this person paid him a large sum of money for several bulbs. Bulbs that are not included in the sale list for the auction."

"So the orphanage director pocketed the money," Emma said.

Alec nodded. "There's a big difference between a ten percent commission and one hundred percent of the profits. Do you know how much he got for those bulbs?"

"Twenty-one thousand guilders," Harold said. "A fortune in those days. And that's not all."

He thumbed through the papers he had brought with him and fished out a couple of them.

"This is unrelated to the auction, but I also discovered that Wouter Winckel didn't die of the plague, as some people say." He held up the pages. "It turns out that the city physician kept meticulous records of every autopsy he performed."

He glanced down at his papers. "Those records clearly show that Wouter Winckel was killed in his own tavern."

"Murdered, you mean? Who did it?" Alec asked.

Harold shrugged. "I have no idea." He looked at his watch and stood up. "Sorry, I have a meeting to go to. I'll be back afterward to see how you're coming along."

When Harold had closed the door behind him, Alec said, "Suppose the orphanage director had something to do with it."

"With Winckel's death?" Emma raised her eyebrows.

"No, no, with the bidding frenzy at the auction. We keep hearing how unusual it was for an auction like that to raise ninety thousand guilders. First Dick mentioned it, then Wolters, and now van Benthum. If everyone feels that way, maybe there really was something fishy going on."

"You think it wasn't just market forces after all?"

"If the orphanage director was really so greedy, he probably wasn't satisfied with the twenty-one thousand guilders he had already embezzled. Maybe he manipulated the auction to inflate the final proceeds—and his own commission." Alec grabbed her by the arm. "Hey, what if that's what happened? What if he planted bidders in the auction hall, who kept raising their bids and driving up the asking prices? All they would have to do is stop in time and let someone else outbid them."

"It's possible," Emma said. "But there was always a risk they would have to buy the bulbs at inflated prices."

"I guess he thought it was worth the risk."

"You may be right. In fact, that could also be why he sold those bulbs before the auction." She sounded excited. "Suppose the tulip dealers found out about that sale. If the news was deliberately spread throughout the Dutch republic, then that would have pushed up prices. It's like the stock market: the asking price depends on the most recent sale price. The dealers would have known in advance that the asking prices at the auction would be astronomical."

He nodded. "If that's true, then before the auction even began, the bidders knew that enormous sums of money were going to be paid."

"And the orphanage director could be certain of much larger proceeds."

"But they must have known there was a chance that prices would plummet after the auction, at least temporarily. If our suspicions are right, then the orphanage director single-handedly orchestrated the collapse of the market."

"But why would he do that? How would it benefit him?"

"I have absolutely no idea."

FORTY-SEVEN

A fierce wind was blowing, and most of the vendors had covered their books with transparent plastic weighed down with stones. Except for a few stray tourists, the book market on the Spui was almost deserted, unlike the café. Damian pushed the door open.

Odors of coffee and toast drifted through the large, dark room. He looked around. Dick was sitting in the far corner, sunk so deep in thought that he didn't even notice when Damian came over to his table.

"Dick?"

As Dick looked up, a hesitant smile crossed his anxious face. His eyes were bloodshot. "Hi, Damian, sit down." His voice was weary. He removed his briefcase from the chair next to him and patted the seat. Damian draped his coat over the back and sat down. Dick was staring into space, rocking back and forth slightly with his hands clasped together.

"Dick? What's going on? You didn't sound like yourself on the phone."

"That's right. I'm not myself."

The waiter came over to take their order. Once he was gone, Dick leaned toward Damian, put his hand on his knee, and said, "Before we begin, there's something I should tell you. Anyone who knows about this could be in danger. Don't ever forget that. You've seen what happened to Frank and Simon. If you boys aren't careful, the same thing could happen to you."

Damian's eyes narrowed. "So you know a lot more than you admitted. What made you keep it to yourself? And why did you ask me to come here alone?"

"Because I want you to decide how much to tell Alec. He was his uncle's pride and joy. Frank would never forgive me if I put him in danger. Alec was like a son to him. So it's up to you to decide what to do with the information I'm about to—"

"You expect me to take all the responsibility?"

"That's right." Dick grabbed Damian by the shoulder and stared intently into his eyes. "You can turn back now if you like. You can choose not to hear my story."

"It's too late for that. Now that we've got ourselves tangled up in this, there's no way back."

Dick nodded and let go of Damian. The waiter brought two cappuccinos. When he was gone, Dick said, "So you're not giving up."

"And neither is Alec."

He nodded. With a deep sigh, he said, "Let's get down to business. I did withhold information from you. Right from the start, I knew what Frank was up to."

"Well, now we know too." Dick's eyebrows shot up. Damian went on, "I assume you mean the Fund?"

"Who told you about that?"

"Tara."

"So you talked to her. Then you know what the Fund was intended to accomplish."

"Yes, we do." Damian told Dick what they had learned from Tara.

"Did she know who else had been involved, besides Frank and Simon?"

"She didn't say anything about that."

"So she didn't tell you that I'm a member."

"You're a member? But I thought the members were—"

"—businessmen with money and connections. That's partly true. I'm involved in a different capacity, as a scholar, a researcher."

Then he leaned forward. Damian could see the fear in his eyes.

"Damian, it's all going wrong. This isn't at all how we'd planned it. We never anticipated this kind of trouble."

"Is that why you're so tense? Are you scared you might be next?"

"That depends."

"On what?"

"On whether Simon or Frank mentioned my name, of course. If they kept quiet, then I probably have nothing to worry about." Dick gazed sullenly into the gloom, pursing his lips.

Damian felt his impatience mounting. Bending forward, elbows on his knees, he said, "What do you want from me, Dick? Are you going to tell me what you know, or aren't you? If not, then I'm wasting my time here. You were the one who wanted to talk to me."

Dick looked him in the eyes. "If you'll give me just a little of your time, and if you can find the patience to hear me out, then I'm sure you'll understand. At least, I hope you will. But remember, this is no game. Just look at what happened to Frank and Simon. If you can't take it seriously, we'd better end this conversation right here and go our separate ways."

He got up and said, in a tone of quiet indignation, "So you tell me. Do you want to know why Frank was killed, or shall we forget the whole thing?"

"Listen, I'm really sorry," Damian said. He stood up and laid his hand on Dick's arm. "I didn't mean it that way. But I'm sure you understand how frustrating this is for us, especially Alec. We're discovering that Frank had a second life that Alec knew nothing about. If Frank had ever talked about it, if he had once mentioned it to Alec, then maybe it wouldn't have come to this. Maybe he'd still be alive today. That's why I lost my temper. Please, forgive me." He looked around. "Shall we sit down again? Everyone's staring at us."

Dick grudgingly slumped back into his chair. "Look, first of all, there's nothing you or Alec could have done. Just put that out of your mind. In fact, if you had tried to get involved, you might have ended up like Frank and Simon."

He fell silent and hung his head, knotting his fingers. When he looked up again, he said, "I understand why you lost your temper, Damian. But remember this. The reason Frank didn't say anything to Alec was to protect him, to make sure nothing would happen to him. That's why we've all kept it secret. None of us have told our friends or families, the people we care about most. And now that our lives are at risk, it's clear we made the right choice."

"So why did Tara know about it?"

Dick shrugged. "I don't know what Simon told her, or how much. She probably doesn't know the half of it."

"But in the end, Frank did get Alec involved, and he must have had his reasons. He probably thought Alec could do something to help. I assume it was connected to the Fund."

"Maybe he did think Alec could help, but of course, at that point he had no alternative. That's why I want you to know exactly what's going on."

FORTY-EIGHT

Alec and Emma looked up as Harold entered the room.

"I see you two are still hard at work," he said. "Can I help you with anything?"

"We've been looking for more information about the murder of Wouter Winckel. Do you know anything else about it? Like the motive? Or the identity of the killer?"

Harold shook his head. "All I know is what's in the autopsy report. His head was bashed in and someone had shoved his pamphlet into his mouth."

"You mean a pamphlet like these?" Emma asked, sliding an open file folder over to Harold.

"Yes, those are copies of pamphlets published that same year."

"So these were the newspapers of their day, right?" Alec asked.

"More or less. In the seventeenth century, pamphlets were the usual way of disseminating information or publicizing your views. They were like today's opinion columns or letters to the editor."

He pulled a few sheets of paper out of the folder. "The language can be difficult to follow. But these have been translated into modern Dutch by a student of historical linguistics. The translations are attached to the copies."

"What about Winckel's pamphlet? Which one is that?"

Harold leafed through the copies and picked one out. "Here it is. It was published under a pseudonym, but it couldn't have been written by anyone else."

"How can you be so sure?"

"Look at the signature."

Emma held it close to her face. "It's hard to make it out, but I think it says Augustus Semper."

Harold looked at them expectantly. Seeing the uncomprehending look in their eyes, he said, "Sorry, I thought you'd know the name. There were a lot of pamphleteers in the Dutch republic, but Wouter Winckel was radical for his day, to say the least. Here's the modernized version. Read it for yourself."

After a few minutes, Alec said, "I see what you mean. He seems to deny the existence of God as a higher power, and then he says that Nature should take God's place. Here he actually writes, 'God is Nature.' His contemporaries must not have been too pleased."

"Wasn't there freedom of expression in Holland back then?" Emma asked.

"Compared to other Western European countries, Holland was reasonably liberal," Alec said. "Religion was a frequent topic of discussion, and there were constant debates. But you couldn't just say anything you wanted. There were limits."

"But the seventeenth century was Holland's golden age of philosophy and natural science. It was the age of reason," Emma said. "Some people even claim that the Enlightenment didn't start in France but in the Dutch republic. We were tolerant—at least, more tolerant than other countries."

"Tolerant, hmm," Harold said. "There are various schools of thought about that. The real difference was that we were a republic. There was no monarch telling people what to do, no sovereign making everyone work for his benefit."

"Other European states kept a close watch on what their citizens were up to, what they said and wrote. But it wasn't like that here," Alec said to Emma.

Harold opened the thermos and poured them all another cup of coffee. "It's true that here, people could talk about subjects that were off-limits elsewhere."

A wrinkle creased Alec's brow. "But the freedom to say or write what you believed was limited. The church was powerful, and political leaders didn't want to hear any complaints from the public."

"You're absolutely right. When pamphleteers knew they were venturing beyond the limits, they used pseudonyms, or published anonymously. Their pamphlets were dropped off at inns or plastered on walls and nailed to doors at night." Harold pointed to the pamphlet. "I have no idea who committed the crime, but this may have been the motive for killing Winckel."

Emma looked at him. "So he was killed because of what he wrote?"

"It could be. He wouldn't have been the first or the last person to be murdered by religious fanatics."

"Now that I've read his pamphlet, I see your point," Alec added. "He takes a fairly extreme position here. It's clear that he wants reform—and not just moral reform, but religious too."

"Exactly. He claimed that the truth about nature and all its secrets could only be discovered if there was freedom of thought, and that meant breaking free of religious dogma. He felt that scholars and researchers had to be at liberty to experiment, and to challenge prevailing theories and ideas."

"Ideas and theories that had always been based on belief in God," Emma said.

Harold nodded. "But this was the seventeenth century, and if your ideas conflicted with those of the church, your life was in serious danger. To make things worse, Winckel emphasized the spiritual side of religion, people's freedom to believe whatever they wanted and practice their faith in any way they chose, any way that suited their needs and preferences. His goal was a true brotherhood of men—and women too, for that matter—regardless of their personal backgrounds. He strongly believed that different religions could coexist in peace. Winckel didn't care what church a person went to. What mattered to him was empathy and humanity."

"That must have horrified the religious hard-liners," Alec said.

"It wasn't just Winckel's theories that had them worried," Harold said. "It was also his fortune. Wouter Winckel didn't spend his money on his own comfort. He had a purpose in mind for the money that he earned by trading in tulips. He gave a large portion of it away. Not to friends and acquaintances, but to—"

"—science."

"That's right, Emma."

Just like Frank, Alec thought. It couldn't be a coincidence. Frank had deliberately hidden the coded message in the very book produced for the auction of Wouter Winckel's tulips. Was Winckel his shining example? Had Frank hoped to raise funds for science through the tulip trade, just like Winckel in the seventeenth century? As far as Alec knew, that wasn't how Frank had made his money. So far, they had no indication that tulips had brought Frank anything but trouble.

In the car on the way home, Alec said, "Suppose someone planned the whole thing and knew in advance exactly what would happen?"

"What do you mean?"

"Well, wasn't it common knowledge that after Winckel's death his children would go to the orphanage?"

"I guess so. What's your point?"

"So everyone knew that if he died, his collection of tulips would be auctioned off, and the orphanage would keep a share of the proceeds. Dick said that was how it always worked in those days. Whenever an orphanage took in children, it got to keep a percentage of their property. Suppose it was all a scheme, worked out in advance?"

"But van Benthum said the motive for Winckel's murder was probably religious. They choked him with his own pamphlet."

"Yes, but what if they just wanted to make it look that way? What if their real objective was to get Winckel's tulips into the hands of the orphanage, for pure financial gain? The next step would be to drive up the prices of the bulbs artificially, so the auction would bring in more money."

"And they could do that by spreading rumors of bulbs that were sold in advance for outrageous prices."

Alec nodded.

"So you think the religious motive was really just a cover? It was all about the money?" Emma frowned. "I'm not so sure. Those were the glory days of Calvinism. The extremists condemned all forms of luxury and excess."

"And the whole tulip craze was based on greed," Alec muttered.

"I can imagine that some people hated the excesses of the bulb trade: all the money that changed hands, and the extravagant lifestyles of successful tulip dealers. Religious fanatics must have been infuriated."

"Emma, if this is true, if that's really what it was like, then it's a revelation. It would explain why the market collapsed from one day to the next. Maybe the tulip trade had enemies, people who wanted to bring it crashing down."

"It's certainly worth considering," she said softly.

"Em, I just thought of something. The pseudonym that Winckel used in his pamphlet. Augustus Semper. We forgot to ask how they linked that name to Wouter Winckel."

Emma picked up her phone. "I've got Harold's card in my bag."

She punched in the number that Alec read to her. Harold picked up right away.

"Sorry to bother you, Harold, but there's something we forgot to ask," Emma said. "That pseudonym, Augustus Semper."

"Yes?"

"Why did Wouter Winckel use that name?"

"It was a reference to the tulip Semper Augustus."

"The tulip?" she repeated. Her eyes widened, and she glanced at Alec.

"Yes, the most precious tulip of all time. There were rumors that

Wouter Winckel owned a Semper Augustus bulb. So everyone knew from the pseudonym that he had written the pamphlet."

"Was the Semper Augustus sold at the auction?"

"No, that's the funny thing. We have the sale list, and it doesn't include the Semper. Emma, before you hang up, there's something else. After you left, I was thinking about Alec's last name. I checked our records, and another man named Schoeller visited the archives a couple of years ago, also asking about Wouter Winckel. I didn't talk to him myself. Another archivist told me that he'd been here. I've found the visitor card that he filled in."

FORTY-NINE

"It all started with the death of Paul Rijen, a good friend of mine. We'd known each other since we were students," Dick said.

"So Frank must have known him too."

"They'd met a few times, sure. A couple of years back, I heard that Paul had committed suicide. It came as a great shock. I felt it was his personal decision, and I respected it, but for some reason I just couldn't get it out of my mind. He'd never seemed like the type to take his own life. He loved life, he had a family, and he was passionate about his work. Of course, you never know what's going on in a person's heart, but I always thought there was something strange about his suicide, something that didn't quite fit. Yes," he mused, "it just didn't add up. The truth is, he lived for his work, and life lost its meaning when it all went wrong. But I didn't realize that until later."

Dick took a sip of his cappuccino. "About two months after he died, his wife wrote and asked me to come and see her. She showed me his suicide note and gave me a CD-ROM. Then she told me what Paul had been doing, the secret project he had concealed from all of us. On the CD there was a document."

He bent over, opened his briefcase, and took out a report. Pursing his lips, he drew circles on the cover with his index finger.

"Is that it?" Damian asked.

Dick nodded. "I was so appalled by what I read that I decided I had to do something. Stupidly, I showed the report to Frank. If I hadn't done that, none of this would ever have happened. Frank would still be alive, and everything would be fine."

He wiped his face. "I should have realized from the start that Frank couldn't leave well enough alone. I knew what he was like. But I let him in on the secret, and that was the start of all our troubles. This report, right here."

Damian picked it up. "'Toward a World at Peace.' Sounds like a noble goal, but what does it have to do with—"

Dick held up his hand. "Bear with me, I'll get to that. Science was everything to Paul. He was an anthropologist, applying the scientific method to human culture, and his specialism was religion. He looked at religion in the broadest sense of the term, including things that we would call cults or superstitions but other cultures take very seriously. He was fascinated by the need for religious faith and its influence on social communities all over the world. Paul knew better than anyone else where religion could lead."

"To war," Damian said ironically.

Dick shook his head. "No, that wasn't his position at all. Paul was a humanist. He believed in the power of love, human fellowship, tolerance, and mutual understanding, and he saw Christian humanism as one expression of those values. His research convinced him that faith could strengthen communities and create a peaceful society where people help and support each other."

"Atheists can build strong communities too."

"I agree, and until two thousand one, Paul felt the same way. It was the attacks on the World Trade Center that changed his mind, just as they changed the attitude of so many people. One of the effects of nine/eleven was that Americans and Europeans started demanding measures to protect Western values, to defend our freedom and our democratic principles." Dick shook his head. "Our world today is ruled by fear, Damian, you know that as well as I do. And a fearful world is quick to turn to religion. People are looking for something they can depend on, something to make their lives seem purposeful and manageable, something to give them hope."

"There's nothing wrong with that, is there?" Damian said.

"Nothing at all. As far as I'm concerned, people can put their faith in anything they choose. They can believe in an intelligent designer, or 'something out there somewhere,' or a man with a white beard who looks down at us from heaven. Whatever they like."

"And Paul?"

"Paul was one of the people who believed we had to take some kind of action. So he decided to found a think tank."

"A think tank? Do we have think tanks in Holland? They're like research institutes, right?"

"That's right. There are lots of them in America, often financed by interest groups who expect to benefit from their findings. The American business sector loves think tanks."

Dick held up three fingers. "In America, private organizations have three ways of influencing government policy. The first is by supporting political candidates. The second is by lobbying, persuading politicians to make laws and policies that benefit your business. The third and most lucrative way is by donating the money a think tank needs for its research. Some business groups go even further and set up think tanks of their own."

"Sounds very cunning."

"When a think tank produces a position paper, it provides scientific arguments, with figures and research results to back them up," Dick continued. "That makes it look like the paper comes from a neutral source, even though it doesn't. What's more, think tanks can stir up public debate."

"Clever. So they influence not only politicians but also public opinion."

"Exactly. Now, Paul set up his think tank as a scientist, independent of political parties and the private sector. But they gave him plenty of support when he reached out to his network. Paul was very well connected. Not just at universities but also in the art world, politics, the media, and business. He asked some of his contacts to join the think tank and help him come up with a plan for peace and a renewed sense of community. To achieve those goals, he aimed to establish a new missionary movement."

"Missionary? You mean they wanted to convert people?"

"Yes, they did. Paul and his associates believed that the values of Christian humanism formed the path to a world without war and aggression. They argued that those values were inherent to Western culture but had been watered down and distorted through the centuries. Paul needed not only collaborators but also donors to finance his project. Thanks to his connections, the money rolled in. Everyone involved was committed to the project and thought that it could bring people together."

Dick looked at Damian. "You're probably wondering what this has to do with Frank and Simon. I want to explain the background, so that you'll understand what they had in mind when they set up the Fund. I think it's important for you to see the big picture. That's why I'm telling you all this."

He held up the report. "This report presents the outcome of their efforts. What it boils down to is this: They concluded that to achieve their goal they had to exert influence on three traditional institutions, which they saw as the basis of civil society—the family, the church, and the school."

"But you can't force values down people's throats. What were they actually planning to do?" Damian asked.

"Their strategy was based on mass psychology and took advantage of people's need to put their faith in something in today's uncertain world. But you're right—in fact, they were declaring a holy war, an invisible war without any casualties. Their plan had several stages. They were going to start with a massive media campaign to promote Christian values and traditions. Then they would recruit 'opinion leaders,' people with influence and prestige, to promote their brand of Christian humanism to their friends and acquaintances. But at this point, Paul discovered that his well-intentioned plan was being twisted to serve a cause that he would never support."

FIFTY

The leaves of the dusty rubber plant brushed against her neck. Dawn swiveled around and toed aside the flowerpot. Peering down the long row of cubicles, she wondered how Ben could work there. The rubber plant was not the only thing covered with dust. Everything was grimy and gray: the walls, the doors, the computers, and even the people. That was the strange thing about the Dutch, she thought, the contrast between their working lives and the way they acted in their leisure time. When they were on vacation, they lingered over meals for hours, sampling each other's food and sharing carefully chosen bottles of wine. But in their everyday lives, it was as if they were doing penance for those indulgences, working their way through mounds of bland potatoes and drinking wine only on weekends. A friend had told her their birthday parties were even worse: "They look like monkeys, sitting in a circle and eating peanuts."

She looked over at Ben, who was still focused on his screen. On top of his monitor were three photographs. The first was of a woman with short red hair, looking cheerful and carefree. The next photo was of a little boy, whose sun-bleached hair stood out against the cool blue of the swimming pool. The last was of the whole family, smiling into the camera, all dressed in orange from head to toe. Ben was even wearing an orange wig. They were in the middle of a large park full of market stalls, between which other vendors had spread out their wares on the grass.

"Football?" she asked, pointing to the snapshot.

"What? Oh, no, that was for the queen's birthday. We celebrate it every year on April thirtieth. Everyone has the day off, and we throw a big party. We wear orange to honor the royal family—the House of Orange."

"What about those vendors?" she asked. "Aren't they working?"

"Those aren't vendors. On Queen's Day anyone can sell things, without a permit. Sandwiches, soft drinks, stuff they find in the attic, whatever."

"So you celebrate the queen's birthday by selling each other your old junk from the attic?"

"I guess you could put it that way. Of course, it's really her mother's birthday."

I give up, Dawn thought. I'll never understand these people.

"Here, I've got it. This is what we know about Versteegen. I'll print it out."

FIFTY-ONE

"But who twisted Paul's plan, and how?" Damian asked.

"As I said, Paul wasn't working alone. He had a large network of advisers and financial backers."

"Sure, but you said they all shared his belief in Christian humanism."

Dick leaned close to Damian and murmured, "Listen carefully. That's exactly what went wrong. Paul found out that not everyone involved shared his ideas or his goal of world peace. Some of them had a hidden agenda."

"What was that?"

"They wanted to propagate Christian fundamentalism in Western Europe, using the plan developed by the think tank. They saw religion as a vehicle for achieving their ultimate goal: the global dominance of the West. And what better place to start than here in Holland, with our Christian schools, universities, hospitals, nursing homes, newspapers, broadcasting companies, and political parties. Of course, our country has all sorts of denominations, from Catholics to mainline Protestants to strict Calvinists, but they all share a common faith. These people wanted to exploit and manipulate that faith, to make the Christian community in Holland not only larger but also more radical."

"So there were fundamentalists involved."

Dick looked at him sadly. "Paul tried to stop them, but he very soon realized he'd lost control. That's when he killed himself."

"Wasn't there anything he could have done?"

Dick ran his hands over his face and replied, "When Paul saw them misusing his life's work for their purposes, his world collapsed. Like any reasonable person, he understood that religious fanaticism is the enemy of individual freedom, that it leads to a world where women are oppressed, where homosexuals are persecuted, and where all sorts of books, films, and music are banned. A world that has no place for dissent and diversity. That had never been Paul's intention. He'd wanted to strengthen our sense of community and believed the only way to accomplish that was through a common faith."

"Dick, do you think that could ever really happen in Holland? Book burning and all that? I mean, this is a pretty levelheaded country. And religion has been in decline here for years."

"If you're talking about the decline of organized religion, then you're right, but at this point in history, people are desperate for the reassurance that religion provides. And there's nothing wrong with that, as long as no one takes advantage of the situation. But that's exactly what's going on now, and it's partly because of Paul."

Dick's face darkened. "In the worst case, our country will see a resurgence of fundamentalist groups hostile to all the liberties we've won over the centuries. That prospect was so repugnant to Frank that he decided to join forces with several wealthy business leaders to oppose the extremists. Frank was the instigator and the mastermind behind this counteroffensive."

"The Fund."

"Exactly. And I believe he and Simon were murdered by the Christian fundamentalists who had infiltrated Paul's think tank. They felt threatened by the Fund and its activities. Frank and Simon were trying to stop the extremist movement that had grown out of Paul's initiative, to uphold the scientific method, and to prevent independent-minded individuals from degenerating into a herd of sheep, living their lives according to religious dogma. The Fund had a lot of money that it could use to find even stronger evidence for fundamental scientific theories, like evolution, and to oppose the ideas of reactionary religious movements." He seemed lost in thought for a moment. Then he continued, in a quiet voice, "When Frank learned that centuries ago Wouter Winckel had defied religious extremism without using violence, he decided to pursue the same strategy."

"Winckel? The tulip dealer?"

"Yes, that was his shining example. And Wouter Winckel paid for his beliefs with his life, just like Frank did in the end."

"But what did Wouter Winckel believe in, exactly?"

"Freedom of action, freedom of expression. And that means the freedom to express your opinion, not the freedom to hurl crude insults at those who think differently, though these days some people don't seem to know the difference. As far as I'm concerned, that kind of abuse has nothing to do with freedom of expression."

Dick nervously picked up a coaster and started tearing it into tiny shreds, which he tossed into the full ashtray.

"We're only human," he said. "We have to make a go of it together." He looked at Damian. "Frank had found something that had once belonged to Winckel. A priceless treasure."

He motioned to Damian to move closer and whispered, "The Semper Augustus."

"Semper Augustus?"

Dick nodded. "The most precious tulip of all. So precious, that for hundreds of years historians wondered whether it had ever truly existed. Apparently, in the seventeenth century there were only three Semper Augustus bulbs. Nobody knew who owned them."

"If it was just that this tulip was so scarce, why didn't they grow more?"

"No, you don't understand, that was precisely the problem. The tulips in the catalog I showed you, with flamed petals, were almost impossible to cultivate. That's why they were so rare and valuable. Seventeenth-century growers just couldn't understand it. An offset from the bulb of a flamed tulip might well produce a single-colored flower, or one with hardly any color at all. What they didn't realize was that the tulips with flamed, or 'broken,' petals were diseased. That came to light only in the twentieth century. The patterns were a side effect of a virus transmitted by aphids: the mosaic virus."

"So it was a harmful virus that produced the most beautiful tulips in history, and then it was the beauty of those tulips that caused so much misery," Damian muttered.

"Three people were said to own Semper Augustus bulbs. Wouter Winckel was supposed to be one of them, but no one ever found out whether the tale was true."

"Surely if he had owned one, it would have been auctioned off with the rest of his collection."

"That's just it. No Semper Augustus was sold at the auction. So everyone assumed it had been an idle rumor. That is, until Frank found the bulb, more than three centuries later." Dick laid his hand on Damian's arm. "Can you imagine what would happen if the Semper Augustus were restored to life? If the latest technology and scientific advances allowed us to clone the bulb?"

"You could make millions."

"Tens of millions. That was Frank's goal." He raised a finger. "Not for himself, mind you. He wanted to use that money to give science a huge financial boost. With those enormous profits, think of all the research he could have funded."

Dick paused for a long moment, brooding.

"I think the people who killed Frank and Simon are after the bulb. They know how much it's worth, and they want it for themselves. They intend to use the Semper Augustus to finance their plans for the worldwide expansion of fundamentalist Christianity."

"But who are they?"

"That's the problem. I haven't been able to identify them yet. In his farewell letter to his wife, Paul told the whole story. He said he knew who they were but would carry their names with him into the grave."

Damian nodded. "To protect his family."

"Exactly. But I'll find out who's responsible. I'm the only one left who can stop them."

Coetzer was sipping his third cup of coffee by now and still had his eyes on page three of his newspaper. He had shuffled his chair toward Dick and Damian, as far as he could without attracting attention. Thanks to the miniature speaker in his ear, he had heard every word of their conversation.

FIFTY-TWO

Tara started at the shrill sound of the doorbell, which echoed through the empty house. She went to the front room and peeped out of the window.

The man at the door was so small that for a moment she thought it was a child. His black coat came down to his ankles. He wore gleaming black shoes and a red knitted scarf tucked into his raised collar. The briefcase he carried had seen better days. When she saw him reach for the bell again, she decided to risk it—he looked harmless enough. She unlocked the front door and pulled it open.

For a moment, his eyes widened in surprise. "Good afternoon." He extended his hand. "Jacob Wolters. I'm here to see Mr. Vanlint."

"He's not in. Come in, Mr. . . . . Wolters, was it?"

"Yes."

"I'm Tara, Alec Schoeller's girlfriend. You're from the auction house, right?"

He nodded hesitantly.

"It's all right, I know what you're here for."

"I, er, do you have any idea when Mr. Vanlint will be back? I should have called before coming over, I suppose. But you see, I was running an errand just around the corner."

"He won't be back for a while. But please, come inside. Have you made any progress with the message from the tulip book?"

He looked relieved. "Yes, that's why I'm here."

"*Tulipa*—that was the code word, wasn't it?"

He nodded.

"Come on, let's sit down."

As he followed her into the kitchen, she turned to glance at him. "Coffee?"

"I'd love some."

Wolters took off his coat and sat down at the kitchen table. Tara brought him a mug, which he grasped with both hands, taking a large gulp of the hot liquid. When she took a seat across from him, he said, "You and your friends were right. The code word is *tulipa*."

"We thought it was. It was hard to imagine it being anything else."

"I don't mean to pry, but I'm very curious how you figured it out."

"So you managed to crack the code?" Tara asked.

Wolters slipped his hand into his pocket and pulled out a piece of paper.

"Shall I read it to you?"

"Please do."

He looked at her uncertainly. "You will pass it on to Mr. Vanlint, won't you?"

"As soon as he gets home, I'll give it to him personally. Don't you worry about that."

He unfolded the paper. "All right, then, this is the message that we deciphered." He read:

> "*Few can resist the allure*
> *Of her divine beauty*
> *She will remain slumbering*
> *In this silver shrine*
> *Until she is awoken*
> *Semper Augustus*"

He looked up. "Does that mean anything to you?"

Tara tried not to let her face betray her emotion. Her heart was pounding so hard that she feared Wolters might be able to hear it. She was glad that she had trusted her intuition, sticking close to Alec until she found out where the bulb was hidden. But not so fast—she wasn't done yet. Not by a long shot.

"Well, at least we know what it says now. It's bound to be more useful than gobbledygook. Thank you very much. Damian and Alec will be glad to hear the news."

She pushed back her chair and stood up.

Wolters looked at her. "Semper Augustus—that's a kind of tulip, if I'm not mistaken."

"Thanks again, Mr. Wolters," she replied coolly, holding out her hand for the sheet of paper. "I'll give it to them as soon as they get home—"

"You'll give us *what*?"

She spun around, aghast to find Alec and Emma standing in the doorway. Forcing herself to remain calm, she said, "Mr. Wolters was kind enough to stop by and let us know what they discovered. Here it is."

Alec nodded at Wolters and took the message from him, his eyes still fixed on Tara.

"Mr. Schoeller." Wolters stood up and groped for his coat, looking uneasy. "I'd better be going. I hope you don't mind that I told your girlfriend about the message."

Alec's eyes bored into Tara. He opened his mouth to speak, but seeing the look on her face, he shut it again. "Not at all," he said to Wolters. "I'll show you out."

When he returned, he made straight for where Tara was standing. She shrank back, lost her footing, and landed with a thud on the chair behind her.

"What are you trying to pull? Why did he think you were my girlfriend? What are you really after?"

"Isn't that obvious? The Semper Augustus bulb. It's hidden in something made of silver," Tara said. Her eyes were wide, and her cheeks burned with an unhealthy glow.

"Damn it! When are you going to come clean with us? You knew Frank a hell of a lot better than you claimed. I'd say the two of you were pretty close. Here, explain this."

He pulled the e-mail from Frank to Tara out of his pocket and threw it in her face. It fell onto her lap, and she pulled it open. A moment later, she looked up, unmoved.

"So now that you know how far we had already come, you must understand how important this is. Did Frank leave you anything made of silver—or could it be locked up in a safe somewhere?"

"Will you shut up about the goddamn silver? Just tell us what's going on and how you fit into it. Now."

She shrugged and stared sullenly into the distance.

Alec kneeled in front of her, placing his hands on her knees. "Okay, let's make a deal. You tell me how you're involved in this and whatever it is you know. Then I'll tell you all about Frank's silver collection. Okay?"

Her eyes lit up. "So he does have one! Does it include any seventeenth-century pieces?"

Alec gave her a stern look.

"All right, all right. Semper Augustus. Ever heard of it?"

"Just this morning, in fact," Emma said. "It was the most valuable tulip in the world. The question is whether it ever really existed."

"Oh, it existed, that's for sure. And it still does. You see, Frank asked me to come up with a method for developing the Semper Augustus."

"Developing? You mean cultivating?"

"No, Em, I know exactly what she means," Alec said. "She was going to clone it."

"Clone it?" Emma said, surprised. "That's not possible, is it? I thought you could only clone living cells."

Tara turned to Emma with a smile. "It's possible for me. I can make an exact genetic copy. When Frank came to ask if I'd give it a try, he gave me enough money to use the most advanced techniques available. In the end, I got the job done."

"But the bulb is hidden in a silver shrine," Emma said.

"That's why I was asking about his silver collection. How about giving me an answer now?"

"Later," Alec said. "I'm not done yet. Why did Frank want to clone the tulip?"

"To make money."

"He had plenty of money."

"Sure, he had lots of money, but not as much as he needed. With the Semper Augustus, he could have earned tens of millions. Through years of careful breeding, modern growers have developed ingenious imitations with flamed petals, but those have nothing to do with the genuine article. They're fakes, phonies. What would happen if the real Semper came onto the market? No other tulip has had such a colorful history. In the seventeenth century, hardly anybody ever saw one outside a tulip book. But today, with the cloning techniques I've developed, we can bring it back to life. Not some cheap knockoff but a direct descendant. A true Semper Augustus."

Emma peered at Tara. "What was in it for you?"

"Respect. Admiration. Above all, professional recognition. Maybe even a major prize. Finally, I could establish my reputation. You don't know what my world is like. Nobody can be trusted. People are always stealing ideas and research findings. They'll run you into the ground unless you can show them what you're capable of." Her voice faltered. "I had done all my research, completed the experiments, analyzed the data, written up the results. Everything was ready. All I needed was the bulb." Almost whispering, she went on. "Frank had it. When he died, he was the only one who knew where it was. He told me he had hidden it, someplace where no one would find it. So when I first saw you, walking up the path to Simon's door, I had a hunch that, without even knowing it, you could lead me to the Semper Augustus."

"Your hunch was right," Alec said.

"Yes," she said guardedly.

"So who's after you?"

She looked bewildered. "After me? Oh, I see. No one, as far as I know."

"No one?" Alec sputtered. "Then who was tailing us on our way back from Simon's house?"

She shrugged. "If I hadn't acted like someone was chasing us, Damian wouldn't have invited me to stay here."

Dick wandered down the stairs, lost in thought. The wind rushing through the underground corridors of the subway station pushed him out onto the deserted platform. A stray leaf crackled under his feet, and a plastic bag danced by. He checked his watch, then stared out at the filthy black wall across the track. The handle of his briefcase clung to his moist palm. The tape he'd wrapped around the cracked hinge was coming undone. He clenched the briefcase between his legs and started to scratch off the traces of glue on his hand.

He heard someone walking down the platform. The footsteps stopped right behind him. Suddenly, he felt a powerful blow as the briefcase was kicked from between his legs, arcing through the air all the way down to the track, where it flew open. Sheets of paper fluttered over the rails and were sucked into the dark mouth of the tunnel.

"What—"

He turned around, dazed. A hand clamped over his mouth. Then came the roar of a subway train, charging ahead at full speed, coming closer and closer. The last thing he heard was a man's voice shrieking. The last thing he wondered was whether the voice was his.

FIFTY-THREE

The front door slammed shut, and a moment later Damian came into the room.

"Wolters came by, and Tara was thoughtful enough to let him in and find out what he had to say," Alec explained. His sarcasm wasn't lost on Damian, whose eyes shot to Tara.

After Alec had told the whole story, Damian said, "So we were right about the code."

"Here, take a look. This is the decoded message."

After a few seconds, Damian looked up again. His expression was strained. "The Semper Augustus. Dick was just telling me about that. So it's really true—Frank had found the bulb. When Dick told me, it seemed too fantastic to believe."

"Is that what Dick wanted to talk to you about?" Emma asked.

"Among other things. I'll tell you all about it in a minute. Alec, didn't Frank have a silver collection?"

"Well, I wouldn't really call it a collection, but he had about twenty pieces. Some of them are lovely."

"Anything from the seventeenth century?" Tara looked at him tensely.

"Yes, I think so."

With a few swift steps, she was standing beside Alec. She gripped his arm so tightly that Alec could feel her nails through the material of his jacket. "We have to go to London and see what we can find there."

Alec laughed scornfully. "You really think we'll find a tulip bulb taped to the bottom of a candlestick?" But when he saw the fire in Tara's eyes, his scorn melted into doubt.

"You self-satisfied prick," she shouted. "That's what the message says, in black and white."

"Will you please spare us the hysterics? Or do you need a glass of water in your face?" Emma gazed archly at Tara, then turned to Damian. "Shall we have the collection brought here?"

He nodded. "Alec, why don't you call Tibbens? Ask him if he'll bring the silver to the airport and give it to our pilot. We can have it here in just a few hours."

"But suppose the bulb really is hidden in one of these objects, and we find it. What then?" Emma asked Alec.

"I don't know yet."

"I do," Tara said.

Alec grimaced. "Forget it. You're the last person I would trust with the bulb. Frank and Simon were murdered for that thing, and you don't even care. It means nothing to you. All you can think about is the tulip. I thought you'd want to help us find out who's responsible for Frank and Simon's deaths. Have you ever taken a good look at yourself? You should try it sometime. You make me sick."

Tara's eyes narrowed in fury. She spat out her words. "I may keep my emotions to myself, but that doesn't mean I don't care. Do you think I'm a heartless monster? What happened to them matters tremendously to me. It's just that right now I have other priorities." She held out her hands and said despairingly, "Can't you see how much this means to me? I don't care about the money; all I care about is the Semper Augustus."

"If that were really true, I think I could begin to understand. But it's not true at all. All you care about is yourself, your reputation."

Tara shook her head desperately and lowered her eyes. In a quavering voice, she said, "I knew I could help Frank carry out his mission."

"Help Frank?" replied Alec with a sneer. "You sanctimonious hypocrite." He turned away from her. "You make me want to puke."

She ran out of the room. The door banged shut behind her.

Damian took the suitcase from the chauffeur and put it on the floor of the living room. Alec kneeled down and opened it. There were about twenty packages inside, covered in bubble wrap and taped shut. About fifteen minutes later, Frank's entire silver collection was lined up on the floor.

"Where could he have hidden it, for God's sake?" Alec looked at the glittering array. "A tulip bulb would be too big to fit in any of these things."

They looked up as Tara entered the room. With bloodshot eyes, she came up to Alec and said, "Everything you just said about me is true. You're right. I just needed a wake-up call. I can't believe the way I've been acting." Her fingers were knotted together, and she held them clutched to her chest like a shield. "You're right, the important thing is to catch the killer. Nothing else matters. I . . . I couldn't even work with the bulb anymore. It's stained with blood." She shook her head. "I don't even want the damned thing."

"Come on," Emma said. "Give us a hand. If our guess is right, the bulb is hidden somewhere in this collection."

Each of them picked up an object. Tara snatched up a candelabrum, turned it upside down, and started to pick off the felt lining on the bottom. After tearing it loose, she squinted into the tiny cavity, then shook her head. "There's nothing in there."

After a while Emma said, "I think I'm on to something. Come and take a look."

She held up a small silver buckle and pointed to the thickest part. "This has a tulip carved into it."

"Let me see." Damian took the buckle and held it close to his face. The slight protrusion in the middle was engraved with a small tulip.

He ran his finger over it, pressing gently. To his amazement, the top of the buckle sprang open.

"You've got it," Tara cried.

They looked on in silence as Damian pushed the top farther open. He peered inside and shook his head.

"Nothing. It's empty."

"There's a matching buckle over here. Let's try that one." Alec picked it up and repeated the process. Again, the buckle sprang open. He squeezed his thumb and index finger into the opening, and when he pulled them out again, he was holding a tiny brown pouch.

"Oh, my God," Tara murmured.

Alec opened the pouch, held it over his palm, and shook out the contents. In his hand lay a small dark brown object, no larger than a centimeter across. It resembled a raisin.

"It's completely dried out," Alec said softly. "There's no life left in it."

Tara said excitedly, "If you only knew how much life I could get out of it."

"What about the other buckle? Why is it empty?" Emma sounded wary.

"The message must have been in that one," Alec replied. "Remember? It said 'in this silver shrine.'"

"So Frank removed it and hid it inside the tulip book."

London

2001

"Just wait for me here," Frank Schoeller told his chauffeur after stepping out of the car. "I won't be a minute." For the past few days, mild mornings had given way to sweltering afternoons, and the asphalt on the Kings Road had absorbed the heat. Frank could feel the warmth rising up the legs of his pants.

He dabbed at his face with a handkerchief. Before entering the antiques shop, he stopped to admire the sideboard on display in the window. It was covered with shagreen, and the granular surface had a silvery luster. The ivory knobs on the doors and shelves looked as good as new. He rang the bell, waited for the buzz, and pushed the door open.

"Mr. Schoeller, how are you?" said the man who came to meet him.

"Fine, and you? How's business?"

"Couldn't be better. What can I do for you today? Are you looking for anything special?"

"No, not really, just nosing around."

"Be my guest. You know where to find me."

Moving from case to case, Frank scrutinized every object: ivory netsuke shaped like monkeys, flowers, and samurai; miniature clocks with finely painted scenes on their enamel faces. Next to the table in the middle of the shop, goldfish were circling in an enormous Chinese flowerpot. He continued to the back of the shop, where the furniture was on display. As he inhaled the odor of wax, the owner came to his side.

"Mr. Schoeller, I have something that may . . . well, you come from Holland, don't you?"

"That's right."

"I don't know whether they'll suit your taste, but they're Dutch, seventeenth century, so I thought . . . wait a moment, I'll go and get them."

Frank heard a rustling sound in the back room. "Here we are," the antiques dealer said, returning with something in his hand. He opened his fingers and unfolded the thin paper.

"I bought these at an auction in Holland just recently. They're magnificent, aren't they?"

"Are they hallmarked?"

"Yes, indeed. If you'll just follow me . . ."

At his desk he turned on the magnifying lamp and placed the two buckles under the lens. Frank leaned over to examine them. They were stunning in their simplicity, their clean curves. Only the tops were decorated, each with a single tulip.

"Here's the mark, see?"

His magnified nail tapped an almost invisible symbol stamped into the side.

"I've done some research. They're seventeenth century—I can't pinpoint the date, but probably around sixteen thirty, or maybe a bit later. They were made by a silversmith in Alkmaar. Ever heard of the place?"

"Oh, yes. It's a lovely old town in the province of North Holland."

"I see."

"May I have a look?"

"Of course, take your time."

Frank sat down, picked up one of the buckles, and examined it carefully under the lens. As he studied the tulip engraved into the top, he noticed a word inscribed underneath it in letters so minute that even when magnified they were barely legible.

"Tulipa," he whispered.

Running his finger over the silver, he imagined a wealthy merchant of ages past wearing the buckles with pride. A pride that many people would have resented. In those days, it was bad form to flaunt your wealth.

"Don't put on airs. Don't stand out in the crowd. For God's sake, don't express yourself," he mumbled. "What a bitter bunch of Calvinists."

When he was done examining the two buckles, he stood up. "The buckles are charming, but they're nothing special. Besides, there's a dent—right there, on this one. But I'm getting sentimental in my old age. You might as well seize the opportunity. What kind of price can you offer a faithful customer?"

Seated at his kitchen table, Frank picked up his glass and downed the last drops of cognac. He slipped his hand into a glove impregnated with silver polish and rubbed gently on one of the buckles, putting a little extra pressure on the decoration to remove the layer of tarnish. Suddenly, something moved in his hand. He put down the buckle, removed the glove, and stared at the opening in amazement. Then he picked up the buckle again and held it in front of his nose. His fingers barely fit into the tiny compartment. When he drew his hand out, a small sepia scroll was nestled in his fingertips.

FIFTY-FOUR

Dick's muffled voice asked Damian to leave a message after the tone.

"Hi, Dick, this is Damian. Could you call me back as soon as possible? I think we're on to something. Please call as soon as you can, it's important."

As soon as he hung up, his telephone rang. He recognized the number. "Dick, listen, I—"

"Sorry to interrupt, sir," a woman's voice said. "I'm calling from the hospital. I saw that you had just phoned Mr. Beerens. Are you a relative?"

"What? No, a friend. What's wrong? Is he in the hospital?"

"I'm very sorry to tell you this, but unfortunately, there's been an accident. Mr. Beerens died about fifteen minutes ago."

"What do you mean, died? That's impossible. I just spoke to him earlier today."

"He was brought into the emergency room an hour ago, after being hit by a subway car. They think he may have dropped his bag onto the rails and gone after it, but he didn't make it back to the platform in time. It's also possible he tripped and fell. There were no witnesses. He was unconscious when they found him."

As Damian hung up, he broke into a sweat. So the murderer's not far away, he thought. In that case, he probably knows who we are, and where we are.

He ran down the hallway and into the living room.

"We have to get out of here. Now. Dick is dead."

Tara and Alec stared in disbelief. Emma let out a cry and stifled it with her hand.

"That was the hospital. Apparently he was run over by a subway. They think he fell off the platform by accident, but obviously that's not what really happened. Look, we're not safe here anymore. We have to get out of town, and we'd better take the Semper Augustus with us."

"Out of town?" Tara repeated. "Where to?"

"To the island."

FIFTY-FIVE

For the third time that evening, Dawn opened Simon Versteegen's file.
She couldn't concentrate. Her hotel room was filled with a booming
noise from somewhere nearby, which never seemed to stop. The low bass
tones were sometimes accompanied by something like music. She began
to look forward to those snatches of melody, which somehow made the
monotonous thrumming more bearable.

She pushed up the window and looked outside. Standing on tiptoe,
she could see a thin sliver of canal in the distance. Below, clutches of
people were talking in loud, slurred voices. A teenage boy staggered
away from his friends to empty the contents of his stomach into a
doorway across from her hotel. Dawn pictured the person who lived
there heading off to work the next morning and stepping right into the
mess. She closed the window. Just as she was about to draw the curtains, she noticed the door opening across the street. Two arms flung
a pail of water over the spot where the boy had vomited.

Flopping down on the bed, she grabbed the file. Versteegen had
been seventy-three years old. He'd come from a large family, had studied law, and risen to become director of a large pharmaceutical company. On top of that, he'd served on all sorts of boards and committees.
He'd retired at the age of sixty—he could have afforded to earlier, since
there was plenty of money in the family, but until then he had always
enjoyed his work. He'd been married twice but never had children.

After the death of his second wife, he'd adopted her daughter from an earlier marriage. Now she was his sole heir.

Dawn spread out the photographs of the crime scene on the bedspread in front of her.

"There has to be something, there has to be," she said aloud.

One by one, she picked up the photos, studied them, and put them down again. When she came to the photo that Ben had described, the one with the streaks of blood on the wall behind Versteegen's bed, Dawn straightened up. She held the photo at arm's length and squinted. That investigator was right, she thought, it did look like a tulip. She pulled the close-up out of the stack, examined it, and frowned. Something about it seemed so familiar. Where had she seen it before? She shook her head and closed the file. Maybe the whole idea of a connection between Schoeller and Versteegen was just a red herring. What if the two murders were unrelated?

She put the file down on the floor beside her and turned on the television. When she had found the BBC, she got up and went to the minibar. As she kneeled in front of the refrigerator, it came to her in a flash. She rushed over to her bag, pulled out Schoeller's file, and began rifling through the photos.

"Where are you? Come on, you must be here somewhere," she muttered as she flipped through the stack. "Aha!"

Schoeller's body lay on the steel table. It had been washed, but the autopsy had not yet begun.

"I knew it, I knew it."

With the blood washed away, it was glaringly obvious. The knife wounds to his upper body matched the pattern on the wall in Versteegen's bedroom. The two topmost incisions joined to form a U. Between them was a deep gash leading downward, like the stem of a flower. On each side of this vertical line was a small diagonal stab wound.

"A tulip?" Dawn whispered.

Her cell phone rang and she reached out for it, her eyes still glued to the photo.

FIFTY-SIX

The bumpy, unpaved track cut through the pastures of Friesland, leading them straight to the dock for the river island. The rain had transformed the broad path into a long, muddy ditch, and Damian slowly edged the car forward, skirting the deep puddles and the swampy shoulders. After a mile or so, he pulled up onto a small patch of asphalt that served as a parking lot.

The cold wind howled across the open fields. As soon as they stepped out of the car, they felt the full blast of the storm. Raindrops pricked their faces. They unloaded the car and filed down the narrow path to the landing. In the distance, a light was swinging wildly back and forth.

"Damian! Have you got enough light?"

The voice was almost carried away by the fierce wind.

"No problem," Damian shouted. "You can stay where you are."

They stepped onto the landing, where a small white boat was docked. A large, burly man stood next to it. His blond hair clung to his forehead, and his waterlogged woolen sweater sagged from his sturdy shoulders.

"I'm glad you could make it out here, Sytse."

"Sure thing, Damian. Come on board, quick, the ladies are getting soaked."

He reached out to steady the boat, which was rocking treacherously on the waves of the canal. They stepped in, and Damian went to join Sytse, who turned his key in the ignition and brought the diesel engine roaring to life.

"The house is fully stocked," he shouted over the engine noise and the beating rain. "There's food in the fridge, and you know where to find everything else. If you need anything, let me know and I'll bring it over."

They set off across the water and ten minutes later were pulling into the dock.

The island covered more than two hundred acres. Many years earlier, Damian had snapped it up at a bargain price. He had torn down the dilapidated barn he found there and then neglected the site for years before making up his mind to build a large house. The local authorities had balked at his modernist design, but in the end he had won them over.

After dropping them off on the platform, Sytse tied up the boat. He stepped into his own smaller craft and roared off into the stormy night. They watched him disappear into the darkness.

FIFTY-SEVEN

Agonizing pain shot through his head and down his spine, forcing him to his knees. He tried to stay upright but toppled over, landing hard on his side. The driving rain filled his ears and stung his eyes, making him squint. Someone grabbed his wrist and started tugging at his fingers. No, he thought, not the key. He balled his hand into a fist and felt the metal teeth digging into his palm. Opening his eyes as wide as he could manage, he saw a man whose face was concealed by a hood, hovering over him like a vague shadow. His hand was abruptly released. Then he felt a sharp tug on the black cord attached to the key, which protruded between two of his fingers. The tugging stopped, and he felt his muscles relax. He tried to focus, but the ache in his head was too distracting. Concentrate, Sytse, concentrate. Then a sudden burning in his hand, unbearable. He screamed in pain. A second blow to the head, and he was silenced. As he sank into the shallow mud, his fingers uncurled.

Each gust of wind pushed the small motorboat farther to the left. Coetzer was slowly drifting away from the narrow channel that led to the dock at the island. He could scarcely see a foot ahead of him. The rain was pelting down with the force of a tropical storm. He swung the tiller and managed to bring the boat back on course. If he could steer it straight ahead the rest of the way, he knew he would end up right where he wanted to be.

Suddenly, something towered up in front of him. He swung the tiller as far as it would go. The boat swung sharply to the right, but he was too late to avoid the buoy. He ran into it with a dull thud. His body shot forward and his chin hit the edge of the small cabin. Cursing, he scrambled to his feet, wiping away the blood.

Squinting against the rain, he realized that he was entering the channel. To the left, the faint outline of the house was just visible. As he pushed down the lever, the roar of the engine faded to a soft chugging. A few minutes later, he was steering the boat carefully toward the dock.

FIFTY-EIGHT

"All right," Damian said, once they were all sitting in the living room. "Now that we've made it here safe and sound, I can tell you what I learned from Dick. Then we'd better decide what to do with the bulb."

After Damian had told them, Alec replied, "I know what we should do. That thing is cursed. Three people have been killed for it already. Do we really want the same thing to happen to anyone else? And what if it ends up in the wrong hands? Besides, would it really be so terrible if no one ever saw it again? If the Semper Augustus remained a legend forever? Who would miss it? No one at all." Alec's eyes pleaded with them. "We have to destroy the bulb."

"How can you even suggest such a thing?" Tara was furious. "You're utterly missing the point. Don't you get it? The work of the Fund is crucial. We can't just abandon it. If you destroy that bulb, you're betraying all three of them: Frank, Simon, and Dick. All of them will have died for nothing."

"Spare me the bullshit. There are lots of ways to make money. Now that Frank's not around, they'll find other benefactors. No, I know exactly what we should do with the Semper."

Alec opened the buckle, shook the pouch out of it, and went over to the fireplace. The flames were rising high, licking the blackened walls and bathing the silver in an orange glow.

"No, stop," Tara shrieked, diving forward and tugging at Alec's arm with all her might.

Damian stepped toward her and grabbed her arms. "Let him do what he needs to do," he said, pulling her away with difficulty. "He's right. Enough is enough."

She panted, trying to squirm free of Damian's grip. "Wait, Alec, listen to me. Don't do it. You can't just destroy the Semper. How could you do that to Frank? He would have wanted you to continue his work. I knew him, and he felt a lot more strongly about this than you people seem to think. You have no idea how important this was to him. It was his sole purpose in life."

Alec showed no sign of turning away from the fire.

"Anyway, it's mine." Her voice broke. "I decide what happens to it. The Semper belongs to me, and it always will."

Damian shook her roughly, shouting, "Wake up, for goodness' sake. That goddamn tulip will bring us nothing but misery. Do you want more people to die? Don't you understand that if they do, it'll be your fault?"

Tara suddenly fell to her knees, and her teeth sank deep into Damian's hand. With a cry of pain, he let go of her, and just at that moment the door of the living room burst open.

They stared in horror at the man in the doorway. The gun in his hand was pointed right at them. He was tall and muscular, his face tanned a deep brown. His smirk revealed a row of perfect white teeth. With his free hand, he wiped a spot of blood off his chin. The look in his bright blue eyes was reserved as he sized them up, one by one. Then his gaze settled on Alec, and the corners of his mouth curled upward.

"So, you must be Alec. I've come here for you—or rather, what you've got there in your hand."

Alec's eyes shot toward the fireplace.

"I wouldn't if I were you. Or are you looking for a bloodbath? It's your choice. You saw what happened to your uncle, and to Versteegen.

Beerens didn't get off any lighter, I can assure you. The same thing could happen to your friends. Do you want that on your conscience? I'll tell you what. Just put it down on the mantelpiece. Slowly. Go on, that's right. Now back away. Just sit down, all of you. Go on, sit down."

He motioned with his gun, and they obeyed.

"It's too bad you weren't around when I worked over your uncle," he said, when they were all seated. "You should have seen it. I must say, I almost respected the man. He's the first person I've ever worked with who managed not to give away anything."

Alec leaped up, but Damian pulled him back down.

"And this must be Damian Vanlint. I know all about you too. So, Alec, have you and your friends enjoyed your little adventure?" Coetzer ran his hand over his face to wipe away the raindrops trickling from his hair, and took another step into the room.

"Who are you?" Damian snapped.

"That doesn't matter."

"How did you get here?"

"I borrowed a boat. Your friend won't be needing it anymore."

"What did you do to him, you bastard?" Now Damian was shouting.

"I can hardly imagine a less important topic." Coetzer smiled. "You see, I have other priorities. You all know what this is about. I'm here for the Semper Augustus."

Alec laughed scornfully. "Then we're all in the same boat. I guess you fell for the same story we did, about the million-dollar tulip bulb." Alec pointed to the mantelpiece. "You know what? Take it, it's yours. Just get that thing as far away from me as possible."

Tara's eyes shot toward Alec.

"He's right," she said, "it's no good to us in this state. I should know. I'm the person Frank selected to clone it."

"You don't have to tell me who you are. Anyway, I can tell you're lying."

Tara shook her head. "I know exactly what I'm talking about. This is the first time I've actually seen it, and I took a good look. It's completely dehydrated. There's absolutely nothing anyone can do with it."

"Wait, I'll show you," Alec stood up and started toward the fireplace.

Coetzer swung his gun toward him. "Cut the shit. I heard your whole conversation just now, and I saw her trying to take the bulb away from you. Why would she do that if it were worthless?"

Alec cursed. "Who are you? Who are you working for?"

The man's sardonic laugh echoed through the room. "That's no business of yours, you pathetic little turd. I'll give you one last chance. Sit down. No, wait, I have a better idea."

In two quick steps, he was standing next to Emma. Grabbing her by the hair, he yanked her head back and pressed the barrel of the gun to her temple.

FIFTY-NINE

Dawn climbed out of the car. Within a few seconds, she was soaking wet. The wind buffeted her toward the water. A raincoat was pressed into her hands, and she squirmed into it, struggling to keep her footing. Pulling up the hood, she hurried after the detectives, who were racing toward the landing. Her shoes squelched through the mud, seeming heavier with each step.

The small landing did not jut out into the water but ran parallel to the bank. Before they reached the platform, the detectives came to a stop. Dawn saw Ben pointing off to the left, and then the two men rushed away in that direction. She ran after them as fast as she could.

"What's going on?" she asked, panting, as she came to a halt behind them. They were kneeling down and peering at a man, lying on his side, his face half submerged in a muddy pool. Ben rolled him onto his back, pulled down the collar of his sweater, and held two fingers against his neck.

He looked up. "This is the bargeman that Vanlint had asked to take us across. He's out cold. We have to call an ambulance."

He turned to his partner and jerked his thumb at the water crashing hard against the landing. "I'll cross to the other side with her. You stay here so you can signal to the paramedics. They'll never find him otherwise."

Dawn couldn't understand a word, but the meaning of his gesture was clear enough. She looked out over the turbulent water to the faint glimmer on the far side.

"How will we get there? We don't have a boat."

Ben rose, and they walked to the landing together. He leaned forward, scanning the water's edge.

"Follow me. There's something lying over there," he shouted.

They pushed their way through the reeds, Dawn dodging the sharp blades of grass that snapped back into her face. By the time she'd caught up with Ben, he was already stepping into a metal rowboat. She took his outstretched hand and hopped into the boat, which began to wobble precariously.

"Careful!" Ben shouted, gripping the boat on both sides to steady it. "Never jump into a boat. You have to *step* inside. Sit over there, and I'll shove off. You take one oar, and I'll take the other."

"Sounds like you do this all the time," she shouted. "Bear with me, I'll do my best!"

Ben pushed the craft into the water and sat down next to her.

"Start when I give the signal, okay? Here we go."

They moved off, slowly at first, but once they had fallen into a rhythm, they picked up speed. The landing soon vanished from sight.

"One, two, one, two," Ben hollered into Dawn's ear.

Now they were shooting forward. Dawn looked over her shoulder and could just make out the island. With every stroke of the oars, it was drawing closer.

SIXTY

Coetzer pressed the barrel of the gun into Emma's temple with such force that she grimaced with pain. He nodded toward Alec. "Bring that thing to me, or I'll blow her head off."

Damian felt adrenaline surge through his body. Don't move. Don't lose your head. He took a deep breath and held up his hands.

"Steady now. Alec'll get it for you. Right, Alec?"

Coetzer's eyes followed Alec as he turned to the mantelpiece and picked up the bulb. In that instant, Damian lunged forward, summoning all his strength to knock Coetzer to the ground. The two men fell to the floor together, with Damian on top. He grabbed Coetzer by the ears and, with all his might, slammed the man's head into the stone floor. With a howl of pain, Coetzer dropped the pistol. Damian hauled him back onto his feet.

"You filthy coward." Damian kicked Coetzer in the crotch, and he fell to the ground, wailing, his hands between his legs.

As Damian was about to pin him down, Tara said breathlessly, "I've got him." She held the pistol aimed at Coetzer. Damian released his grip and stood up. No sooner had Tara taken a step forward than Coetzer, in one fluid motion, reached down and drew a knife from its sheath around his calf. He lifted his arm, the blade glinting in his clenched fist.

The shot rang through the house. Coetzer's head flew backward.

His left eye was wide open and staring in utter surprise at the ceiling. His right eye was a gory hole. His head slowly slumped to one side.

Alec and Damian gaped at Tara. She was staring, as if in a trance, at the pistol, which she held in a white-knuckled grip. Alec inched toward her, extending his hand.

"Just give it to me, go on now, it's all right."

She shook her head savagely. Turning to Alec and Damian, she pointed the gun at them, jerking it back and forth from one to the other. Her hands were trembling. "Emma, move over and stand next to them, please? Okay, Alec, hand it over."

"No."

"No?" When he remained perfectly still, she said, "Well, then, I guess I have no choice."

Her finger slowly curled around the trigger.

"Stop! Police! Drop your weapon and turn around slowly with your hands up."

The detective had his sidearm trained on Tara. She released her grip, and the pistol clattered to the floor. Without lowering his own gun, he walked over and kicked it in Dawn's direction.

Alec stared at her. "What are you doing here?"

"He called us," Dawn said, looking at Damian. "This is Detective Inspector van Dongen of the Dutch police force."

"Pleased to meet you," Ben said.

"Is the bargeman all right?" Damian asked.

"He should be on his way to the hospital now. We found him unconscious when we got here."

"Hold on a second," Alec said. "Damian, what's going on? I thought we agreed we wouldn't involve the police."

"After I heard Dick was dead, I called Scotland Yard and spoke to Wainwright. I told him everything I knew and persuaded him that we should set a trap for the killer. He got in touch with Sergeant Williams, who happened to be in Amsterdam."

Alec swore. "You used us as bait? What were you thinking? We could have died."

"Alec, if he hadn't got his hands on Sytse, the police would have been here in time."

"Oh, God." Tara stared at her hands in bewilderment. Had that really been her waving a pistol at those people just a few moments ago? She started to shake uncontrollably and slowly crumpled to the floor. Someone draped a blanket over her shoulders. She looked up to find Alec kneeling beside her.

"Are you okay?"

Tara shook her head. Then she leaned to one side, supporting herself with her arms, and threw up. Tears ran down her cheeks, and spasms rippled through her stomach. She felt a wet cloth on her forehead and pressed her hand against it. Cool water ran down her face.

"What have I done?" she whispered.

"Quiet now. It'll be all right."

She lifted her tear-streaked face to look at him. "I'm so sorry. This isn't anything like how I imagined it."

Alec nodded. "It's all right. We're safe now."

"Alec, what are we going to do with the Semper? We can't just throw it away or destroy it. It would be such a waste. At least we agree about that, right?"

SIXTY-ONE

Tucked away in the London suburbs, Kew Gardens is an oasis for tourists in search of peace and quiet. Formerly the private gardens of King George III, the site has been open to the public since the late nineteenth century. Covering more than three hundred acres, it holds over forty thousand species of plants, as well as dozens of historic buildings.

At the gate in the towering wrought-iron fence, Tara and Alec gave their names and strolled into the park. It was almost closing time. A few lingering tourists ambled past them on their way out.

"I think this is the ideal solution," Alec said.

Tara nodded. "The Semper's in good hands here. I'm glad you all felt the same way I did."

During the journey back from the island to Amsterdam, Tara hadn't said a word. When they arrived at the house, she had gone straight up to her room. The next morning she had told them about her plan for the Semper Augustus. That same day she had called Karl Peterson, the director of Kew Gardens. She recalled a symposium where he had given a lecture about the Millennium Seed Bank Project, which he had launched in 2000. From the very start, his enthusiasm had impressed her. In Wakehurst Place, West Sussex, not far from Kew, tens of thousands of seeds from flowers and plants all over the world were in storage in enormous underground vaults. They were intended not only for posterity but also to prevent famine in the aftermath of a natural or man-made disaster. Many of the seeds preserved in the subterranean complex came from vegetables and other food crops.

When Tara had told Karl Peterson what they wanted to contribute to the seed bank, he had been beside himself with joy and had guaranteed her that the Semper Augustus would always be in safe hands with him.

Alec and Tara paused at the intersection of two paths.

"Left, or right, or straight ahead?" Alec asked.

"Let's see. I haven't been here in a while. Oh yeah, his office is over that way, next to Temperate House—that big greenhouse you can see from here."

They left the main route, following a narrow path that wound among ancient trees and shrubs toward the gigantic Victorian plant house. The lower part of the building was made of whitewashed stone, and the windows were so large that the walls seemed to consist entirely of glass, rising straight up to a pair of high metal beams. Above that point, the large panes of glass slanted inward, meeting to form the roof of the fifty-foot-tall building.

At the entrance to the greenhouse, they followed a path to the left, which led them to a redbrick building whose door was held ajar by a small leather sandbag. Alec followed Tara inside.

The tall grandfather clock in the entrance hall was ticking softly. The building smelled like incense and furniture polish, and the parquet floor gleamed with age. The walls of the room and the staircase were lined with prints of flowers and plants in small gold frames.

Alec pointed up the stairs, turning to Tara with raised eyebrows.

"Don't ask me," she said. "I've never been here before."

"Should we ring the bell? He knows we're coming, doesn't he? Hello? Is there anybody there?"

Above their heads, they heard the creak of floorboards and then the scrape of a chair being pushed back. A moment later, brisk footsteps followed, coming to a halt at the top of the stairs.

"Are you here to see Karl Peterson, the director?" a voice droned. "He's been expecting you. Please come upstairs. His office is the first door on the right."

The room was decorated in a bright, contemporary style. The large white desk was furnished with a monitor and a large carnivorous plant whose traps sagged from its stem, full of small insects the plant had lured in. Next to the filing cabinet behind the desk, the wall was covered with diplomas and certificates. At the sound of the door closing, they turned around.

"You must be Alec Schoeller and Tara Quispel."

They nodded. The man was well over six feet tall. His thinning gray hair was plastered to his scalp, and where he had combed it, the lines were still distinctly visible. He scrutinized them through the lenses of his glasses. A scar slanted down his nose and lip.

"The director asked me to meet you," he said in a nasal voice. "I understand you have something you'd like to donate to the Millennium Seed Bank Project?"

Alec nodded. "Isn't the director in today?"

"Certainly. He's in a meeting right now, but he'll be here in a moment. We'll wait for him if you like."

"We'd actually prefer to give it to him in person, if you don't mind."

"As you wish. We can wait for him here." The man waved a hand at the chairs facing the desk. "Have a seat." He made no move himself, but remained standing next to the desk with his arms folded. "So you've brought us the Semper Augustus. What a marvelous addition to our collection. I'm sure you can imagine how thrilled we are."

"I hope you won't have any reason to change your mind," Tara said. "It's brought us nothing but bad luck."

The man raised his eyebrows, gave a curt laugh, and sat down at the desk. "Indeed? Are you telling me it's cursed?"

"No, of course not," Alec said. "We're just happy to be rid of it. If you know anything about it, I'm sure you'll understand why."

"You're referring to its value?"

"That's right."

"Tomorrow the tulip will be deposited in the Seed Bank at Wakehurst Place, behind lock and key forever," the man said, rummaging in his desk drawer. "Then it won't be of use to anyone—and that would be most unfortunate."

Tara grabbed Alec's hand. A silencer had already been fitted to the barrel of the pistol pointed at them. The buckle in the inside pocket of Alec's jacket seemed to throb against his heart like a living being.

"So, who's got it?"

Alec suppressed his fear and tried to look nonchalant. He leaned back. "You don't seriously think we'd just hand it over to anyone who asks for it? After all we've been through? It's the director or no one, you arrogant son of a bitch."

"The director's not coming. Haven't you figured that out yet? You must be even more stupid than I thought. I don't think you realize who you're dealing with."

"That's true, I have no idea," Alec said. "But it doesn't interest me. I'm fed up with this whole business."

"Give me that thing." The man held out his hand and stepped toward them.

"No, you can't have it." Tara stood up, tightly clutching her purse. The man turned to face her, and at that moment, Alec leaped out of his chair and rammed him with his shoulder like a football player. The man fell backward, slamming his head against the wall. The gun flew out of his hands and slid to the other end of the office.

Alec grabbed Tara's hand and pulled her out of the room. Out of the corner of his eye, he saw the tall form sliding to the floor. The man's head fell forward, and his arms hung slack at his sides.

SIXTY-TWO

"What are you thinking about?"

Damian turned to Emma, who was lying beside him, and smiled. "I was thinking that Frank would be happy with this solution. So would Wouter Winckel, probably."

She sat up. "Can you imagine what it must be like to live in a country where you can put your life at risk just by expressing your opinion?"

"Or even just by having the wrong beliefs. You're right, we're lucky to live in a tolerant place like this."

"For as long as it lasts."

Damian stared at the ceiling. "It always fascinates me how people fight for their rights, only to lose them again later. It seems to go in waves. We get a taste of freedom, then it's all taken away from us again."

"Maybe the tide turns when some people decide the limits of freedom have been reached."

He looked her in the eyes. "Have *you* ever reached the limit?"

"Yes, I know exactly where my limit is. You want to know why?"

"Why?"

"Because I had the freedom to discover it for myself, and you gave me that freedom. That's why I love you so much."

As he was leaning in toward her, the telephone rang.

"Don't answer it," she whispered.

He smiled and took her in his arms. The ringing stopped. A few seconds later, his cell phone started buzzing.

"Perhaps you'd better answer it after all," she said.

He sighed and picked up the phone. "Vanlint speaking."

"Mr. Vanlint, this is Inspector Wainwright. Sorry to bother you, but I have some news. We've discovered the identity of the man who killed Schoeller and Versteegen and held a gun on you."

Damian straightened up. "Well, who is he?"

"It wasn't easy. He uses multiple identities. Interpol's been searching for him for years."

"Interpol?"

"That's right. He was a hit man."

Damian sat bolt upright.

"But that means—"

"—that whoever hired him is still on the loose. That's why I'm calling you. Where's the bulb?"

"Alec and Tara took it to England. They've arranged to drop it off at Kew Gardens this evening."

"Why Kew Gardens?"

"They're donating it to the Millennium Seed Bank," Damian blurted out. "You'd better get over there, fast."

SIXTY-THREE

Panting, they came to a stop. Darkness had fallen, and the park was deserted. From where they stood, dimly lit paths branched off in all directions.

"Which way?"

Behind them heavy footsteps boomed down the stairs.

"That way," Alec said. "Follow me."

They ran toward Temperate House and up the steps. Alec pushed open the narrow glass door and pulled Tara in after him.

The tropical heat closed in on them. Alec looked around, intent on finding something to barricade the door. He wrapped his arms around a terra cotta pot as large as he was, but he couldn't budge it.

Tara looked outside. "He's coming," she shouted. "Which way do we go?"

The man had reached the steps. Alec surveyed the interior of the greenhouse. It was clearly organized: between the rows of plants, two tiled paths ran in parallel over the entire length of the floor. The only place they met was right at the center of the building, where Alec and Tara were standing.

"Look," Alec said, pointing to a wrought-iron spiral staircase. "Come on, up those stairs."

A shot rang out, and they heard the sound of breaking glass. For an instant, Alec could feel the rush of air. The bullet had struck a palm tree about ten feet away. They ran to the staircase and up the winding stairs.

"What now?" Tara asked, gasping for air. Her forehead was beaded with sweat. They were standing on a high metal walkway that extended along the entire perimeter of the greenhouse, so that visitors could view the plants from above. "We've walked into a trap," she said. "Look, Alec, it loops all the way around. There's no place for us to go."

Alec leaned over the edge and looked down. The man had run off in the opposite direction. To his horror, amid the greenery in the distance he could make out another staircase. No matter which way they went, they were sure to run into him. All they could do was go back down the stairs, but that was equally pointless. Their pursuer would notice right away and be there waiting for them at the bottom.

Heavy footsteps pounded up the metal steps. A few seconds later, he was directly opposite them. Across a gap of almost a hundred feet, they stared at each other over the tops of the trees, waiting to see who would make the first move. Even at that distance, Alec could see that the man was having trouble breathing. His chest heaved up and down. Alec made a quick decision.

He took Tara's hand. "At the count of three, we'll run as fast as we can along the right-hand side, okay?"

"And then what? He'll be right there waiting for us."

"Just trust me."

She nodded. Alec counted down, and they charged down the walkway. In the distance, Alec could see the man letting go of the railing and calmly striding in their direction, his pistol at the ready.

"Alec, no," Tara yelled. "We're running straight toward him."

"Stop, right here! Jump!"

They vaulted over the railing and into the treetops, crashing through the foliage of the fifty-foot palm tree and landing on the soil with a thump. Tara looked around with a dazed expression and then felt her elbow with a moan. Alec pulled her upright and placed a finger to his lips. She followed his gaze upward. The footsteps were receding into the distance. Alec and Tara tiptoed back onto the path. At the bottom of the staircase, Alec pointed to the recess underneath the steps. They scrambled into the small space, pressing themselves as close as possible to the wall. They could hear the man descending. Then, suddenly, he stopped. Through the wrought-iron above their heads, they saw the soles of his shoes scrape lightly over the landing. After a moment's hesitation, he slowly continued down the stairs. Just as he reached the bottom step, Alec leaned forward, seized his ankles, and gave a sharp tug. With a yelp, the man pitched forward, his face smacking into the floor. The pistol fell out of his hand.

"Tara, grab it," Alec shouted, climbing on top of the man and pinning him to the ground. She handed the pistol to Alec, who slowly rose to his feet.

"Get up."

The man looked at them. Blood was streaming from his nose, which was cocked at a grotesque angle to his face. He pushed himself up from the floor and onto his knees, then collapsed again. Groaning, he brought his hands to his face.

"Now it's our turn," Alec said. "Who are you?"

The man shook his head and chuckled.

Alec kicked him in the leg. "Who are you? And what were you planning to do with the bulb?"

When he smiled, Alec saw he had lost a tooth. Blood trickled from his mouth. He spat and said, "I've got the money. Thirty-two million euros. I've got it, and you can have it all, if you give me the Semper."

"Was that you? Was it you who took the money from the Tulip Investment Fund?"

The man slowly nodded. Drops of blood fell to the damp floor and spread into stains.

"That's right. I needed the money to buy the Semper."

"So were you also the one who set up the fund?"

"I was one of the founders, yes."

"Did you want the Semper so that you could pay back the investors?" Tara asked.

The man laughed drily. "Of course not, you stupid twat. Those investors were rolling in money, they could easily afford to lose a little. I thought it was a handsome price for a single tulip bulb. But when Frank found out where I'd got the money, he backed out of the deal."

"And paid for it with his life?"

The man nodded. "He knew too much and wasn't willing to keep it to himself."

"And now you really think I'll take your offer?"

"Everybody's different."

"And Simon?" Tara asked.

He looked up. "Simon was in financial trouble because he had invested in the fund. He had no idea it was me who had embezzled the money. He thought I was one of the investors who'd been defrauded, just like him."

"You and Simon were working together to get your hands on the Semper?" Tara asked in a shaky voice.

He nodded. "Yes, at first. But Simon changed his mind. He tried to back out, but he knew too much."

"So you had him eliminated? And what about the director? Where's Peterson? Don't tell me he's—"

The man slowly pushed himself up from the ground again. Still reeling, he straightened his back and spread his arms. "I have a different proposal. How about this? I'll give you the money, and you let me go. You can keep the bulb. You know what you could do with all that cash? Tara? You could fund your research. It's everything you need, and it's in your grasp."

Tara shook her head. "You're too late," she said. "If you'd come to me a week ago, I might have accepted your offer. But not now."

"But why? What's changed?"

"Me, I've changed."

All at once a bright light shone straight into the man's face, which he reflexively shielded with his forearm. Alec pulled Tara toward him. Someone was shouting, grabbing hold of the two of them, and pulling them outside. Heavily armed police officers ran past them, pointing their guns at the man in the spotlight, who had his hands in the air.

They left the greenhouse under police escort. To his surprise, Alec saw Wainwright waiting for them.

"Well, Mr. Schoeller," he said, "I bet you never thought you'd be happy to see me." At his side stood Dawn, looking at Alec with a smile.

SIXTY-FOUR

Damian uncorked a bottle of champagne and filled their glasses.

"Well, then. I guess it'll be a while before Sytse can get back to work, but I'm glad he's recovering so quickly. Let's hope no unexpected visitors will be dropping in tonight."

"Yes, and let's hope it's really, truly over," Emma said. "Alec, was that man really just after the money he could make with the Semper Augustus?"

"Apparently so. Wainwright tells me that the people Dick was talking about, the ones involved in the think tank, had nothing to do with Frank and Simon's deaths. Coetzer was hired to find out from Frank where the bulb was. Coetzer killed Frank when he wouldn't talk, then realized I might know where Frank had hidden the bulb."

"Now I understand why Simon said that if anyone knew anything, it would be you," Tara said. "And I fell for it. He wanted to use me to find out where the Semper was."

"Tara, Simon must have been desperate," Damian said. "I'm sure he never wanted to put you in harm's way. Besides, in the end he regretted the things he had done. If he hadn't, they wouldn't have killed him."

"Maybe you're right. Anyway, I'm glad Karl Peterson has placed the Semper Augustus safely behind lock and key. The bulb is where it belongs."

"Yes, and I'm glad Mr. Peterson's still among the living. Did he think the bulb was worth it?"

Tara smiled. "Of course. It's a one-of-a-kind acquisition for the institute. He had it taken to Wakehurst Place right away."

"Speaking of tulips, I don't understand why Coetzer made those tulip drawings on Frank's chest and Simon's wall. What on earth possessed him?" Emma asked.

"I was wondering the same thing," Damian said. "Wainwright thinks he wanted to send the police on a wild-goose chase by giving the impression there was a serial killer who used the tulip as his signature."

Alec stretched out his arms. "Well, I just hope one thing: that the Semper Augustus will remain at Wakehurst Place forever."

Tara nodded. "And this time its shrine won't be made of silver but of impenetrable steel."

Wakehurst Place

One by one, the other researchers trickled out of the office, until finally he was alone in the high-security zone of the complex. For several weeks, the young scientist had been the last to go home, so no one had been surprised to see him still at work.

As soon as he was certain that everyone else had left, he opened the door of the laboratory and walked down the broad hallway that led to the vaults. At the second door, he typed in the code known to only a small circle of staff members at the Millennium Seed Bank Project. When the light turned green, he lowered the heavy handle and entered the vault.

Every wall was filled with metal drawers, and on each drawer was a numbered label. He went to the wall on the right and kneeled down, knowing exactly which drawer he needed and sliding it out of the wall. As he brought it to the table in the middle of the vault, he gently stroked the label and whispered, "You are my future."

There it was. For a moment, the sight took his breath away. It was almost unimaginable that the wrinkled brown thing in front of him held such divine beauty within, or that it was worth so much. He smiled. The thought that they had chosen him to get the bulb for them filled him with pride. They'd described how they'd been waiting for the bulb for more than two years and had almost given up hope of ever laying hands on it again. They'd told him that the he was the chosen one, the only person who could aid them in their quest.

The young man knew the risks, and he knew that his job was on the line, but those considerations were outweighed by his sense of adventure and the enormous sum of money they had promised him. Their plans for the bulb didn't interest him one bit. This was a once-in-a-lifetime opportunity.

He slid his hand into the pocket of his lab coat. His fingers clasped the shriveled bulb that he'd placed there earlier that day. At first sight there was no difference between that bulb and the Semper Augustus. It would be years before the seed bank realized that the precious bulb had been replaced with a worthless substitute.

After he'd made the exchange, he replaced the drawer, thinking of the sum that would be transferred to his secret bank account the next day. From that moment on, he would be free. Then he could set up his own lab, do his own research, and purchase whatever his heart desired.

It took all his strength to shut the massive door on his way out. He scanned the deserted hallway as he hurried back to the lab.

"Well, well, young man, working late again?"

"Oh! You startled me."

The security guard looked at him benignly. "I can see that. Sorry, just making the rounds. Anyway, isn't it time that you were getting home? It's Friday night. The city of London awaits you! A person your age should have more in his life than just work. Seize the moment, right?"

The guard spread his arms wide and let them drop. Then, lifting a finger, he added, "Because before you know it, it'll be over. Take it from a wise old man. You have to enjoy life to the very fullest."

He nodded amiably at the guard as his hand slipped into his pocket. Gently stroking the bulb, he said, "I know just what you mean. And I will enjoy myself. Don't worry about that."

ACKNOWLEDGMENTS

Without the support, inspiration, and confidence of my beloved husband, parents, mother-in-law, relatives, and friends, I would never have made it through this. I am deeply grateful to all of them. The same can be said of my readers Godelieve and Liliane, whose willingness to comment on my draft version was a sign of true friendship. I also owe a tremendous debt of gratitude to my agent, Paul Sebes, as well as to my editor, Juliette van Wersch, for her encouragement, her suggestions, and her patience.

Mike Dash's wonderful book *Tulipomania* was a rich source of inspiration for me. In addition to the print and online sources that I used, a number of people kindly took the time to answer my questions. My thanks go to Bert Stoop and Simon de Waal of the Amsterdam-Amstelland Police Force, Harry de Raad at the Alkmaar Regional Archives, and Jan Pelsdonk at the Royal Dutch Mint's Money Museum.

The Tulip Virus is a work of fiction. Its characters and plot are based in part on historical events and recent news stories but have been adapted to suit my own narrative purposes. My website, www .daniellehermans.nl, describes the facts that inspired the novel and the sources I consulted.